THE WEEPING WOMAN OF PUTTEN

A WWII NAZI CRIME STORY

ALYCE BAILEY

ISBN: 978-1-5356-1746-8

Published in the United States of America
with the assistance of BookFuel.com

Contents

· · · · · · · · · · · · ·

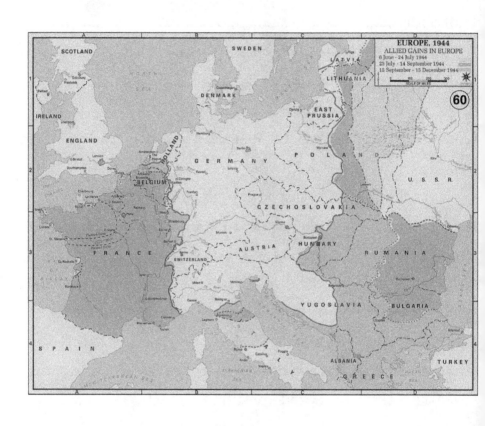

EUROPE, 1944
ALLIED GAINS IN EUROPE
6 June - 24 July 1944
25 July - 14 September 1944
15 September - 15 December 1944
SCALE OF MILES
60

Prologue

· · · · · · · · · · · · · ·

AT A BEND IN THE HIGHWAY, close to the Oldenaller Bridge, Witvoet was hiding in the brush, armed with a loaded pistol and a flashlight. From where he crouched, he could see traffic approaching from either direction. He could also see the full moon, which he feared might give them away. As he anxiously waited, the minutes crawled by, and he remembered the concern voiced by some of his friends in the resistance. At the time, he'd dismissed their worries, but now he wasn't so sure.

The moon had broken through the cloud cover, illuminating the road and revealing the faint outline of a small truck parked backward, just beyond the bridge. Witvoet could even vaguely make out the figure in the bed of the truck. Vehicles from the west surely wouldn't spot it, he thought, but someone approaching from the east might notice their truck in the light of the moon. Too late. Everyone was in place.

Headlights approached from the west, jolting him back from his thoughts. He watched, heart pounding, but the car passed without incident, not even slowing as it approached their parked truck. There were only soldiers in the car, not officers. So the waiting dragged on. His throat grew tight and dry despite the cool dampness of the dark autumn air. It was Saturday, just before midnight, September 30, 1944. It was also dangerously past curfew, he realized, far too late for him or any Dutch civilian to be out...let alone on the road. Only German vehicles moving to and from their posts were likely to pass by now.

As he continued to wait and watch, Witvoet thought through the orders his group had received, making sure he had it all straight. He, as the leader, had chosen seven other men from the resistance to help intercept German vehicles. Their orders were to strike quickly and retrieve anything that might prove useful. The Dutch resistance were fighting, along with the Allied troops, to help free the Netherlands from Hitler's tight grip. They needed new information on German troop movements to the front.

Another vehicle approached, again from the west, and Witvoet watched carefully, trying to discern the passengers inside. When the moonlight glinted off an officer insignia, Witvoet was ready to move. He signaled to their truck with his flashlight to set their plan in motion. When the vehicle rounded the bend by the bridge, Oosterbroek turned on the brights, and the oncoming driver slowed in the blinding light.

Tex, manning a machine gun bolted to the bed of their truck, aimed at the German vehicle with the steady precision for which he was known. The gun misfired. Immediately and with the same precision, Tex aimed again and fired.

A stream of bullets struck the approaching car. It veered to the left, slid into the ditch, and came to rest against an old cement post. A scream followed by yelling and swearing came from the German car. Tex remained crouched and watched as several figures jumped from the car and ran toward the woods, firing back at the truck as they fled.

Other resistance fighters emerged from the brush on the side of the highway and ran toward the car in the ditch. Shots were exchanged. Oosterbroek chose this moment to shut off the truck lights and, under the cover of fire, attempted to slip out of the truck cab, unnoticed. Instead, he found himself under fire, but he kept on moving, slipping quietly down the side of the truck until he was nearly flat on the ground. He moved stealthily toward Tex, who was at the back of the truck. Together, they were now both reasonably shielded.

"Who's shooting at us? Doesn't seem to be coming from the German vehicle," whispered Oosterbroek.

"Well, I'm not entirely sure," replied Tex.

A shot flashed and rang out, barely missing Oosterbroek, and he panicked. "Where is Witvoet? We need him to make sense of this!"

"Shhh," whispered Tex. "Quiet down. Haven't heard a word, so I don't know. Could be he's been shot. You're next in charge, so for now, I guess you'd better tell us what to do."

Oosterbroek took a deep breath to regain his composure before cupping his hands around his mouth and calling out as loud as he dared, "Hold your fire and take cover!"

All fell quiet but the rustle of leaves on the trees. After a long, uncomfortable moment, they heard a low moaning from the direction of the ditch.

Oosterbroek took his time to assess the situation before calling again to the men, "Make your way back to the truck!"

Only four men showed. Oosterbroek muttered, "We are missing Witvoet and Slotboom." Speaking up, he said to the men, "Has anyone seen them? Witvoet and Slotboom?"

When no one reacted, Oosterbroek ordered, "Tex and I will search the German vehicle and the surroundings. You four, look for Slotboom and Witvoet. Regroup here in fifteen."

As they neared the German car, the faint sound of moaning grew louder. Oosterbroek and Tex moved in with their pistols drawn. They soon saw that a German soldier was lying on the ground, slumped over, holding his stomach. He didn't seem to have a weapon and was only barely conscious.

Tex held the German at gunpoint while Oosterbroek checked the car. No one else was inside. Three grenades and a pistol were in the back, but Oosterbroek found no maps, no documents of any kind in the car. It was all for nothing.

Tex tried to help the wounded German to his feet, but the man cried out in pain and collapsed. Tex picked him up easily, carried him across the highway and laid him down in the bed of the truck. Before making his way back, Oosterbroek reached inside the car and grabbed the pistol and grenades.

By then, their search party had located Slotboom. He had been shot and was found on the other side of the road. They lifted him into the truck and laid him gently beside the wounded German. While the group was tending to the two injured men, a vehicle approached. Everyone ducked for cover, but the car sailed by, oblivious to both the truck and the bullet-riddled car in the ditch.

Under the cover of night, the moon somewhat subdued by the low passing clouds, Tex stayed behind to guard the German soldier while the others continued the search for Witvoet. They quickly combed the immediate area, spending as much time as they dared, but it produced no sign of Witvoet or any clues as to what might have befallen him after their attack.

Oosterbroek called off the search, and everyone returned to the truck. They discussed what to do with their German prisoner. Witvoet had ordered any captured Germans to be killed on the spot, no questions asked. But Witvoet was not there. After some deliberation, all agreed that the wounded soldier should receive medical attention.

With nothing left to do there, the four who had come to the bridge by bicycle uncovered their bikes and left. Oosterbroek and Tex got into the truck cab and headed toward Putten in search of a doctor willing to tend their enemy soldier.

Chapter One

. . . .

SUNDAY, OCTOBER 1, 1944

AFTER THEY FINISHED MILKING THE COWS and doing their other morning chores, Papa and Henk headed back to the house for breakfast. Janneke gave her father a peck on his cheek as he entered the kitchen. She nodded at her older brother Henk. He smiled and nodded in return. She glanced at the clock and said, "It's too late for the first Sunday church service if you want to eat your breakfast now. Shall we go to the later service today?"

Papa agreed, "Yah, sure. Without Willem and Gerrit here to help, it took us much longer to get everything done today. I think, tomorrow, I will ask our guests if the men can help us with our work."

Janneke studied her father's face. "Are you sorry you sent the boys up north? I know they're out of harm's way, but it is much harder on you and Henk now."

"No, I am not sorry, daughter. It was the right thing to do. They will be much safer up there, far from this endless fighting. I do wish the Allied troops would cross the rivers at Arnhem soon. They would probably have us free in a day. If they don't, who knows how much longer this war will drag on. It is such a strain on us all. Not just the fighting, also the constant uncertainty of what they may do to us next. I have heard rumors of another roundup coming, that they will take more of our young men for their factories."

Henk chimed in, "Yah, I heard it, too, Papa. The Germans may come back into Putten to do this soon. I'm glad Willem and Gerrit aren't here. They're too young to be hauled off for laboring."

"But what about you, Henk?" Janneke asked. "You may be the eldest, but you're only twenty-six, young enough to be picked up yourself."

"I need to stay here to help on the farm. I'm not leaving Papa to handle all this alone." Henk gestured toward their barn, the stream, and the surrounding pasturelands bordered by woods.

Papa stood thoughtfully at the sink, his mind far away while he washed his hands. He was weighing the certainty of farm and family needs against the seemingly endless risks of occupation and war. Queen Wilhelmina and their Dutch cabinet, who were exiled, had been ruling from London for four long years now.

Food was scarce, except for farmers like himself who were still living on their own land, food that had not yet been confiscated to provide them some sustenance. The Allied troops had only just begun their efforts in the Netherlands, and who knew how long it would take for their village to be liberated?

At last, he turned back to Henk and said, "I appreciate your willingness to stay, son, and I thank you. You are a man now, and you are right to take your place beside me. But you are also young and still inexperienced in the ways of war. Do not venture far from the farm and always remember to be careful."

After a pause, Papa added, "Maybe I should change my mind. I am not feeling good about asking our guests to help us on the farm. It is a practical idea, but they have already been through too much since the evacuation. Their houses and businesses have been confiscated. Their futures are all so uncertain now. With all the fighting around Arnhem, will their homes even be standing when all of this is over? I don't like to add to their burdens."

"But, Papa, it might be a welcome distraction for them to do some work on the farm," Janneke suggested. "Their days must go so slowly, especially with nothing but worry to fill their minds and no work to keep them busy."

"Maybe you are right, daughter. I know that, if I was in their shoes, I would want something to help keep my mind off this war. It is hard enough on me, living in my home, just hearing the bombing to the south. It keeps me awake at night, worrying about what's to come."

Mama came into the kitchen. "I thought I heard you talking in here. I am waiting with your breakfast. Come. Sit down. Janneke, would you fetch the milk and tea?"

Without the younger boys' usual chatter, they passed their breakfast in near silence. Henk and Janneke finished first, but they remained seated until Papa stood up. Then, Mama rose to clear away their breakfast. Janneke stood up as well, ready to help her. The women continued their silence as they washed the dishes, each deep in their thoughts, until a sudden loud banging brought them back to the moment.

Mama wiped her hands on her apron and moved to the kitchen door. Janneke remained at the sink, waiting. Mama opened the door slowly and was surprised to find Jacob, a young farmer from up the road, hat in hand, trying to catch his breath. Gasping out his words, he said, "Good morning… ah…I'm so sorry to disturb your quiet Sunday morning, but…well, when I came back from milking, I saw armed German soldiers walking on the road. They were coming from the direction of the highway, and I worried the rumors about a roundup may be true. I ran away from them as fast as I could. I can't go home, and I didn't know what else to do. Yours is the first farm I came to, and I don't believe they saw me. Please, do you have a good place to hide me until this is over," he pleaded. "I can't go to work in Germany. Papa is too old to manage the farm alone, and my wife and children need me, too."

Was this really happening again? Janneke looked at her father in disbelief, but her mind was already racing. Before he could speak, she said, "Papa, I think all the men in this house would be safer at Pieter's house. It's away from the highway and well hidden in the woods. I think you should go there now and wait until we know what this is about."

Papa looked from Janneke to Henk and, finally, at Mama, who nodded her head almost imperceptibly. They had always communicated like this, Papa and Mama, and it was no different now, even though the world they knew, and had trusted, kept slipping further away.

Janneke's strong independence often amazed her father. It was so unlike the women of his generation. Shaking his head, he knew he had no better idea. He nodded his agreement and said, "Henk, quickly let our male guests know what is happening. Tell them they should join us immediately. It is no longer safe for them here. Jacob, we will get word to your father as soon as we can, but first we must be safe."

Janneke, then, suggested, "If I wear my uniform, I can probably ride toward the highway without causing any suspicion. Maybe I can find out what's going on." She noticed her father's hesitation and spoke before he could protest, adding gently, "Don't worry, Papa. I'm sure the soldiers will let me through if I'll tell them I'm on my way to help a sick child."

The plan made sense, and there was no time to argue, so Papa nodded in agreement. Pulling his coat back on, Papa went off after Henk to tell the men.

Without waiting for them to leave for Pieter's, Janneke ran upstairs to her room and closed the door to change. As she was dressing, Mama barged in. "I am so afraid, Janneke. Please do not leave me here alone. What is going to happen to Papa, to all of the men? What if the Germans are able to find them? Oh, Janneke!" She was crying now. "I am afraid for them all, and I am afraid to be here without Papa and Henk."

Janneke buttoned the white cape at her neck as she turned toward the door.

"Please, Janneke, do not go," Mama pleaded. "I need you here with me."

Janneke reached for her mother's hands and led her gently but firmly down the stairs and back into the kitchen. "Mama, I have to go. I need you to be strong. Please, go get the mothers and the children. Bring them into the kitchen and stay here until I get back."

Janneke straightened her uniform, grabbed her cap, and strode through the door to her bicycle. Pushing off quickly, she rode as fast as she could toward the spot where Jacob had seen the soldiers. When a shiver ran down her spine, she wondered if it was fear or simply the rush of the air.

As she neared the spot, she heard shouting as two gunshots echoed through the woods. She slowed as the woods cleared, unsure of which way to go now. When she saw the people standing in the pasture beside the highway that led from Nijkerk to Putten, she stopped. She scanned the group for familiar faces and was surprised to see that there were also women and children. In that instant, she knew this was more than another roundup of

German factory workers.

Her mind flashed back to the women and children she'd just left behind. Worried now for their safety, Janneke turned her bicycle to head back to the farm and nearly ran into a young German soldier. He had been running toward her from behind, waving his gun in the air. As their eyes met, he yelled, "*Halt!* Where are you going? What are you doing here? *Ausweis bitte!*"

Janneke calmly presented the identification card he demanded. Continuing to look him in the eye, she replied in perfect German, "I live nearby. I am on my way to treat a sick child. Is there a problem here?"

Taking in her nurse's uniform and caught off guard by her excellent command of his native tongue, the soldier slid his gun back into its holster. Still, he scrutinized her ID card and looked her over slowly. She realized, with some surprise, they were probably the same age. When he finally handed her card back, he answered her question. "One of our cars was attacked on this highway last night. You say you live near here. Did you hear anything?"

When Janneke shook her head, he continued, "One officer was badly wounded in the attack, and another is still missing. We believe he is being held prisoner in one of the farms around here. Do you know anything about this incident? Do you know where they have taken him?"

"No, I don't know about any of this," Janneke replied evenly, struggling to remain calm, despite her growing fear.

"We have orders to search all the farms in the vicinity," he informed her. "We are to round up everyone and hold them until we receive further instructions from headquarters."

He began to say something else but was interrupted by another soldier who came running out of the woods, calling out, "Hey! Is she a nurse? Someone has been shot."

The soldier told Janneke to leave her bike and follow him immediately.

Worried she would never see her bicycle again if she left it behind, she simply followed him without answering. Half-walking, half-running beside her bike, she dodged tree branches and tried not to trip on the uneven, leaf-covered path. When the trees began to clear, she realized they were coming up to Jacob's family farm.

"Oh, my God," she exclaimed. "Who...who was shot here?"

"A young girl," answered the soldier. "She tried to run away. She would not stop running. One of our men tried to warn her, shooting over her head, but one of his bullets struck her in the back."

He led Janneke around the old barn to a ditch. There, the sight of Jacob's middle daughter, lying in a pool of blood, was just too much for Janneke. She knelt down beside little Janna and felt for her pulse, though she doubted she would find one. Her long-controlled calm gave way to tears as she thought about Jacob and his family and all the pain and hardship the Germans had wrought upon her people. Suddenly, unable to contain her anger any longer, she jumped up. "You damn brutes! If I had a gun, I would shoot you both. Do you enjoy killing little girls? Is that why you are soldiers?" she demanded. "You barbarians! Animals! Wasting such an innocent life, and for what?"

Though her tirade was in Dutch, speaking to the Germans that way was dangerous, a risk she shouldn't have taken. Their steely blue eyes met hers, and even if they didn't understand her words, they clearly understood her tone. The young soldier looked away for a moment and then back at the lifeless child. He nudged the other man's arm, and they both backed away.

Janneke released her breath without realizing she had been holding it and knelt back down beside Janna. After examining Janna's body carefully, she thought the bullet had probably punctured her lung, causing her to die quickly. She hoped, wanted to believe, that the girl had not suffered for long.

The young soldier who had first stopped her earlier came toward her. He took off his coat and covered Janna's body. Janneke saw something, maybe in his face or in the way his shoulders seemed to have slackened, that suggested he wanted to console her. Instead, he simply said, "I think you had better leave here and go care for that child you mentioned before. After that, your help may be needed in the village."

"What do you mean?" Janneke asked, bewildered. "Has there been another incident?"

"I started to tell you the rest earlier, before we were interrupted. We have surrounded the village. All people must go to the square and remain there until we find the missing officer."

"I thought you said the search and roundup were only around here where the attack occurred. Were people hurt in the village roundup?"

He simply asked for her ID again and wrote *exempt* on it, along with his name and rank. As he handed it back to her, he urged, "Go now. This will get you through if you are stopped."

As the Germans turned to go, Janneke walked back to her bike. She took her time straightening her hat and uniform, waiting until they were well out of sight. Then she leaned the bike against an old lilac bush and went to Jacob's door. No one was home. In a daze, struggling to comprehend all that had happened, she ran back to her bicycle and headed for home, hoping her mother, the women, and their children would all still be there. Had she really left them only an hour ago?

She arrived to find the house totally deserted. She could only assume they were now among the people guarded in the pasture by the highway.

While thinking about her family and the people in the pasture, she remembered the atrocity at Oradour-sur-Glane in France. Oh, no, not here, she thought frantically. Please no. Surely that could not be happening here.

She had read about it in an underground paper earlier that summer. The farming village in France was much smaller than Putten. Yet the two places were very similar. After the French resistance had sabotaged the movement of German troops, the SS had rounded up and murdered the entire village, more than six hundred innocent men, women, and children, in retaliation. The men were driven into barns where machine guns awaited them, shot in the legs so they could not escape, then covered with hay and burned to death. The women and children were locked inside the village's Catholic church, which also was set ablaze, killing everyone inside. The SS then looted the village, and before departing for the Normandy front as planned before the sabotage, set the remaining buildings and homes in the town on fire. It was said not a single structure remained after the massacre of Oradour-sur-Glane.

The thought of that happening in Putten pushed Janneke into a further panic. She had to talk to Pieter. She could only hope that the seclusion of his old forest ranger house had kept him hidden from Nazi eyes.

When, at last, Pieter's house came into view, the panic rose in her throat until she could barely breathe. There was a white sheet hanging from a second-floor window. What on earth could that mean? Without thinking of the risk, she dropped her bicycle in the yard and ran around to the back of the house. She threw open the door, burst into the room, and stopped in an instant when she saw the startled men looking at her from the kitchen table.

"Oh! What a relief! You're all here!" she exclaimed as she looked at the men – her father, her brother Henk, Jacob, and five others. Pieter came running down the stairs when he heard Janneke's voice.

"You all have to hide somewhere, immediately. The Nazis are coming! They're searching all the farms, rounding up everyone all around Putten, even the women and children," she said, still trying to catch her breath. "An SS car with two officers was attacked on the highway last night. One officer died, and the other is still missing, so they're holding everyone until he is found."

Her father looked down and shook his head. Some of the men groaned in disbelief as they realized this was more than a roundup of laborers for German factories.

Pieter pulled Janneke in to hug her, wrapping her in his strong arms. In his protective embrace, she broke down, weeping at last. She felt so safe with this man.

Janneke had been taken with Pieter from the first time she had seen him, four long years ago. He had come to their farm to introduce himself as the new forest ranger. It wasn't very long before they were spending their free time together, grooming the horses, riding in the woods, hunting birds and rabbits, picking mushrooms and blueberries, or just bicycling into Putten for market or church.

In the beginning, Mama disapproved, unsure of this stranger who was spending so much time with her daughter. Over time, as she came to know him better, Mama softened. When, after two years, Pieter asked Papa for permission to propose, Mama was fully in favor. They had become engaged on Janneke's twenty-first birthday, but war had a way of interfering with plans, and their marriage had been on hold ever since.

Pieter focused his clear blue eyes on hers as he peered out from under his dark unruly hair, the usual lock falling over his eyes.

"I was very worried about you," he said softly into her ear. "I'm relieved to see you and know that you're safe." Turning away, he, then, addressed the men and Janneke, too, "We are all safe here for now, I think. It's unlikely this house will be noticed any time soon. It's so far from Putten and out in the woods. Please, sit down, Janneke. Rest and gather your thoughts. I'll pour you a cup of tea, and you can tell us what you've learned since you left your farm."

Janneke looked around the kitchen; all eyes were now upon her. She smiled at her father and brother, but when she looked at Jacob, she felt the tears start again.

"I, I...hardly know where to begin," she said, brushing away the tears. "When I neared the highway, I saw entire families, not just men, standing in the pasture, guarded by armed German soldiers. Papa, I...I'm afraid for Mama. When I went back to our house, no one was there. I'm afraid they have taken her and the evacuees from our farm to the pasture."

"Oh, dear God," uttered Papa. "Please let them be safe."

"Did you see my wife and daughters there?" Jacob asked Janneke as Pieter set the teacup in front of her.

Pieter noticed her hesitation in answering Jacob's question and pressed on gently, "There is more, isn't there?"

Janneke nodded, looking down at her tea. She lifted her head back up to look Jacob in the eye. "I am so very, very sad to have to tell you this, Jacob, but...your little Janna has been shot."

Jacob was shocked. "Wha...what? But why? How?"

Janneke reached for Jacob's hand and continued, "The soldiers went to your farm, too, Jacob. Apparently, Janna tried to run away. They ordered her to stop, but she kept running. A bullet meant as a warning hit her in the back. One of the soldiers took me there to help her, but..."

Janneke took a deep breath, her voice trembling when she spoke again, "Janna had already passed when I reached her. I am so sorry, Jacob."

All the blood drained from Jacob's face, and Pieter, who was standing next to him, had to grab Jacob's arm to keep him steady.

"Wha-what," he stammered. "What a-bout my wife? What about my other two daughters? My father? Where are they?"

Janneke felt such sorrow for Jacob. She felt miserable for having to give him the news and wished she could have, at least, reassured him about the rest of his family. "I'm sorry, Jacob. I don't know. I was able to look inside your house after the soldiers left me, and I saw that no one was there."

Before anyone had time to stop him, Jacob grabbed his coat and ran out of Pieter's house. Henk ran after him, yelling for him to come back, but Jacob kept on going, quickly disappearing from sight. When Henk came back inside, everyone gathered around the kitchen table again.

Janneke turned to Pieter. "We've got to figure out what to do from here, but first I want to know why the white sheet is hanging on the outside of the house. What does it mean?"

"Ah, good, you noticed," started Pieter. "The soldiers will see it, too, and pass this house by as having already been searched."

"But has it?" Janneke asked. "I had hoped they wouldn't even find your house."

"No, they haven't searched it, and hopefully now, they won't. Just before you arrived, a German soldier came here alone, just as I stepped outside for firewood. He had already seen me, so I stood there and watched as he walked around the house to get a drink from the hand pump. He was so much older than most SS soldiers. I'm sure I've not seen him before. I walked over to ask if I could be of help, hoping to draw his attention away from the kitchen window. I was almost certain he saw the men inside." Pieter paused and took a sip of his tea while remembering. "He looked at my forest ranger uniform, and instead of answering my question, he said, '*Achso, polizei.*' He smiled, which put me at ease, and then told me the same story you did about the attack and the search for the missing SS officer. He told me, together with the other '*polizei*' inside, to go to the village police station because we would probably be needed there."

Janneke asked, "What about the bedsheet?"

"Oh, yes. About that," Pieter continued with a bit of a chuckle, remembering. "The old soldier started to walk away but stopped and looked up at the house. That worried me, but he just said I should go get a white bedsheet. When I asked what for, he said to hang it from an upper window before we left. He told me that, if other German soldiers came around, they would know this house had already been searched, so they would not interfere with our duties.

"What he didn't tell me, though, was that the whole village was being surrounded. Between that and what happened to Janna, we are all in great danger now. I agree, Janneke. We need to make a plan quickly to keep everybody here safe."

Everyone nodded in agreement and waited for Pieter to provide direction.

Nervously, Henk asked, "Is it, maybe, okay to stay here, at least, until after dark?"

"Yes." Pieter nodded. "But we have to think about where you all can hide until this is over. It could be days. They're sure to keep patrolling the area until that officer is found."

Janneke jumped up, remembering something. "I know of a great place where I'm sure they'll never look. Papa, remember when I was a little girl, and I didn't want you to find me? I played in the small cave below the waterfall… well, that is until the pigs found it and started taking shelter there in the winter." She turned to Pieter and continued, "The stream that runs through our property has a little footbridge over it with a small waterfall on one side. Under the bridge behind the waterfall is the cave I'm talking about. It is probably big enough to hide all the men."

Janneke saw Henk holding his nose, but before he could say what was surely on everyone's mind, Janneke laughed and said, "Don't worry. There haven't been any pigs on the farm for well over four years now. It should be quite tolerable in there, I think. Right, Papa?"

Papa, standing behind Janneke, reached for her shoulders and squeezed them lovingly. To Janneke, his touch was as important as Pieter's hug. In her family, love was rarely shown physically in public.

"How ever did you remember that? It's been so long," he said, remembering those long-ago years when his children were just babes. The farm was dear to his heart. It had long provided for his family, and it held so many cherished memories—of his parents, his siblings, and now, too, his family. Coming back to the present, he said, "Yes, I do agree. No one would know a cave is there or even think to look."

Papa and Henk turned to discuss going back to the farmhouse and the supplies they should bring for their hiding. Janneke gestured to Pieter to go outside with her. She needed to speak with him alone.

Once they were outside, she started, "I think we need to get a warning to Enny's Estate. I was there a few days ago to deliver some coded messages, and Mrs. Pouw told me to take them to the attic where several resistance men were meeting. I asked her about them when I came back down, and she told me that they were leaders of various resistance groups that have been working independently in this part of the Netherlands. Prins Bernard and our exiled government recently sent word from London that they were to unite, so they asked if they could temporarily reside in her attic. She told me she and her husband agreed to let them to stay there because they had the room, and with as many mouths as they were already feeding, a few more wouldn't make much difference. She did say, though, that she was getting worried about the increasing resistance activity."

"Yes, I know," Pieter answered. "I, also, was at Enny's Estate the day before yesterday. I found a British soldier walking in the woods and took him there. He was a paratrooper who'd been captured by the Germans behind the front near Arnhem. The Germans were transporting him by train to Germany, but when the train slowed down near here, he managed to jump out and escape. I agree that the people at Enny's Estate need to be warned. There are many there who are of special interest to the Germans and must not fall into their hands."

Janneke pulled out her ID and showed Pieter what the German soldier had written on it earlier that morning. "I will go," she told him. "This should get me past any checkpoints. After that, I'll head for the village square. I was told to go there to see if medical help was needed. I can look for Mama while I'm there."

Pieter, not at all surprised by the courage of his beautiful, strong-willed fiancée, took her face in his hands and kissed her. "Okay then," he said obligingly, "but please be very careful. I would rather go with you, but you probably have a better chance of getting through if you go alone. Better leave now. I'll explain to your father that you have left to check on your mother."

Chapter Two

. . . .

ENNY'S ESTATE

JANNEKE RODE HER BICYCLE TO ENNY'S Estate, which was tucked deep in the woods, south of Putten. As she pedaled along beneath the colorful canopy of old beech trees, she remembered, with a smile, how much she had liked working for the Pouws. They were truly nice and generous people. Mrs. Pouw had grown up in Germany, but Mr. Pouw came from a very old Dutch family in Amsterdam. They had built their estate early in the century, and it had been their family home ever since. She wondered for whom the estate had been named, thinking, "Funny. In all the time I was there, I never learned their first names. Perhaps Enny was Mrs. Pouw's given name, or maybe it was an old family name."

Janneke had many sweet memories of Enny's Estate from throughout her teenage years. Every summer vacation, she would work for the Pouws in their home. She would also tend to the dachshunds they bred. She had found it interesting how life on Enny's Estate had so contrasted with life where she had grown up on her family's farm. Those had been the best summers of my youth, she thought fondly.

When she had first begun working there, she loved to pretend she was a baroness living in a mansion, and she had always wanted to be like Mrs.

Pouw. She had continued her summers there until just before the war began. When she started working for the doctor, her visits to Enny's Estate ended.

Janneke reflected on how different her life had become since then. Not only did she work for the doctor, she had Pieter in her life. Unbeknownst to her family and most of the town, both she and Pieter aided the resistance. Janneke served as a courier whenever they needed her and she could get free. Just last week, they had asked her to deliver coded messages to Enny's Estate, and she had happily accepted the assignment.

She had been so excited at the thought of seeing Mrs. Pouw again, and the pleasure had clearly been mutual. Mrs. Pouw had invited Janneke in for a cup of tea, not even stopping to ask the nature of the unusual visit after these many years. They were soon chatting away like the dear old friends they were, and Janneke had realized how much she had missed talking with Mrs. Pouw.

Over tea, they had talked first of little, neutral things, the weather, pleasant memories from their past, but the conversation eventually turned to the difficult reality of their lives under German occupation. Mrs. Pouw had told Janneke how, after the Nazi's bombed Rotterdam in 1940 and the occupation had begun, she and her husband had opened their home to anyone needing shelter from the occupying Germans. Over the past four years, they had housed many fugitives: Jewish families, deserting German soldiers, and downed Allied pilots and paratroopers. Most recently, underground resistance fighters had been added to their endless list of house guests.

In turn, Janneke had told Mrs. Pouw that, although her parents and Henk were well, her younger brothers had gone north to avoid the roundups and that she missed them. To Mrs. Pouw's surprise, Janneke also told of her own part in the resistance. After a reflective moment, Mrs. Pouw had taken Janneke's hands into her own, brought them to her heart, and kissed them.

Pedaling up the long drive and seeing the great main house peeking through the trees brought Janneke's mind back to the task at hand. She parked her bicycle beside the impressive marble and granite entrance. The massive wooden front door stood wide open, so she invited herself in. She found suitcases and boxes cluttering the floor of the black and white tiled entrance. People she didn't know were running up and down the stairs. Wondering at the commotion, she peered into the front sitting area with its heavy antique furnishings and the Pouws' hunting trophies on the walls.

When she did not see Mrs. Pouw in the room, she walked through the hallway and entered the formal dining room, then continued on to the kitchen. Finally, through the window, she saw Mrs. Pouw at the edge of the garden, talking to a man she did not recognize. She went quickly through the door and down the neat path to where the two stood beside the rose bushes. Mrs. Pouw introduced Janneke to Tex Banwell, the same British soldier Pieter had taken to the estate.

Tex took one long step forward and shook Janneke's hand, his serious face brightening into a broad smile.

"It is a pleasure indeed, miss."

"Janneke. My name is Janneke," she replied in her rusty English. "Good to meet you, Mr. Banwell. My fiancée Pieter told me about bringing you here."

In high school, she had never understood why she was made to learn German, French, and English, but now it was all serving her very well. Admittedly, her English was a bit rough from disuse, but she could manage.

"Well then, Janneke, please do call me Tex." He returned and continued, "Yes, Pieter did indeed bring me here. Good man. Did he send you to speak with me?"

"No, actually I came to speak to Mrs. Pouw about something quite urgent. I apologize for interrupting, but please, would you excuse us for a moment?"

Mrs. Pouw spoke up, "Janneke dear, you may speak freely in front of Tex. He is a part of the resistance, a part of all of this now."

For Tex's sake, then, Janneke continued in English, telling Mrs. Pouw that she had come to warn her about the roundup in progress all around Putten. Janneke knew she was carrying an enormous load on her shoulders, and it was beginning to show. She was sorry to have to add to it with this news. Mrs. Pouw took a deep breath and let out slowly, between pursed lips, a soft but audible sigh. "Yah, the German motor car attack, very unfortunate that was for us all. It is causing such upheaval in Putten and also here, as you can see," she said, nodding toward the house and to the activity within.

Surprised at Mrs. Pouw's knowledge of the attack, the commotion she had seen in the front hall now made sense. "Then, you must also know about the missing officer."

"Yah, I do know," Mrs. Pouw answered. "In fact, he is here at the estate. We want to return him to the Germans as quickly as we can to put an end to their search. The men have worked out most of the details, but they must take great care to leave no trail and to be certain the lieutenant cannot lead them back to us. The Germans must not find Enny's Estate before the many lives we are protecting have had time to flee and find new shelter. Many of these people would be at risk of being put to death if they are found."

"But how did the officer end up here?" Janneke looked at Mrs. Pouw, then at Tex, hoping for some explanation.

It was Mrs. Pouw who replied.

"The short answer is, he was injured during the attack last night. German or not, our men did not have the heart to leave him there to die. The full answer is longer, and I can tell what I know of it if you would like."

"Yes, please. Maybe what's happening in Putten will make more sense if I understand the details."

"It begins with the resistance group you brought messages to. They have been meeting here since then because one of those messages came from the top resistance leader in our area. It carried a directive to begin attacking German vehicles. The objective was to find information on German troop movements and other activities behind the front. You remember Witvoet, yah?"

"He was the man I gave the messages to, yes? He said he was a deserted police chief, I think, from a small town up north. He told me he refused to work with the Germans and came to Putten, hoping to hide."

"Yah, that is Witvoet," continued Mrs. Pouw. "He took the lead on the new directive and assembled a team with Oosterbroek and six others to plan their first attack. Then Pieter found Tex and brought him here. When Oosterbroek learned he was an expert with British weapons, Witvoet added him to the team, so they could use the British Bren machine gun for the attack. The resistance has an ample supply from all the Allied weapon airdrops. With the team and weapons sorted out, the men were able to move forward immediately and planned the first attack for Friday night. But when the time came, the night sky was clear, and the moon was too bright, so they rescheduled the attack for last night."

Janneke's eyes had widened as she listened. It was not just that Mrs. Pouw had known about the attack. Janneke was standing here in front of the man who may have shot the missing officer. She didn't realize that, while she tried to process this information, she was staring impolitely at Tex.

"So, you…you were there at the highway last night?"

"Yes," Tex answered simply.

Janneke hesitated before responding, not sure whether she wanted to thank him for helping the resistance when he was, at least, partly to blame for the roundup and for putting her family and Pieter in danger.

"What on earth happened?" she demanded more sharply than she had intended.

Seeing Mrs. Pouw's chiding look, Janneke fell silent and let her friend speak. "Yah, I have the same question, Janneke. This is what we were discussing before I introduced you to him. Tex, please, would you continue the story and tell us what happened last night?"

"I'm happy to tell you all I know," answered Tex, "but may we sit down, perhaps on the benches over there? This will take a bit of time for the telling, and to be honest, I could do with a little rest after being up most of the night."

"Of course, a good idea," said Mrs. Pouw. "And we will all be more comfortable there in the sun. Janneke?"

"Yes, definitely. Since innocent people are being punished for it, I would like to understand how the attack could have gone so wrong." She was looking pointedly at Tex.

"All right then," he began as they walked toward the benches. "Last night, eight of us left here on bicycles, carrying handguns and the Bren machine gun. We rode part of the way together and then split up as planned. Four men went ahead to the highway bridge where the attack was planned."

"The Oldenaller Bridge, yes?" interrupted Janneke. "I saw several armed German soldiers there this morning, guarding a large group of people. At first, I thought it was another worker roundup, but then I saw there were women and children, too."

"Yes, I believe that's what Oosterbroek called the bridge. So four men rode on to the bridge while Witvoet, myself, and the other two went into Putten to get a small truck we had hidden earlier. We bolted the Bren to the bed of the truck, covered it with straw and a tarp, then rode quickly to the bridge. The others had surveyed the area and determined the best place to set up the truck. When we arrived, we quickly got the truck in place and took up our positions."

Tex went on to tell about the attack, searching for Witvoet, and finally their return to town.

"We drove into Putten with Slotboom and the wounded German officer, and we called on two different doctors for help. Both of them told us to take the men to the hospital in Ermelo."

"Did you call Dr. van Gulden?" Janneke asked with some concern.

Tex glanced at Janneke. "Yes, I think he was the doctor we first called. Why do you ask?"

"Because I work for him. Did you tell him how the men got wounded? I mean, well, if you should ever speak with him again, please don't mention that you met me. I don't want him to know I have anything to do with the resistance. If he finds out, I won't be working there anymore."

"I would never mention you to anyone other than resistance workers and, even then, only if necessary. But to answer your question. No, Oosterbroek didn't mention the resistance involvement to the doctors. He just said we found two men with serious gunshot wounds and were trying to find immediate care for them."

"Oh, I am relieved to know that. So then what happened?"

"Since we couldn't take the wounded men to the hospital, we had no choice but to bring them here. Mrs. Pouw knew of a nearby doctor from Voorthuizen, and he agreed to come quickly. He treated them both and dressed their wounds without question."

Mrs. Pouw sighed again as she turned to Janneke, taking over the story from there. "We watched over the two wounded men through the night while we waited for Witvoet to return. He never showed. Then early this morning, Slotboom died."

Janneke heard the grief and pain in Mrs. Pouw's voice as she brushed away tears and went on. "Tex helped me wrap Slotboom's body in a blanket, and together we buried him under the old oak tree…over there, beyond the garden."

Janneke looked to where Mrs. Pouw was pointing and saw freshly turned soil beneath the tree. Resting a hand on Mrs. Pouw's lap, she wished she could undo this day and all the suffering it had brought.

"Mrs. Pouw, I am so very sorry this has happened to you. Of all people, you should not have to live through such things. I wish I could assure you that all will be well, but I think you and Mr. Pouw should leave the estate with the others. You are not safe here either, at least, not until the Germans have their officer back and hopefully send everyone back home."

Mrs. Pouw could not speak as a single sob escaped her. She put her hand over her mouth, but the tears fell, unchecked, down her weary face. Janneke put an arm around Mrs.Pouw, felt her strong shoulders shaking with emotion. She was surprised by Mrs. Pouw's breakdown. Such a strong woman, she had always been the one to console others.

Before the war, Janneke would not have believed that a day would come when Mrs. Pouw needed to be consoled, let alone that she would be the one to do it. Sitting here beside her now, she understood all too well the strain of living with war and occupation. It broke even the strongest of people. Janneke hugged her briefly, then softly pressed on, "And what about the wounded German soldier?"

"His name is Lieutenant Eggert," she replied tearfully, trying to regain her composure. "He is badly wounded, but his life is not in danger. Mr. Pouw is watching him upstairs until the men are ready to return him, which must be soon. I suppose you are right. Mr. Pouw and I should leave, too. It is only a matter of time before the Germans find Enny's Estate, whether or not they have their officer back."

"That is a terrible thought, but I do believe it is best," Janneke encouraged. "What a pity, such a tragedy, all of this is. I wish I could stay to help you and the others, but I need to go into Putten to see if I can find my mother. I think she was picked up by the Germans, along with our neighbors. Now, I wish we had sent her and the women away with our men this morning. They would all be hiding safely at Pieter's, at least, for now anyway. I also need to offer medical help if it is needed in town." Janneke rose from the bench but added, "Before I leave, would you like me to look in on Lieutenant Eggert?"

Tex stood, his long shadow falling across Janneke. "No, that is not a good idea. The fewer people the lieutenant sees here, the better. We don't want him to be able to identify anyone after he returns to the Germans. Besides, he is stable for now and doesn't need any further care here. You go on your way and care for your family and the people of Putten. You are needed there more than here. Mr. and Mrs. Pouw need to pack and prepare to leave, and I will cover signs of our stay here, starting with poor Slotboom's grave."

"But, Janneke, before you go," Tex continued, "I want you to know that I'm truly sorry our plan went awry and that it is causing so much trouble. I just tried to do my duty as a soldier. We all did. Please know that I admire your great courage. May God be with you."

Mrs. Pouw stood and embraced Janneke tightly before she asked with concern, "Will you be safe going to Putten by yourself? I am certain you will encounter checkpoints, and even a nurse will be stopped."

"With this, I think I'll be okay." Janneke showed Mrs. Pouw that the German soldier had written *exempt* on her identification card and, also, his name and rank. "Besides…" She winked. "My nurse's uniform seems to impress those soldiers. They always let me pass when I say I'm going to see patients."

"Yah." Mrs. Pouw smiled wryly. "The Germans do favor uniforms, do they not? Okay. Well, please be careful, dear, and I do hope you find your mother."

"Thank you, Mrs. Pouw. I'll come back to check on you when I can," she promised and turned to walk away. Just before rounding the front of the house, Janneke turned back and waved. Mrs. Pouw and Tex, still standing by the benches, waved good-bye in return.

Chapter Three

· ·

ROUNDUP

JANNEKE PARKED HER BICYCLE AT DR. van Gulden's house. She was just a few blocks away from the old village square, and judging by the sunlight angling through the golden leaves, it was mid-afternoon. On her way to town, she had been stopped several times by armed German patrols. Most had let her pass with a curt nod. A few had repeated the young officer's earlier directive to go to the market square to assist those needing medical attention.

She climbed the tile steps of the doctor's large front porch, stopped before the massive, dark blue door, and lifted the heavy iron knocker. She let it go, watching it bounce against the metal plate, thinking about her employer as she waited. She heard the shush from above her before she saw Mrs. van Gulden leaning her kerchiefed head out an upstairs window, her index finger against her lips. "Shhh…the children are napping. I'll be right down."

Janneke nodded that she understood and that she would wait. Looking up at the stately brick home, high windows framed in heavy old wood and graced with white lace curtains, she thought, Just like Enny's Estate. Such a contrast with the simple buildings of our farm.

After she swung the door open, Mrs. van Gulden exclaimed, "Oh, Janneke, thank goodness you are here. Come in please. I'll make us some tea."

Janneke knew Mrs. van Gulden quite well because she frequently brought coffee and tea for the doctor and his staff from her kitchen into the attached medical practice. On occasion, Janneke had also cared for their two small children when Dr. and Mrs. van Gulden had gone out for an evening together.

Normally, two crystal chandeliers shone brightly in the hallway, but today, it was dark within. The Germans kept cutting the electric lines on this side of the front. The light of the petroleum lantern Mrs. van Gulden was holding made the shadows of the chandeliers dance on the walls and ceiling in intricate little patterns.

Janneke was indeed thirsty, and the tea would be so soothing, but much as she wanted to go inside, she declined. "Thank you for the offer, Mrs. van Gulden, but I cannot stay. I was wondering if I could leave my bicycle here. I have to get to the square before it gets dark, and I don't think it's a good idea to park it there where it might be confiscated. You and the children are well, I hope? Is the doctor home?"

"Yes, the children and I are well, but the doctor is away, and I am worried. He was on call this weekend and left very early this morning for an emergency house call in Ermelo. He phoned this morning before the electricity went out and said some very alarming things about the rumored roundup taking place. He felt it unsafe to come home just yet because he saw German trucks loaded with armed soldiers going toward Putten. He also saw a group of people held at gunpoint, standing in a field, at the edge of the village. Do you have any idea what is happening?"

Janneke didn't want to worry Mrs. van Gulden, so she shook her head, but she thought, "If the doctor saw activity on the north end of the village, opposite from where I had come, then the roundup wasn't limited to where the attack took place."

Mrs. van Gulden continued, "My husband told me to stay inside with the children. He said he'd be home as soon as it was safe."

Janneke nodded in agreement. "I have to believe that your husband is right, that he should stay away for now. I will come back to check on you."

She left on foot for the market square. Lined with linden trees, their lower branches trained horizontally and long since intertwined, it was a very old marketplace, bustling with vendors on market days. Today it will be empty, she thought, as she rounded the corner onto the main street through Putten and abruptly stopped short. Janneke had caught sight of armed Germans spurring on men, women, and children in the direction of square. She quickly stepped back into the quiet side street behind her and walked around through an alley. When the square came into view, she was astounded by what she saw. Manned machine guns were positioned on each corner of the square, pointing at the people corralled in the center. Hundreds of men were lined up there already, and more were pouring in. The women and children were separated from the men and directed to the front of the square where they were ordered to enter the Dutch Reformed Church.

She felt frozen in place, unsure of what to do. Oradour-sur-Glane flashed back through her head, and she felt her heart pounding as panic threatened again. Her eyes darted around the square and took in a group of men separated from the rest. They were clothed in their Sunday best and were lined up alongside Café-Restaurant De Heerdt, across from the church. They stood eerily still with their arms at their sides, faces turned grimly to the wall. Manned machine guns were fixed on their backs. She looked away, trying to collect her thoughts, sifting through her options, until she decided on a plan.

Suddenly, her purpose resurfaced, and she crossed the square. When the soldiers seemed to ignore her, she entered the church and began to search the gloomy late-day interior, looking for her mother. After a quick, fruitless scan of the poorly lit interior, she started down the outside aisle, looking down the pews as she passed. Most of the women were in their traditional Sunday clothes, while others wore simple coats. Children were everywhere; infants were in arms, and toddlers were holding tightly onto their mothers' legs. She passed a group of teens, apart from their mothers, talking quietly among themselves. She saw the baker's wife and could see she'd been crying, but she continued down the aisle, peering down each pew, looking for her mother in the traditional cap and dress she had worn in the morning.

Making her way back up the center aisle, Janneke spotted her mother at last, standing among a group of women in the far back corner of the church.

She quickened her steps, but before she could get to her, she was pulled aside by a German soldier and led back to the doors of the church leading to the square.

"Nurse! Go check on the man who collapsed over there," hollered another soldier stationed just outside.

Janneke saw the elderly man lying on the cobblestone. Someone had covered his chest with a coat, and a man she recognized from the bank was holding the poor man's head in his lap. She stooped down next to him and found that he was unconscious. As she checked his vital signs, he began to come to. She asked if he was in pain; he said no, but he still felt dizzy, and he was quite hungry. She helped him sit up, and he continued, "I am worried about going so long without my medication. I am many hours late now."

"I'll see what I can do, but for now, you need a warm place to sit. Do you think you can stand?"

"I will try."

Janneke and the banker helped him up slowly. When she was sure he was strong enough to stand with her support, she thanked the banker and told the man to come along. She walked him over to the German soldier positioned outside the church and explained that the old man was sick. That was evident to the soldier, and she quickly convinced him that the elderly man should be allowed into the church to sit down. When he nodded his assent, she walked the man inside and had him sit on the nearest vacant pew. She knew now what she had to do. "I need to leave you now, but I will be back to check on you later."

He nodded and gave her thanks by way of a weak smile. She hoped her words had offered, at least, some measure of comfort, but if nothing else, he was seated now, instead of standing endlessly out in the chilly air.

She made her way back out to the square and surveyed the line. The patrols seemed unconcerned with her moving about as she continued to help the sick and elderly men into the church. She returned several times, looking for anyone who might have medical problems that would prevent them from tolerating the forced lineup. Because they had been standing for so many hours, it was easy to spot the ones who were unsteady on their feet. Walking toward a middle-aged man who was beginning to reel backward, Janneke stopped dead in her tracks. She had heard a familiar voice softly calling her name. She turned, hoping she was wrong, but she was not.

"Oh, Jacob! Not you, too! What happened?" she asked in a whisper, searching his face as if she could divine the answer there.

"I'm sorry, Janneke. I was so worried about my family. I couldn't stay there at Pieter's and do nothing. I know it was headstrong, but I felt I should be with my family. I was sure they needed me, and I could not think beyond that. I still don't know where my wife and daughters are because I was picked up by a German patrol before I got to my house. Please tell me, have you seen them inside? I have seen you going in and out of the church. Are they there? Do you know, are they well?"

"No, I'm sorry. I haven't seen them. I did see my mother inside, but I haven't spoken with her yet. When I go back in to check on her, I will look for your family."

Jacob impulsively grabbed Janneke's hand as she began to step away. "Thank you, Janneke. I am so sorry if I added to your burdens. I should have stayed with the men at Pieter's house. I might have been of more help to my family by keeping myself safe."

Dusk was creeping over the village. Janneke looked around again, taking a mental inventory of the square. The men seemed even more uncomfortable now, hands under arms or in pockets, hunching their shoulders against the rising breeze. German soldiers were moving men at one end of the long listless line into the school that bordered the back of the square. At least, they were being given shelter against the coming cold of the night.

An open police motor car nosed its way slowly through the crowd of people around her. When it reached the center of the square, the uniformed Dutch officer turned off the motor, and after a couple of stuttering chugs, like last gasps of breath, it died with a little cloud of smoke. Picking up a loudspeaker, he clambered onto the hood of his car. His amplified voice bellowed out over the crowd, "Hallo! My name is Otten. I am here to find witnesses of an attack on a German motor car last night. It happened south of Putten, near the border of Nijkerk. If you saw this attack, if you saw anyone running or driving away from this area, if you know anything at all about it, you must step forward now! A German officer is missing, and as you can see, this is very serious. Anyone with information on the whereabouts of this missing officer should step forward immediately. The punishment for all people of Putten may be less severe if the truth can be found out quickly!"

While he was speaking, Janneke made her way closer to his car. When he lowered the loudspeaker and scanned the people in the square, Janneke shouted out to him boldly, "Mr. Otten, may I ask you a question?"

"Yes, but be quick. Many lives are at risk."

"Do you know what will happen when the missing officer is found? Will everyone be allowed to go home?"

"Command in Germany has not said what will happen when the officer is found, but their eyes are on Putten now, and they are furious. The attack gave them reason to believe this is a *partizanen* nest, and they want it cleaned up," he answered. Then, he went on to say, "Commandant Fullriede is in command here, and even he does not know yet. He is waiting for further orders from Germany, regarding the fate of your people."

"Mr. Otten," she pressed on angrily, shouting loudly so others might hear, "do you know whether the commandant realizes the people of this town are innocent? Does he care? Or are we to be like those poor, innocent people of Oradour-sur-Glane?"

"Dear God, I hope not. Do not even mention such a thing. Have you ever seen the commandant? I have had several meetings with him, and from his gray hair and demeanor, he appears to be much older and, hopefully, wiser than most of the German soldiers we have encountered. I think we may be right to hope that this man has a heart."

"Just one more question," Janneke implored. "Do you know why the men at the wall are being kept separate?"

Otten held her gaze just a moment too long, then looked to the wall, where more than thirty well-known Putten businessmen and bureaucrats stood, silent and still. He answered, "The German patrols call them death candidates. They are to be shot immediately if the people do not follow orders."

Janneke shivered and looked away, thinking, What barbarians the Nazis are. She turned to survey the square, and Mr. Otten did the same, hoping to see someone coming forward with information. No one did. Mr. Otten climbed off the hood and reluctantly got back into his car. He started the motor, and after a repeat of the chugs and smoke like from before, it started up, and he slowly drove out of the square.

Janneke had not heard about this Commandant Fullriede mentioned by Otten before, so now she was curious. However, she had other, more pressing matters to attend to, so she returned to the church to find her mother. As she entered, she took a moment for her eyes to adjust to the low light and to take in the unusual scene before her. So many women and children without so much as a single man but the patrols at the doors. Many of the women were wearing their traditional long black clothing—their Sunday best—heads topped with their white starched caps, the backs of which always looked to Janneke like white ponytails trailing behind. Many children were also in their Sunday dress, frightened and hanging onto their mothers or playing with others their age, too young to understand.

Going to church on Sunday was a ritual in Putten, a serious event for most of the people of this very religious village. Nobody would have thought at breakfast this morning that this was how their day would unfold.

Finding her mother still in the back corner where she had seen her earlier, Janneke moved close and hugged her. Mama felt so much smaller as she cried in Janneke's arms. "I am so glad you are here, but no…did they pick you up and bring you here, too? Oh, Janneke, what did we do to deserve all this? What will they do to us here? Where are Papa and Henk? Did they make it to Pieter's house? Are they still there? Are they here, too? Outside? Who will take care of the animals tonight?"

Janneke let Mama cry for a few minutes. Without knowing it, she was rocking her ever so gently back and forth. She whispered, "Papa and Henk are still at Pieter's. Tonight, they will make their way back to the farm and hide under the bridge until this mess is over. I came here on my own, Mama, after I found you gone from the farm. I needed to make sure you were okay and also to help anyone who needs medical attention. So far, the soldiers are allowing me to come and go, to give help, and to move the sick and elderly into the church. I will go home soon to make sure the men have arrived and promise to tend the animals if they haven't."

"Thank you!" Mama whispered back. "I am so proud of you, Janneke. I wish I had your strength and courage."

"You do, Mama. You just don't know it yet." She tenderly kissed her mother on the cheek and said goodbye. She scanned the church for Jacob's wife and daughters and, indeed, spotted the three together. Janneke went outside to tell Jacob, but he was no longer in the square. She assumed he had been moved into the school and made her way to its entrance. As she approached, the soldier guarding the door called out, "*Halten zie.*"

Unlike the others, he did not care that she was a nurse and would not let her go inside. Not knowing what else she could do in the square, she headed back to the alley that had led her there and walked toward the doctor's house.

* * *

The house, like all the others, was completely dark. The mandatory black-out curtains obscured what little light it held inside. However, to Janneke's great relief, the familiar white sheet was now hanging from a second-story window. She pulled her cape around her and dropped the heavy knocker. Petroleum lamp in hand, Mrs. van Gulden cautiously opened the door but relaxed and opened it wider when she recognized Janneke standing there in the dark. After a furtive look up and down the street, she brought her inside to the kitchen. The children were seated with their dinner, looking warm and cozy in the amber glow of more petroleum lamps.

"Please sit with us and share some dinner, Janneke. We have only just now sat down." Mrs. van Gulden gestured toward her table and the food that had been set on it.

Janneke had not eaten since breakfast and smiled, welcoming the plate of ham, carrots, and potatoes Mrs. van Gulden placed in front of her. The smile faded as quickly as it came, though, as images of the people she had just left behind flooded her mind. Reaching for her fork, she guiltily thought, They have not eaten all day, either. Still, her hunger won out, and she dug in, even as her sorrow welled up for all those poor people in the square.

"Thank you, Mrs. van Gulden. I had no idea I was so hungry."

Mrs. Van Gulden's precocious three-year-old son outstretched his arms toward Janneke. "Miss Janneke, may I sit on your lap? Please?"

He looked to his mother, who nodded, giving her approval. Janneke moved his plate closer to hers and ate while balancing the small child on her lap.

"Miss Janneke, bad soldiers came to look for Dada. Dada is not here. Is Dada coming back soon?"

Janneke assured him that he was and turned to Mrs. van Gulden. "I saw a white sheet hanging outside. Was the house searched?"

"Yes, several German soldiers came inside, accompanied by local policemen. They were here twice this afternoon asking the whereabouts of the doctor. I told them he was not here and that I did not know where he was or when he would be back. They threatened me in front of the children, said, if he was hiding somewhere in the house and they found him, there would be severe consequences. After the second time, when they still did not find him, they believed me and said to hang a white sheet from the second-story window. When I asked if it meant I was surrendering, they said no, it meant the house had been searched, and I could stay at home with the children for now."

Janneke talked with the children for a few minutes and assured them, as best as she could, that their father would, indeed, be back. While she helped Mrs. van Gulden wash the dishes, she filled her in about what was happening in the square, omitting her conversation with the motorized policeman Otten so as not to worry her too much.

"I think it's wise for the doctor to stay away until we know what the Germans intend to do with the people in the church and school. I want to go back to the square, but first, may I please use your telephone to call my fiancée Pieter?"

"Of course. Help yourself. I need to put the children to bed, so take your time. Oh, will you stay here with us tonight? I would welcome your company and would feel safer with you here. I will ready the guest room before I come back down. It will take no time at all."

"Thank you, Mrs. van Gulden. That is very kind of you, but it depends on what Pieter has to say. The animals on the farm need to be tended to tonight. The cows must be milked early in the morning. If my father and brother have not made it home, I will have to go there to take care of it all."

"Well, all right then. I do understand, but I will ready the room anyway, just in case."

Grateful for Mrs. van Gulden's offer and, also, for the privacy she had been given, Janneke picked up the phone receiver and dialed Pieter's number. He answered on the first ring, as if he had nothing better to do than stand next to his phone and wait for her to call. It was so comforting to hear Pieter's voice. Safe within the warmth of the van Guldens' home, full from the hot dinner, she suddenly felt that, with Pieter in her life, she could move mountains. Looking back at her day, it surely felt like that was what she had been trying to do.

"Hello, dear. Just checking in with the most handsome man I know."

"So glad you think so, my lovely lady. I am relieved to hear your voice. Are you okay? Did you find your mother? Is she okay? What is happening in Putten?"

"Whoa! Slow down there, Pieter. Yes, I am fine, but a lot is happening here in Putten. I'll tell you all about my day, but first, please tell me, are Papa and Henk still there?"

"No, as soon as it was dark, they went home to get supplies and to take up residence in their hiding place. You are still in Putten? Where are you calling from?"

"I am with Mrs. van Gulden. The doctor is not here. He was away on an emergency call in Ermelo when all of this started, and he did not think it was safe to come home. We know now that he was right to stay there. He most certainly would be one of the death candidates now if they had found him here."

"Death candidates?" Pieter inquired, concerned.

"Yes, to make sure all the people follow orders."

Janneke did not really want to relive it all again, but of course, Pieter needed to know. So she recounted her day for him, starting with Enny's Estate. She told him what Tex Banwell had told her about the attack and about the death of Slotboom, the wounded German officer, all the people in the square, talking to Otten, seeing Jacob, and, lastly, talking to her mother and promising to tend to the animals if the men couldn't do it.

Pieter had listened without interrupting while Janneke recounted the details of her day. "That is a lot for anyone to go through in a single day, let alone a single woman with Nazis all around. I am rather in awe of your ability to face it all so head-on. I'm still surprised the Germans let you move so freely among the people in the square and church, even if you are 'Nurse Janneke.' It must be that authoritative confidence you wield so well when you are doing your work. So what do you plan to do next?"

"Well, I plan to go home to see if I need to tend to the animals, but first, I want to go back to the square to be sure no more medical help is needed."

"Can you stay at the doctor's house if I tend to the farm? I think your assistance is needed more in the village. And I would also feel better knowing you are there with Mrs. van Gulden, instead of being on the road after curfew and riding your bicycle in the dark."

"Actually, Mrs. van Gulden offered to get the guest room ready for me, so, yes, I will take her up on that now. Thank you so much, Pieter. I am truly blessed to have you in my life. You have just taken a heavy burden off my shoulders." She sighed tiredly and continued, "There is something else that I need to discuss with you. It's been weighing pretty heavy on my mind. Mrs. Pouw told me they are trying to find a way to return the wounded officer to the Germans. I asked Otten, if they found him, would they let all those innocent people go home. All he said was that he didn't know. He said the Germans see Putten as a *partizanen* nest, and they are going to clean it up. Since I know where the German officer is or, at least, was, do you think I have a moral obligation to tell them? It might lessen the punishment for the village, but wouldn't I be betraying all the people at Enny's Estate and everyone fighting underground for our freedom? Oh, I don't know..."

Her voice trailed off as they both fell quiet for a moment.

Pieter spoke first, "I understand the inner struggle about your allegiance versus your moral obligation. In my opinion, though, the Germans will continue with their punishment of Putten, even after the officer is returned. Referring to us as a *partizanen* nest sounds like they plan to shake things up for everyone, not just the resistance, to serve as a severe warning to not cross them again. I'll contact the police station tomorrow, see if they have any news about what the Germans are up to."

Janneke was grateful for Pieter's opinion. "Ah, thank you for sharing your wisdom. I don't feel quite so guilty keeping my secret from them now. That allows me to keep my focus on helping as I did today. I know I cannot be everything for everyone, but I do wish I could be everywhere at the same time…in the church with Mama, in the cave with Papa and Henk, in the school with all those innocent men, at Enny's Estate with Mrs. Pouw, but most of all, there, safely there with you. Oh, Pieter, I just want this stupid war to be over, so we can be together."

"My dearest love, you ask too much of yourself. You have done so much already, and I am so very proud. And yes," he said, emphasizing that last word, "there will be an end to all this madness. The front is so close now. I think we can even dare to hope it will be soon."

Janneke was fighting back her tears but managed to keep her voice steady. "I sure hope so. I love you so much, and sometimes, I just don't know how I can continue on this way. I am so tired and so worried for my family and you, our friends, everyone. How can I manage to wait any further for that day?"

"I love you, too. Just keep looking toward that day, and you will surely find the strength and courage to continue, just as you have done. Give my regards to Mrs. van Gulden and my thanks for keeping you safe within her home tonight. Tomorrow, please be careful out there and keep in touch, so I don't worry overly much about you."

"I will, Pieter. Goodbye."

"Love you, my courageous lady! Good night," Pieter said before gently hanging up the phone.

Even after saying her goodbyes, Janneke continued to hold the receiver, lost in thought after the phone went dead, thinking about her conversation with Pieter. When Mrs. van Gulden came down the stairs and looked at her questioningly, she quickly hung up and said, "Thank you. Yes, I will be staying the night."

Mrs. van Gulden was pleased and said the guest room was ready so that she could retire as soon as she came back from the square.

* * *

A crowd of women was walking toward Janneke on the main street, coming from the direction of the church and the square. Her heart skipped a beat as she wondered, Had they been let go? Oh, the joy, if that were true. Lifted by the buoyancy of hope, she stopped a woman and asked what was happening.

"Oh, hello, Janneke," responded the woman Janneke now recognized as one of Dr. van Gulden's patients.

"Did they let you...did they let...everyone...go home?"

"Yes, they let everyone in the church go home. A German named Fullriede came into the church with a Dutch policeman who translated for him. He told us to speak up if we knew where a missing German officer might be. He said that it could lessen the punishment that was coming to Putten. When no one spoke up, he told us to go home with the children but to come back tomorrow morning at ten with food for our men. He said he also expected to have further announcements then."

"That is wonderful news," Janneke exclaimed, and she was relieved to learn that the sick men she had taken into the church had also been allowed to leave. "But what about the men in the school?"

"That is all we know. We have seen no men but Germans since we left the church." She paused for a moment. Then, she said, "Well, we had better go. We have almost an hour of walking in front of us. God bless you, Janneke!"

Janneke was now even more curious about this Commandant Fullriede and wondered whether she could get close enough to talk to him. Continuing toward the square, she kept an eye out for her mother but did not see her. Hopefully she, too, had already passed by.

* * *

The square and the church were dark. The bright moon hung low in the clearing night sky, creating an eerie, discomfiting scene. The silhouettes of manned machine guns and rigid armed soldiers patrolling the church and school like mindless machines all seemed like a nightmare from which Janneke could never awaken. The hostages were still standing at the wall. The guns were still trained on their backs.

As she looked around, two rows of German soldiers began to take shape, forming a line from the school to the now-empty church. A long procession of men emerged from the dimly lit school doorway. They walked quickly, quietly, between the two rows of armed soldiers, disappearing into the church, until not a one was left in the square. Once again, only the eerie square, the Germans, and their machines were left behind, as if the Putten men had never been there at all.

She tried, one more time, to get close to the death candidates but was stopped short by the same young soldier who had sent her away earlier that evening. However, Janneke knew now that her fluency in German had helped put him and the other soldiers she had encountered at ease, and she did not hesitate to use both her uniform and her good looks to her advantage. The young soldier returned her smile, looking a bit friendlier than before, as she moved closer and requested, "Could you let me check on the men at the wall, please? I have been instructed to care for anyone who may be weak or sick."

"No, I cannot do that. I have orders to let no one near them."

"Do you know what will happen to all the prisoners?"

The young man shrugged his shoulders but answered, "I am not sure I should tell you this, but our orders were to put all the men of Putten in the church and to keep men from outside of Putten in the school until morning. These death candidates, we are to lock them up separately in that hall over there." He pointed, and Janneke's eyes followed his gesture.

"The Eierhal? Would you believe that, before the war, all of Putten's eggs and chickens were traded in there?"

"Thank you for that very interesting historical fact." He smiled, took a pack of cigarettes from his pocket, and offered one to Janneke.

"No, thank you," she said. "I have to go now. Have a good evening."

"Will you be back tomorrow?"

"Probably. Good-bye," Janneke said as she walked away with just enough bounce in her step to suggest a little flirtation.

With nothing more to be done at the square that night, Janneke started back to the doctor's house. Mrs. Van Gulden let her in and quickly turned away, motioning for Janneke to follow her into the kitchen. Mrs. Van Gulden retrieved the receiver, which was off its hook, and continued her conversation.

Janneke sat at the table, waiting patiently. While she waited, a heavy weariness overtook her, and she could feel herself nodding off.

"Janneke, Dr. van Gulden wants to speak with you." Mrs. Van Gulden was holding the phone and pointing it toward her.

Janneke, startled back to wakefulness, got up from the table, took the phone from Mrs. Van Gulden, and placed it against her ear. Then, she updated the doctor on all that was going on. She begged him to stay away from the village until they knew what would happen to the men. The doctor told Janneke that he was very concerned for the safety of his family now and that he would send for them as soon as he believed it was safe. When he heard how "Nurse Janneke" had been able to move around the square and church, he said he would contact the other Putten doctors and ask them to send their nurses to the square tomorrow. If they could also move around freely, perhaps they could get medicine and even food to the men. When they ended their conversation, Janneke saw Mrs. Van Gulden had already left the kitchen, so she said goodbye and hung up.

Before heading upstairs, she called Pieter as she had promised. She learned her mother had made it home safely and had taken food to the men in hiding. Pieter said he would return to the farm in the morning to help her mother with the animals, so there was nothing more for her to be concerned about that night. She made her way up the steep stairs and closed the door to her room.

Exhausted, Janneke fell asleep.

Chapter Four

· · · · · · · · · · · · · · · · · · · ·

Monday, October 2, 1944

THE SUN HAD NOT YET CLEARED the rooftops, but the men of Putten were back on the square, cold and anxious. Death candidates remained at the wall, and a small group of nurses huddled nervously to one side.

"*Goedemorgen.* Thank you for coming," Janneke addressed the women, looking them over as she put her back to the breeze and wound her scarf closer to her neck. Janneke held up her medical kit. "Was anyone able to bring along emergency supplies or medicine?" In response, several of the women held up their kits. "Good. Let's team up so we can share our resources as we work. Okay. Now, please follow me quietly toward the men at the wall. Do not speak."

Janneke strode confidently toward the guard and found it was the same soldier. He held up his hand to stop her but greeted her respectfully enough, "Good morning, nurse. I see you brought back-up, but I still cannot let you through to attend to these men."

"I know," she answered with a warm smile. "But that is not what I came to see you about. Can you tell me who I should talk to about setting up a nurses' station? Who is in charge here at the square?"

"A nurses' station?" His shoulders softened just a little, and he nodded in seeming approval. "Well, then, I suppose you need to talk to Obersturm-führer Raschke. You will find him by the church entrance," he offered as he gestured in that direction.

Janneke nodded her head in thanks and left with the nurses to find this officer who was in charge. She approached the most important-looking soldier and asked in her best German, "Good morning, sir. Are you Ober-sturmführer Raschke?"

"Yes. What do you want?"

"My name is Janneke, and I have a team of nurses ready to assist you with medical needs. Where would you like us to set up the medical station?"

Startled by Janneke's directness and command of his native tongue, Oberstrumführer Raschke hesitated. Looking around, he seemed to ponder the best location. "Over there, perhaps," he began, pointing toward the back of the square. Suddenly, he looked back at Janneke. He glared at her. Then, he stood straighter, taller. "Wait. I know nothing about a medical assistance station. Who ordered you to do that?"

"The doctors of this village."

"Are those doctors in charge here?"

"No, sir, you are. The doctors told us you wanted any medical support that could be spared to report to the square. I, myself, was ordered here by your soldiers yesterday. The doctors assumed that, in so large a gathering of people, you believed there might be medical emergencies that would require attention."

"I do not know why they should care if they cannot bother to come help themselves. Still, they are right. You can set up in that hall over there." He pointed at the Eierhal where the death candidates had been held overnight.

"Thank you, sir," Janneke said. She moved as if to go, then looked toward the wall of hostages. She brought her gaze back around to the officer. "Sir, shall we check on the group at the wall over there before we go to the hall?"

"*Nein!*" he shouted, his face tightening into a grimace as he looked at Janneke in disbelief. "Have you not been told they are death candidates? They are your important men, yes? So they are there to ensure everyone will follow my orders. For every person who escapes or makes trouble, one will be shot. No one is to go near them. *Verstehst du?*"

"Yes, sir, I understand," Janneke said, clenching her teeth and repressing the urge to shout back even louder. She knew better, of course, than to pursue anything more with this officer. She motioned for the nurses to follow her to the Eierhal, and as they moved toward the hall, a couple more arrived and fell in step. A German patrol posted at the entrance searched their medical kits and bags before allowing them to pass.

Once cleared and inside, they found a side room with a table and chairs where they quickly set up their makeshift station. Janneke briefed the nurses on what she had experienced the day before.

"Our objective is to save as many of these men as we can from whatever atrocity these soldiers may have in mind. Anyone who is sick, bring them here and treat them as best as you can. Keep them here. Don't send them back out. We will begin with the school and the church. When finished, meet me back here."

Janneke sent three nurses to the church, asked a fourth to accompany her to the school, and instructed the others to remain at the station to treat the men as they were brought in.

A horrible stench greeted them as they entered the school. A stream of raw sewage was coming from the bathrooms, and it was flowing into the halls. The filth was nearly intolerable. Janneke wrapped her scarf around her nose and mouth while she ventured further inside. Most of the men had been removed earlier to the square, leaving only the teens and elders inside.

Janneke asked, "Is anyone here in need of medical help?"

An elderly man answered, "No, at least, I don't think so. They may even let us go. They told all the men between eighteen and fifty to go outside. The rest of us, they said, should stay here until further notice for supposedly when they release us."

Some of the men nodded in agreement.

One of the teens spoke up, "Yeah, it's better now, but we spent the night with so many in this stench hole that there was no place to lie down or sit. We couldn't even go to the bathroom. When I tried to go outside to pee, one of the guards stuck his gun in my face and yelled at me in German. I yelled back at him in Dutch, so he wouldn't understand, but my dad pulled me back inside."

"Good thing," Janneke replied. "Glad you're okay."

"You will let us know when we can go home, right?" the boy asked Janneke when she started to leave.

"Unfortunately, that won't be up to me. If I could, I would send everyone home now, including the men outside. I promise we will check back on you later. That's the best we can do."

"But we're hungry," he shouted as she and the other nurses walked away. "Bring us some food when you come back."

As Janneke and the nurses passed by the guard at the door, she called back over her shoulder, "I know you are hungry and I am so sorry."

The sun was over the rooftops now, though largely obscured by the low hanging sky offering little in the way of warmth or comfort. Janneke met up with three of the nurses emerging from the church. There, too, only boys under eighteen and men over fifty remained. Their main complaints were hunger and thirst. Only a few had asked for medicine, which the nurses dispensed if they had it in their kits.

On the square, the Germans had lined up the men in groups, five rows of twenty each. Janneke counted six full groups and another roughly half that size. She assigned a group to each nurse and left the balance to whomever got to them first. They began pulling men from the lines almost immediately, many barely able to walk. The German soldiers stopped the nurses almost as quickly as they took the men aside. Only they would decide who could leave their line for the medical station; however, they were quick to ask the nurses to remove anyone thought to be contagious. As soon as one man was taken from a row, the soldiers would send a replacement from the smaller group. Apparently, precision was important.

Janneke had chosen the group furthest from the nurses' station. Among them, she found her uncle Hans. He was married to her father's sister, and they had three small children.

"Uncle Hans," she whispered, "act like you are sick and come with me. Lean on me as if you can't walk."

"But I am fine, just hungry and thirsty," he whispered back.

"I know, but I may be able to get you out if they believe you are sick. Tell them you have influenza."

He put his arm around Janneke's shoulder and limped a bit as they walked toward the nurses' station.

"Janneke, if this does not work, will you please look in on my family? Tell your aunt Gerrie that I do not know why they are detaining me. I had nothing to do with any kind of attack. Once they understand I am innocent, they will surely send me home. Tell her I love her and the children very much."

Before Janneke could reply, a German soldier stopped them. He looked Uncle Hans over and sent him back to the line.

The soldier snarled at Janneke, "He certainly doesn't look sick to me. Do not overstep your bounds, nurse. I will be watching you."

Uncle Hans returned to the line, and Janneke went back to check on others in her group, finishing her uncle's row and moving onto the next. When she was just behind her uncle, she turned to his shoulder and whispered, "Uncle Hans, I'm so sorry it didn't work."

He whispered back, "Me, too, but thank you for trying. Oh, last night inside the church, I talked to your uncle Johan and cousin Dirk. They should be somewhere on the square, too."

"I will look for them. May God be with you, Uncle Hans."

* * *

Around ten o'clock women began to arrive on the square with supplies. All brought food, some also brought warmer clothes, and others brought medicine for their men. However, to their great disappointment, they were not allowed anywhere near their men on the square. The soldiers ordered them to take the food and supplies into the church.

Janneke followed the women into the church, thinking she may be able to collect medications for the men outside. She stepped back as hungry boys, who had spent the night in the church, grabbed for the food the women had with them, some grabbing it right out of their hands. Janneke intervened in some of the fights, as the women were determined to hang on to the food in hopes of getting it to their men outside.

One can hardly blame them, Janneke thought, after yesterday, standing in the square and then the night locked up in the church. They must be ravenous and terribly parched from thirst. Looking to distract them, Janneke climbed up onto a pew and shouted, "Listen up!"

She clapped her hands and shouted even louder, "Quiet please!"

This time, she got the attention of the people immediately surrounding her. They, in turn, shushed the people behind them.

"I will be in the front of the church to take in any medications that you have brought. The nurses will attempt to dispense them to our men on the square. Only medications, please. At this time, we are not allowed to take food or clothing to the men. Please form a line in the aisle."

Janneke took a seat in the front row. Before she could even talk to the first person in line, she heard a scuffle behind her. When Janneke turned around, she saw her aunt Ellie pushing her way to the front. Her teen daughters Ria and Hennie followed closely behind her. They apologized for their mother's rude behavior as they moved through the crowd to keep up with her.

"Janneke," exclaimed her aunt, "you've got to help us. Johan and Dirk are out there lined up on the square like prisoners. The soldiers won't even let me give these to them."

She held up two overcoats and a bag of food. Janneke saw other women holding up things they had brought, as well. To avoid further chaos among the villagers, she quickly said, "Aunt Ellie, please come sit next to me with the girls. I could use your help. For now, all we can do is get medication to our men. You three can help me list them. We will have to wait until later to see if we can get these other things to them." She took a notebook and pen from her kit and handed them to her aunt Ellie. "I'll tell you what to write down."

They took in medications for thirty-eight men, one unfilled prescription, and three doctors' work release forms. Before Janneke took these items to the nurses' station, she assured her aunt that she would check on Johan, her uncle, and Dirk, her cousin.

At the nurses' station, Janneke divided the medications among the nurses and instructed them to find those men and to try to bring them to the nurses' station. If the patrols would not allow that, they should hand the meds to the men, so they could hopefully take them later. Janneke took the unfilled prescription and the doctors' notes and started her rounds. Passing through one of the groups, Janneke heard someone frantically say, "Nurse! Nurse? Please, can you come here?" She made her way to the gentleman who whispered, "I am Mr. Pereboom, principal of the high school. I am carrying the payroll for all the teachers and need to get it to the school. Can you help me please?"

Janneke opened her bag, and the principal smiled as he discreetly transferred an envelope from his pocket to her bag.

As the nurses completed their rounds, Janneke made a second pass through the rows and found Johan and Dirk.

"Uncle Johan," she whispered, "Aunt Ellie and your daughters are in the church. They know you are here. I am so glad you and Dirk have been able to stay together."

Dirk showed her his fist and chimed in. "Yeah, just let them try and separate us. I'll…"

Johan grabbed his son's fist. "Easy, Dirk, easy. Please. We don't want any trouble." He turned to Janneke. "Sorry, Dirk is…well, cranky and hungry. I guess we all are. Once the missing soldier is found, surely they will let us go, right?"

Janneke shrugged her shoulders, but only because the soldier who had sent Uncle Hans back earlier was coming toward her now. He gestured that she should move on.

"I've got to go. That soldier is watching me."

Uncle Johan had seen the soldier as well. "Yah, okay, sure, go, Janneke. Tell my wife and daughters not to worry. All will be okay."

"I will. Good luck to both of you."

* * *

The church bell sounded twelve times over the square. The nurses had been able to move more than a dozen men into the station.

Janneke saw the same car she had seen the night before drive into the square. It was Otten's open car, but this time, there was a distinguished gray-haired German officer in the passenger seat. They stopped alongside the church entrance. From Otten's description the night before, the passenger had to be Commandant Fullriede. She started to make her way over to the car, hoping she could talk to him, but she was stopped short by a patrol. Otten's passenger stood up on the seat of the car, and Otten translated for him. "I am Commandant Fullriede. Orders from Germany are to transport all men between eighteen and fifty years old to Kamp Amersfoort. They will be held there until further orders are received. I am handing over the command for this transport to the SS soldiers."

An SS officer saluted Commander Fullriede and promptly began his task.

Janneke watched as thirty well-known dignitaries, who had been held as death candidates, were moved from the wall to the other side of the Dorpsstraat. They were ordered to lie down on the sidewalk with their faces to the ground.

On the square, each group of one hundred men was ordered to take a quarter turn to the left forming twenty rows of five wide in each group.

The procession moved out of the square and into the Dorpsstraat, passing by the death candidates on the sidewalk. Janneke could hear some of the men in the procession moan as they walked by that frightful sight. She, herself, felt like crying. She knew most of these men lying there, face down, with machine guns pointing at them.

Otten and Commandant Fullriede had disappeared into the church. Janneke and the nurses entered there just in time to hear Fullriede's announcements, which, once more, were translated by Otten. Standing on the second-floor balcony in the back of the church, they bellowed, "Saturday night, an attack on a German vehicle took place between Putten and Nijkerk, causing the death of a German officer. Anyone with information about this event is ordered to step forward."

He paused and looked around. Janneke heard some whispering among the women, but no one came forward.

"Well then, I have just ordered for the men on the square to be transported by train to Kamp Amersfoort, a prisoner holding camp. Furthermore, my orders are to evacuate the village and burn every single building. A farm near where the attack took place will be spared. They cared for a wounded German officer, bandaged him, and stopped one of our cars on the highway to take him to the hospital. This farmer will receive a *bescheinigung*, a notification that his house is exempt from destruction. Also, to the homes of policemen and others who are known to aid us in this war, a *bescheinigung* will be delivered. This document will be signed by me. It should be posted on the front door of the house. It serves as a sign to the soldiers who are carrying out my orders that the house is exempt and should not be set aflame. Anyone not receiving such a notification must leave the village before five o'clock this afternoon."

People, initially, were stunned. Then panic broke out. Women and children cried. Men moaned in total disbelief. In total horror, Janneke watched as people stormed out of the church. Some said that they were going to the train station to try and give their loved ones the food and warm clothes they had carried. Others said they were rushing home to gather important papers and personal items.

Janneke grabbed her medical kit and ran to Mrs. van Gulden's house to fetch her bicycle. All she could think was that she needed to go home to help her mother prepare for this horrible fate.

* * *

Mrs. van Gulden and a woman she did not recognize were loading an ambulance.

Janneke cried, "Mrs. van Gulden, you've got to leave immediately. The Germans are going to burn the whole village to the ground after five o'clock today."

Mrs. van Gulden stared at Janneke, bewildered. Finally, she uttered, "My husband called this morning to let me know he was sending an ambulance. He said to pack some clothes and things for the children for a few days, but if the house will be burned, there may be other things I need to take. Oh, Janneke, what should I take?"

"I don't know, Mrs. van Gulden. You need to call your husband and ask him."

Janneke mounted her bicycle. "I wish I could stay to help you, Mrs. van Gulden, but I have to go home and warn my mother. Thank you so much for letting me stay here last night."

"Of course," replied Mrs. van Gulden, "and thank you for all your help, Janneke. May God keep you safe."

Panicked and overwhelmed by guilt, Janneke pedaled out of the village. Would things have been different if she had spoken up about the whereabouts of the German officer? Commandant Fullriede had said a German officer died. Was he talking about Lieutenant Eggert who had been at Enny's Estate? Was there another officer who had escaped the attacked car? She needed to talk to Pieter.

* * *

Janneke was so out of breath when she arrived there that her words flew unchecked as soon as she was in his arms. "I feel like this is all my fault. I should have said something. I didn't, and now the Nazis are taking our men to Kamp Amersfoort, and they are going to burn down the village tonight. I, you…you need to pack and leave. I need to go home and help my mother pack."

While hugging her even tighter, Pieter replied, "Whoa! Slow down. None of this is your fault. Besides, only houses within the village borders are targeted to be burned. I am sure we will be okay out here. In fact, all of us living outside the residential area have been asked to open up our homes and farms to take in some of the people who have to leave the village."

She looked at him through her tears. "But…how…"

"I just got off the phone with the Putten police, and that is what they told me. They told me to notify neighboring farms and deliver that message."

"Then, would it be safe for Papa and Henk to come out of hiding?"

"No, not yet. German soldiers are still patrolling the area."

They held each other closer, now in silence.

"Feel better?" Pieter asked after a long moment.

"Not really," Janneke replied honestly. "I keep thinking of all those innocent families that are being ripped apart by the actions of these brutes. I just wish I could do more."

"My beautiful, courageous lady, you have already done so much. How many men were you able to get out of the lineup this morning?"

As she started to tell Pieter about the nurses' station in the Eierhal, she brought her hand to her mouth and exclaimed, "Oh, my God! I hope the men we took out were able to go home. I left the square in a panic after Commandant Fullriede's announcement. I don't know what happened to them."

Trying to keep her from blaming herself even more, Pieter asked, "Didn't you say there were men left in the church and the school as well? Maybe they left with them."

"Yes, I hope so. Thank you, love. You are so good for me. I think I can go on now." Janneke kissed Pieter goodbye and got back on her bicycle to ride home.

* * *

After she helped her mother get ready to take in some of the villagers, if needed, Janneke took food to the men in hiding. On her way to the bridge, she heard the singing of marching soldiers, first very faint, then getting stronger as she walked on. Next, she heard the pounding sound of boots on the road, coming closer and closer. She looked around and realized that it was still light enough for them to see her. How was she going to explain the food in her hands? She dove into the bushes which flanked the path she was on. Ouch! She forgot that these were berry bushes with very sharp thorns. There was no time to look for a different place to hide, so she endured the thorns.

The soldiers did not see her as they walked past. Before even attempting to get out of the bushes, she listened until she heard the sounds of their footsteps fade away. Scratched up and slightly bleeding, she continued on her way. At the bridge, she whistled, and Papa came out to meet her. He took one look at her and uttered, "Who did that to you? Have you been in a fight?"

"No, no, Papa. I had to hide because there was a German patrol on the road, and I chose the wrong bush to jump into. I really am fine. I have brought food for all of you because Pieter thinks it is better that you stay in hiding tonight. As I just experienced, the Germans are still patrolling this area."

"But," started Papa, "I need to be at the house to help your mother. How is she holding up?"

"She is doing okay, Papa. She is handling everything quite well. Let's go inside the cave, and I'll tell you about all that has happened today."

Janneke and her father entered the small cave where Henk and the two evacuees were huddled around a petroleum lamp. They had wrapped blankets around themselves to fend off the chill. She repeated that it was probably best for them to stay in hiding for another night. She told them about the men who were going to Kamp Amersfoort and that one of those men was Jacob.

The men gasped.

It was Henk who spoke first. "I am so sorry that we weren't able to stop him from leaving Pieter's house. Good thing the rest of us stayed."

Janneke looked at her father, who was shaking his head. He simply said, "Why him? He is a good man."

Janneke took her father's hands in hers and continued, "Papa, I also saw Uncle Johan, Cousin Dirk, and Uncle Hans on the square. It was my intent to take them out of the lineup to the nurses' station, but I didn't succeed. The last thing I need to tell you is that tonight those Nazis are going to burn down the residential area of the village. The people of Putten, who are left, have been ordered to leave by five o'clock. We will be okay out here. In fact, some of the people of the village may come to spend the night here at the farm."

Janneke had never seen her father cry before. Tears streamed down his cheeks as he pulled his hands from Janneke's and made them into fists. "I feel so helpless. There must be something we can do. Those brutes. How can we stop them?"

"Papa, the best thing we all can do right now is stay alive, and maybe in the future, we will be able to get some justice."

"Janneke, promise me that you will check on the families of Hans and Johan. Bring them to the farm if you can."

"I will, Papa. I'll see you tomorrow." She kissed her father on the cheek and inconspicuously put a handkerchief in his hand.

"I am so proud of you," he muttered before Janneke said good-bye to the rest of the men and left the cave.

While walking back to the house, she realized that she had to do one more thing that day, and that was to check on Mrs. Pouw at Enny's Estate. Janneke talked it over with Pieter, and he agreed that she should, but only if he could accompany her.

* * *

At Enny's Estate, things were much quieter than when Janneke had stopped by the day before. They found Mr. and Mrs. Pouw and Tex Banwell in the kitchen, eating dinner. Mrs. Pouw led Janneke and Pieter to the table. "Please join us. We just started."

Mrs. Pouw quickly set two more places and invited the two to help themselves to the stew that was simmering on the sturdy country kitchen stove.

"It's deer," she said, "shot on our property by yours truly just a few days ago. I am so used to cooking for an army, but there's no one left to cook for, so please help us eat it."

Pieter observed, "It is indeed very quiet here." Then, he inquired, "Where is everyone?"

"Well, I will spare you the details, but we were able to move all the people staying here except for my housekeeper, who insists that she is safe because she is German, and this gentleman, Mr. Banwell, who insists on staying here to protect us to the bitter end."

Janneke had noticed that, since they'd arrived there, all that had been spoken was English for Tex's sake. During her last visit, she had become more comfortable with English, so she chimed in, "Thank you for the good food. I did not realize how hungry I was." Then, Janneke turned to Mr. Pouw and asked, "How is Lieutenant Eggert?"

Surprised by the Janneke's question, Mr. Pouw looked at his wife. Mrs. Pouw explained, "Janneke knows. She was here yesterday when we were trying to decide what to do with Eggert."

"Well then," he started, "this morning, we blindfolded Lieutenant Eggert and took him to Voorthuizen, the town just south of here. We deposited him on the side of a road near a dairy farm with a note attached to his coat. The note was in Dutch and in German, explaining who he was. We took cover and waited. Soon, a farmer on his way to milk his cows found Eggert and put him on his cart. We can only assume that he took him to a German patrol post as the note requested."

Mrs. Pouw added, "By now, the Germans have to know that Lieutenant Eggert has been returned. Since he was blindfolded, we don't think he should be able to show anyone where he was held, but the Germans have their ways. Yesterday and today were spent clearing Enny's Estate. Mr. Pouw and I are leaving for Amsterdam in the morning."

Janneke, who could feel their sense of loss, replied, "It's so terribly sad that you have to leave this beautiful place on account of those brutes. But I have to think that you are doing the right thing. Today at the square, Commandant Fullriede mentioned a German officer who had died. Was Lieutenant Eggert wounded badly enough to have died, or was Fullriede talking about another officer who escaped from the attacked car?"

"That could not have been Lieutenant Eggert," Mr. Pouw answered. "He was in good shape and good spirits when we left him on the side of that road. He actually thanked us for caring for him and promised us that he would not let his superiors know where he had been held."

Tex jumped in and added, "According to Lieutenant Eggert, there were four soldiers in the car, two corporals and two officers, including himself. He said the two corporals immediately jumped out and ran into the woods. The other officer was also wounded but was able to walk away from the disabled car. They must be referring to the other wounded officer. Most likely, the two corporals made it back to headquarters and reported the attack. We are sure that their reports of what took place caused the Germans to surround the village so early on Sunday morning."

After hearing this, Janneke recounted all her experiences on the square that day to Tex and the Pouws. When she finished, she turned to Tex and said, "I believe I saw van Heesen lined up in the square. He was one of the resistance fighters in your group Saturday night, correct?" As Tex nodded, Janneke continued, "I only met him once. It was when I came here to deliver messages. I couldn't be sure it was him because I never was able to get close enough to him to talk to him."

Mrs. Pouw chimed in, "Van Heesen came here after the attack, but he insisted on going home in the middle of the night. He lives in Putten, so it could be entirely possible that he was picked up during the raid. You said, though, that no one came forward after repeated requests about knowledge of the attack. I truly appreciate and respect his silence. Things for the resistance and all of us here at Enny's Estate could have turned out quite differently if he had spoken up. I don't believe that it would have made a bit of difference to the Germans. The outcome for Putten would most likely have been the same."

"I sure hope so," Janneke responded, reflecting a bit of her own guilt about not speaking up.

Not knowing how they could be of any more help at Enny's Estate, Janneke and Pieter said their goodbyes after dinner and the day's update and left to go home.

* * *

Trying her best to stay on the narrow bike path beside the dirt road, Janneke rode behind Pieter through the dark woods. The bright moon lit up their path only once in a while when it peeked through the tree canopies high above them. Their bike lights, which were set up across the center of the handlebars to only shine down in order to not be seen by anyone, gave off very minimal light.

Janneke thought about the resistance fighters who must have used this same route to get to the place of attack on the highway. That was only a few nights ago, but so much had happened since then, and it seemed more like weeks ago. When they came to a large clearing in the trees, Pieter abruptly stopped, and Janneke nearly ran into him.

"Look!" Pieter gasped.

The grim truth of Fullriede's statements earlier that day faced them as the sky had taken on an orange-reddish color, and a huge black cloud of smoke towered upward, clearly visible against the blue night sky for miles around. Putten was burning. Horrified, they watched for several minutes, staring at the town in disbelief, despite the warnings that had come earlier in the day.

Janneke looked up at the sky. "I hear airplanes."

Arm in arm, they stood aghast as Allied planes, drawn to the light of the fires, circled over Putten. The sound of the droning planes combined with their relentless firing at targets in Putten made the whole spectacle even eerier.

Pieter felt Janneke shiver as she uttered, "Good God, the people who were exempt from the burning of their homes and stayed in Putten must be spending a very frightful night in their basements."

Janneke and Pieter watched the awful scene a while longer, and while walking close together back to their bikes at the side of the road, Janneke said, "Pieter, I promised my father and my uncles that I would check on their families. Will you go into the village with me tomorrow morning to see where they are and if they need help?"

Pieter's arm around Janneke's shoulder was immensely comforting to her. Their physical interaction was so rare that she savored his slightest touch when it did happen. It was usually interrupted by Pieter's nearly obsessive sense of duty, as it was this time. "Yes, of course, I will," he answered. "And if there is a police station left standing, I am sure they can use my help as well."

They mounted their bicycles and rode the rest of their way home without speaking, listening to the sound of the planes.

Chapter Five

TUESDAY, OCTOBER 3, 1944

AT DAYLIGHT, JANNEKE AND PIETER, BOTH dressed in their respective uniforms, rode their bicycles into the village. Each was lost in their thoughts about the eerie-looking sky from the night before, the orange of the fires mixed with black pillars of smoke against the backdrop of the moonlit dark blue sky. It was a sight they would never be able to forget. Both were wondering about what they would find in the village upon their arrival.

At the German checkpoint before entering the main part of the village, they showed their identification cards, stated their purpose, and were waved right through. This early in the humid chilly morning, the village was mostly deserted. The stench of wet burned wood hung heavy in the air. To Janneke, it smelled like a campfire that just recently had been doused.

Where the residential area began, a whole block of houses had been burned. Their roofs had collapsed onto the still-smoldering rubble. Parts of blackened brick walls and chimneys remained standing and stood out eerily against the sky. Some houses still stood, seemingly unaffected, but others were gone completely. Overnight, the war had become a reality to this peaceful village. It was heartbreaking to see the resulting damage.

To Janneke's and Pieter's great relief, many houses and businesses in the center of the village had not been torched. In the Dorpstraat, most of the buildings were intact, although many store windows had been smashed, and it looked like the stores had been looted. Thankfully, Dr. van Gulden's house had escaped the flames. At the square, the church, the school, and the Eierhal were untouched, but Café/Restaurant De Heerdt had been destroyed. Just yesterday, the hostages had stood there, facing the wall. Today, only partial walls were left standing. Here, too, the rubble was still smoldering.

The village shopkeepers had started to arrive in the heart of Putten, to assess the damage to their establishments. They were obviously relieved their stores had not been burned. They were standing in the street, commiserating with each other. Even though the buildings had been saved, the damage caused by the looting German soldiers was substantial, and there would be so much to clean up and repair.

After their tour of the village, Janneke and Pieter made their way to the police station. Fortunately, it was also untouched. They found Otten, the temporary head of police, in the station. He was meeting with a group of policemen but waved them in and finished his briefing.

A preliminary count suggested that around one hundred houses had been burned, most of them on the southeast side of the village, the opposite side from where Janneke and Pieter had come.

Otten was functioning as the temporary police chief because the former German-friendly chief had left his post on *Dolle Dinsdag* or Mad Tuesday, the day early in September 1944 when the Dutch thought the war had ended. He had not returned to the village.

Otten told Janneke and Pieter that, the day before, Commandant Fullriede had indicated that he did not have enough fuel to burn the whole village and that he had to get the soldiers back to their posts to continue fighting the battles at the front around Arnhem. Otten argued that he had pleaded with Commandant Fullriede to do everything in his power to spare, at least, the core of this historic village. Fullriede had responded that, although he did not personally want to burn the village, those were his orders.

Janneke soon left to fulfill her promise to her father that she would check on the whereabouts of his sister's and brother's families. Pieter stayed at the police station to lend a hand with the overwhelming tasks they would face that day. First Janneke went to Aunt Gerrie and Uncle Hans's house, which was closest to the police station. She was relieved to find that the houses in this area seemed to be mostly untouched. She parked her bike against the wall of the large industrial structure that housed Uncle Hans's construction business and walked the brick path that led through a substantial, well-kept garden to the house.

The backdoor stood open, so she walked in and found her aunt sitting at the kitchen table, sobbing and praying, seemingly unaware that someone had entered the kitchen. Janneke gently touched her shoulder.

Aunt Gerrie jumped up and let out a fearful scream. When she realized that it was Janneke, she exclaimed, "My heavens, Janneke! You scared me. Where did you come from?" She hastily hugged Janneke. Then, she nervously continued, "No telling who may have been in this house last night. I found the kitchen door wide open, but nothing seems to be missing."

Janneke, knowing that it had to be very difficult for this proud and stoic woman to show others her pain, responded, "Aunt Gerrie, I am so glad to see that you are okay and that the house has been spared. Last night, Pieter and I watched from outside of Putten as the sky turned orange and then black from smoke. The village had been set ablaze. We rode in this morning to check on family. I am here to make sure that you and the children are okay. Where are the children?"

Bewildered, Aunt Gerrie answered, "The children are fine, but I haven't a clue what might have happened to your uncle Hans. He left for church on Sunday while I stayed home with the children. He never came home. Oh, Janneke! What has happened out there? My neighbors told me about all the men that were rounded up and marched off to the train station. Is he one of them? If so, why? He most certainly did not do anything wrong! It just cannot be. We need him here. When will he be back?"

Janneke, wanting to temporarily get her aunt's mind onto something else, interjected, "Aunt Gerrie, could we have some hot tea, please?"

She looked at Janneke as if she had not realized her presence before. She uttered, "Oh, my gosh, dear, where are my manners? How do you take your tea? Please sit down, and I'll have tea for us in a minute."

She rushed around, and pretty soon, two steaming cups of tea and a plate of cookies were put down on the kitchen table. The fragile and familiar porcelain teacups and saucers were such a contrast to the cold reality of what Janneke was about to tell her aunt.

Janneke put her hands over her aunt's hands, which were clenched together in front of her on the table.

"Aunt Gerrie, I spoke with Uncle Hans yesterday on the square. He was indeed one of the men who were marched off to the train station."

Aunt Gerrie's eyes teared up. She freed her hands, jumped up again, and asked, "What were you doing there? And what did he say? Do you know when he'll be back?"

Janneke felt an unimaginable sadness come over her. She so wished she had been able to bring her better news. She continued, "The Germans rounded up over six hundred men in Putten as punishment for an attack on one of their motor cars, killing one German officer and leaving another one missing. The men of Putten were brought to the square and kept overnight in the church while the soldiers waited for orders from Germany about what to do with them. I was in the square because the German soldiers allowed some nurses to be there to help sick people. They are afraid of catching illnesses, so they let us remove the sick. I ran into Uncle Hans and tried to get him out, but we were stopped by a German soldier who said that he did not look sick. Since I did not have anything to prove that Uncle Hans was sick, he had to return to the lineup. Uncle Hans asked me to tell you that he loves you and the children very much and that he will surely be released when the Germans realize he has not done anything wrong."

To give her aunt just a sliver of hope, she added, "With the front so close, the war could be over soon. I would hope that the Germans would then return these men to Putten."

While she listened to Janneke, Aunt Gerrie paced back and forth, wringing her hands, tears rolling down her cheeks. She finally uttered, "I will leave it in God's hands to return Hans to us."

Janneke recently had started to doubt there was a God. She quickly changed the subject. "Where are the children?"

Aunt Gerrie sat back down at the kitchen table. "The children are with friends in Ermelo. Yesterday afternoon, my neighbor came to tell me that we had to evacuate the village. After she found out that Hans had not returned on Sunday, she offered to give us a ride on their horse-drawn cart. In the little time I had, I grabbed some things for the children...a couple of blankets, some food, and a box with our important papers. It was awful, but I had to be strong for the children. I told the children we were going on a short vacation. Annie kept asking when Father would be back and if he was coming with us on our vacation. Robbie and Sammie, because they are younger than Annie, were less aware of their father's absence. They thought it was great fun to travel on a cart pulled by a horse."

Janneke was relieved that the children were safe and well cared for in Ermelo. She asked, "When do you plan to bring them back here?"

Aunt Gerrie hung her head and sighed, "I truly don't know. That is what I was praying about when you came in. If I bring them home, they will notice that their father isn't here. Our friends in Ermelo also have small children, so they are fine there, but I don't want to take advantage of their kindness for too long. Besides, I need to be here in case Hans does come back."

She started praying again, asking God to bring her husband back soon and to give her strength. Before Janneke left, she prayed with her aunt. Janneke understood that her aunt received her strength from her trust in God and, because of that, she would most likely be fine, regardless of what happened.

* * *

Next, Janneke set out to check on Aunt Ellie and her two teenage daughters. In this section of the village, many houses had burned. Just yesterday, these houses were pristine with shiny clean windows, small manicured yards and well-tended gardens behind them. Most had completely collapsed. Gray ash and debris covered the whole area. Discouraged, Janneke got off her bike and walked the rest of the way to her aunt's house.

The scene was surreal. Women were consoling each other in the streets. Children were crying, and pets were running around, apparently lost and without their owners. As Janneke walked on, her sadness changed into anger toward the horrible people who'd done this. But knowing that her anger wasn't going to solve anything, a feeling of helplessness and great empathy took its place. These poor people were totally innocent and disconnected from the events of a few nights ago on the other side of the village. How could humans be so cruel to other humans?

She found her aunt and her two teenage cousins gathered together in front of their burned home. Janneke broke down and sobbed with them. Suddenly, Aunt Ellie burst out and started cursing. Janneke had never seen her aunt this way, and it also frightened the girls. Aunt Ellie lifted her arms, and with clenched fists, she motioned to the sky and yelled, "You! You so-called loving God! Is this how you show your love? You take my husband and my eighteen-year-old son away from me, and now you leave us with nothing, no place to live, no food, no clothes?"

Janneke took her aunt's fists and held them close to her until her aunt relaxed. In a soft voice, Janneke said, "Aunt Ellie, I did get to speak with Uncle Johan and Dirk in the square yesterday. There was no way to get them out of the lineup."

Janneke had not expected her aunt's angry reply. "Oh, great, how are we going to live? I had just finished canning for the winter. Now, all the food is gone. How are we going to eat, and more importantly, where are we going to live? We are left with only the clothes on our backs because we could not make it back in time from the train station to get anything." She cursed again. Then, she looked at Janneke, bewildered, and asked, "What are we going to do?"

Janneke turned to her teenage cousins, Ria and Hennie. "Do you still have your bicycles hidden anywhere?"

They shook their heads. During the past few years, the German soldiers had claimed most modes of transportation like bicycles, motorbikes, and horses from the people in the countries they occupied. Some people had been able to hide their bikes, but most could not. Janneke had been able to keep hers because her *ausweis* (ID) stated that she was a nurse, which gave her permission to have a bicycle.

Hennie, who was sobbing now, said, "Janneke, we looked for our dog

Peppi, and we can't find him. He must be so scared. Will you help us find him, please?"

Janneke hugged the girls. She could only imagine the loss they must have been feeling. She offered, "Dogs almost always come back to the place where they belong, so we will come back and look for Peppi later. Right now, though, we have to get you to a place to get some food and to be safe."

Janneke turned back to her aunt. "Aunt Ellie, take the girls to my parents' farm. Papa said to please come and stay there. There is plenty of food and room for all three of you. I know it's a long walk, but if you leave right now, you will get there by mid-afternoon."

"Oh, Janneke, you have to come with us," exclaimed Aunt Ellie. "I don't want a repeat of this morning. Those Nazis at the checkpoint coming back into the village were drunk. They whistled and groped at my girls, joking and laughing about how last night, before they torched Café/Restaurant De Heerdt, they partied and drank almost all the alcohol and what was left they took with them. They are scum. If they even try to touch my girls, I will hurt them where the sun doesn't shine."

Janneke wanted to smile at her aunt's use of metaphor. She could certainly understand that it must have been a frightening experience for her aunt and the girls. She explained, "Aunt Ellie, I won't be able to go with you all the way to the farm, since I need to go back to the police station, but I will walk with you to where the highway begins at the edge of the village. Past there, you most likely won't encounter any checkpoints."

The girls were visibly relieved. Janneke was their cousin, not all that much older than they were, but to them, she exuded authority, and they felt safe with her. On the way, they went on about visiting the farm and playing with the animals. They couldn't have imagined that their time at the farm would not be temporary; instead, it would become their home for a long time.

* * *

With a heavy heart, Janneke said good-bye when they reached the highway. In parting, she said that she would see them at dinner that evening. Janneke returned to the police station where she looked around for Pieter.

A police officer, who was using one of the desks, told her that Pieter had gone out on patrol with some of the other officers. He handed her a note from Dr. van Gulden.

The doctor had called that morning to check on the situation in Putten. Upon hearing the news that the Germans had mostly pulled out of the village and that his house had not been burned, he had stated that he would immediately return to his medical practice. The scribbled message asked Janneke to round up the rest of the staff and to have them all be back at work in the morning.

Janneke climbed back on her bicycle to deliver the doctor's message to her three coworkers. She then rode to the doctor's house.

The same ambulance that was there yesterday to pick up Mrs. van Gulden and the children was parked in front of the doctor's house. After climbing the tile stairs, she lifted the door knocker. Even before it bounced in its receptor, Dr. van Gulden opened the door and heartily greeted her, "Janneke, I saw you coming. It's so good to see you. Thank you for helping my wife these past few days. I am so grateful that you could be here when I could not."

"Oh, you are welcome, doctor. That's my job," uttered Janneke, humbly, even though she knew that it was way beyond the duties of her job.

"Are your wife and children back as well?"

He waved her into his house and answered, "No, I left them with our friends in Harderwijk. I will bring them back when I know with certainty that all is safe. Did you receive my message about going back to work tomorrow?"

"Yes, I did," she replied. "I went by the houses of the rest of the staff, which, fortunately, were also spared from the fires, and they will be here tomorrow at the usual starting time."

"Great. Thank you, Janneke. I anticipate that we will be very busy."

He walked toward the kitchen and went on to say, "I have to unload the ambulance. Would you have time to stay to make some coffee and prepare some sandwiches? I have not eaten since early morning, and you must be hungry as well?"

When the doctor and Janneke sat down to eat, she updated him on all that had happened over the past few days, of course, omitting the details about the attack and about Enny's Estate. If it became known to him or in the village that she had any knowledge of the resistance movements around Putten, she would not be able to carry on her job at the medical practice any longer.

The doctor echoed what Janneke had heard earlier at the police station— that the resistance was the cause of this terrible crime and that, if the perpetrators had immediately come forward, this punishment could have been avoided or, at least, been much less severe. Janneke did not react to that statement.

Before she left, she asked the doctor if he knew what might happen to the men that had been transported to Kamp Amersfoort. He said that rumor had it they would be taken to work camps in Germany, but he hoped that before that happened the war would be over. He said that, for now, the most urgent thing was to help the people who were left in the village, especially those who were left homeless.

Chapter Six

· · · · · · · · · · · · · · · · · · ·

KAMP AMERSFOORT – NETHERLAND

THE SOUND OF HUNDREDS OF FOOTSTEPS echoed eerily through Putten's otherwise deserted streets. Dirk and Johan, along with so many unfortunate innocent men, were led away like prisoners. Dirk saw curtains moving at some of the houses as they passed. Until they were pulled away by their mothers, children were curiously peeking out to see what was happening.

Dirk kept whispering to his father about making a run for it, but between the many soldiers surrounding them and the manned machine guns that had been placed at each intersection, they could not see clear to do it.

At the train station, the procession crossed the railroad where the men were ordered to sit under the large trees, out of sight of any circling allied reconnaissance planes. Women and children, many carrying food and coats, were arriving at the train station, hoping to be able to say goodbye to their husbands, sons, and fathers. The German soldiers had closed the crossing gates to keep them away from the prisoners. Dirk spied his mother and sisters among them. At the thought of their carrying food, he jumped up and waved his arms, yelling, "Mom! Hennie! Ria! Over here!"

Johan pulled him down as one of the guards started to come their way.

Before the guard reached them, he said, "Son, you are going to get us in trouble. Sit down."

"But, Father, they have food. I am hungry."

"We are all hungry, but please be quiet. That guard is coming for you."

Dirk grudgingly stayed seated. He hissed under his breath, "Not fair. I bet these soldiers haven't skipped a meal. They must know that we are starving."

The approaching soldier could not have been much older than Dirk himself. He stopped and looked down at Dirk. "Is there a problem?"

"Yes, there is a problem. I'm hungry."

The soldier nodded and offered, "I don't have any food for you, but if you promise not to give me any more problems, you can have these cigarettes." Dirk eagerly accepted the cigarettes. He had run out the night before. After the soldier went on his way, Dirk offered his father a cigarette.

Johan shook his head. "No, thanks. You were lucky not to get a beating, son."

Dirk offered cigarettes to those immediately around him. This temporarily took his mind off his grumbling belly. He lit his cigarette and after a few moments, his father decided to take one after all.

Late in the afternoon, orders were barked for the prisoners to stand up and form the same groups as when they arrived earlier. Train cars that were normally used for cattle had been joined to a locomotive, and the train was waiting on the track.

With SS soldiers pointing their loaded guns at them, approximately fifty men were loaded into each rail car, standing room only. Dirk secured a place in the corner, just to the left of the door opening in the car. "Over here, Father, we can see outside through the wooden slats."

Johan heard women's voices over the shouting German soldiers. "Listen," he said. "It sounds like the women are coming closer. They are shouting something. What are they saying?"

The guard at the door of the rail car grinned from ear to ear, and in perfect Dutch, he said, "They want you to know that tonight my good SS buddies are going to have a bonfire in your village. Everything will be burned. Not a house will be standing. I wish I could be there."

Johan had to hold Dirk back from decking the guard. Most men in the rail car had heard what the guard said. As the train started to move, some brave women were running on the platform beside the train, shouting, confirming what the guard had so smugly announced.

The train took off, on its way to Amersfoort, passing farms and villages so very familiar to the men from Putten. The mood among the prisoners was very subdued until Dirk grabbed the crossbars of the freight car and started shaking them with all his might. "This is not fair. We did not do anything to these Nazis. We've got to get off this train to stop them."

A guard turned around and pointed his gun directly at Dirk. "Quiet, or I'll shoot."

Dirk felt his father's arm around his shoulder. His father firmly said, "Calm down, son."

Dirk looked at his father, desperation filled his eyes with tears. "But, Father, how can you stay so calm? They are going to burn our houses. We did not do anything wrong. Why are these Nazis doing this to us? We need to get out of here."

"I know, son. I am worried, too," he said solemnly as he felt around in his pockets and found a small notebook with a tiny pencil attached. He took it out and handed it to Dirk. "Here. Write a note to your mother. Let her know that we are together. Tell her we love her and that we will be okay."

Dirk scribbled, tore off the page, and wrote his mother's name and address on the back. He stuck his hand through the slats of the freight car and let it go. He saw others do the same thing. A number of notes had been tossed from the train.

After traveling for about twenty minutes, the train stopped in Amersfoort, just short of the train station. The SS soldiers pushed the prisoners, shouting at them to quickly get out of the train cars, "*Heraus. Schnell. Schnell.*"

The prisoners jumped from the freight cars, onto the tracks. Dirk looked around and whispered to his father, "Maybe…here…we can make a run for it."

Johan whispered back, "Son, there are too many armed soldiers watching us. Maybe there will be an opportunity later."

As soon as the words were out of his mouth, Johan received a blow to his ribs from one of the SS soldiers, who warned him to be quiet and not to talk, "*Schweigen man. Es ist verboten zu sprechen.*"

With his hands made into fists, Dirk started to move toward the soldier who had hit his father, but Johan again was able to hold him back. He whispered, "If you keep this up, we will be shot right here. Please, son, stay calm."

The Nazi punk smirked at them and moved on down the line.

After everyone had disembarked the train, they were ordered to walk between the rails, away from the station. The procession of well over six hundred men, still guarded by SS soldiers, started moving.

The soldiers urged their prisoners on, constantly yelling at them to hurry up ("*Schnell. Schnell. Mach schnell.*") and by ribbing them with the butts of their guns. The yelling made the chilly evening feel even colder as they walked toward a crossroad. Dirk began to wonder if the Germans ever talked in a normal voice.

At the beginning of the long procession, a prisoner stepped from between the rails and started running away from the tracks. Immediately, a shot rang out. It did not hit him, but it did make him stop.

While the rest of the group walked past, several soldiers were working him over. The poor man received such a beating that Dirk abandoned his thoughts of escaping for now.

After they had passed the scene of this gruesome beating, Dirk made sure there weren't any soldiers near to hear them when he said to his father, "When we get away from these brutes, I'm joining the resistance and fighting them any way I can. I'd like to kill me a few of these Nazis now."

Johan, worried that Dirk's mouth would eventually get him in trouble, said, "Son, from here on out, I wish you would speak in our dialect. Some of these guards speak Dutch."

Dirk grumbled, "Even worse, some of our own are joining the Nazis. I hope that, after the war, we get to work over those deserters and make 'em beg for mercy before we put bullets through their heads."

The procession turned left at the crossroad. The journey continued through the city of Amersfoort. Like that afternoon in Putten, the side roads had been blocked off by German military trucks manned with soldiers holding machine guns at the ready.

As the darkness of the night started to set in, the procession arrived at the camp.

"Why are they taking us here, Father? What is this Kamp Amersfoort?" whispered Dirk.

Johan whispered back, "Before the war, this was a Dutch army camp. Then the Germans took it over, and during the first three years of the war, they used it to confine Jewish prisoners before they were transported to the concentration camps in Poland and Germany. I heard that they now use it as a Nazi police transit camp for Dutch prisoners from many forbidden and blacklisted groups."

"People like us, who didn't do anything wrong?" inquired Dirk.

"Yes, mostly. Anyone not agreeing with the Germans or working against them, like captured resistance fighters, illegal butchers, black-market traffickers, homosexuals, gypsies, and non-German friendly Protestant and Catholic clergy—"

"But, Father," interrupted Dirk, "we aren't any of those. Why are they taking us here?"

"Well, son, apparently the Germans feel that we did something to work against them."

As the men entered the camp, a guard at the gate hollered at the accompanying SS soldiers, "Great catch. Who are they?"

Dirk could not understand the answer because of the shouting of other guards around them, something about turning in identification papers and receiving a colored patch to attach to their clothing.

Dirk and Johan were both surprised that they did not have to hand over any personal belongings at this time. But the heavy barbwire fence surrounding the camp, the prison towers, and the armed guards were a sure sign that they were imprisoned, locked up like criminals.

While the men waited on a plaza to be assigned to barracks, they got a taste of what was to come. Someone asked a guard if there would be food. The brute laughed, pulled him out of the line, kicked him to the ground, and yelled, "You are concerned about food? You should be concerned about your life."

Elsewhere in the line, a man collapsed. Two guards picked him up and threw him to the side, to be put on a stretcher and taken away a few minutes later.

Finally, the men were allowed in the barracks. They were spread out among several of them. Once they were inside, they found rows of wooden bunk beds with straw mattresses and thin cotton blankets. Other prisoners were already in some of the bunks. There weren't enough for everybody to have their own, so they had to double up.

Dirk and Johan shared a single bunk. The two sat down on the side of the bed. As soon as the guards were out of sight, Dirk felt his father's hand on his shoulder. "Son, just a few words of advice to survive this hell," he started. "Blend in with the group. Don't try to be a hero. Cooperate, even if you are told to do something you don't want to do. I know that will be very hard at times. Always remember that our revenge will come but only if we stay alive."

While listening, Dirk had been scratching his legs. He pulled up his pant leg and saw several fleas crawling around on his leg. He jumped up, outraged, stamping his feet as to shake them off, but to no avail. The whole barracks was infested with fleas and, as they soon found out, lice as well.

The guards came through, yelling, "Lights out in fifteen minutes."

From the bunk above, a head peeked over the edge. "You'll get used to them…the fleas, I mean. Where are you all from?"

"Putten," Dirk replied.

The man, dressed in only his underpants, jumped down from the upper bunk.

"So am I. My name is Bram."

"Nice to meet you, Bram. I am Dirk, and this is my father, Johan."

The men all shook hands as Bram told Dirk, "I overheard your father's advice, and he is right. I have been here for a few weeks. It's better to lay low. If you have any questions, let me know." Bram then turned to Johan. "My brother and I are contract butchers. We were picked up for illegally slaughtering pigs for farmers who did not want to share their meat with the Germans. What brought so many of you here?"

"Retaliation for a deadly attack on a German car at the Oldenaller Bridge," answered Johan.

"All of you were involved in that attack?"

"No, none of us had anything to do with that, but no one claimed responsibility for the attack, so the Nazis are punishing the whole village for the death of only one of their officers."

"Sure seems extreme, but they have done that in other countries just to make a point."

Bram looked around. "I wonder if there is anyone in your group who has word about my family. Right now, though, it's lights out, so you'd better turn in. Those guards love to beat on us."

"One more thing you should know," said Johan as Bram started to climb back up to his bunk, "Tonight, the Germans are burning down all houses in Putten."

Bram's fist hit the frame of the bunk so hard his knuckles started to bleed, and all he could utter was, "So helpless. I feel so helpless."

A guard, bouncing a bat off his hand, entered the barracks to make his last round for the night. Dirk and Johan had no time to undress. They jumped fully clothed into the single bunk and wrestled with the small cotton blanket, in an effort to hide that they still had their clothes on.

The guard stopped a few bunks before theirs. He pulled one of the new arrivals from his bunk onto the floor and yelled that they were to undress and for him to do it now. So far, his bat had only been hitting the side of the bunk, but as soon as the poor man was undressed, the bat landed several times on his naked body. He collapsed, screaming for mercy.

Dirk and Johan took advantage of the guard's diversion and quickly took off their pants, which they put in plain sight at the end of their bunk next to their jackets. It worked, the guard passed them by and turned off the light. In pitch-black darkness, their stomachs growling, the two tried to find a way to finally get some sleep.

* * *

After a miserable night of tossing, turning, and scratching, morning came all too soon. The light flicked on, and the guard started hitting the sides of the bunks while yelling for the men to get up fast, "*Heraus! Schnell! Schnell!*"

Bram jumped down from the bunk above them, fully dressed this time.

"Hurry," he said. "The earlier you go outside, the more likely you are to get your piece of bread. They will probably run out, since all of you just came in last night."

"Bread?" Dirk's eyes lit up. "Where?"

"Just outside that door. They'll hand it to you when you go outside."

"Why are we going outside? It's only five-thirty in the morning."

"Ah, another thing to get used to," explained Bram. "This happens every morning. We have to line up outside for roll call. The patch you received when you arrived, do you have it?"

"Sure," Dirk answered and pulled it out of his pocket.

"Very important. You've got to put it on your clothes, where they can see it. See the color? Once you are outside, find the people that have the same color patches and get in line with them."

When they were dressed, Dirk and Johan followed Bram outside. Fortunately, they had not run out of bread yet. Dirk devoured his as soon as it was put in his hand. It was the first thing they had eaten in two days. Johan ate half of his and gave the other half to Dirk. It, too, disappeared in no time at all. Their next concern was to find something to drink. The bread felt like a huge lump in Dirk's throat. He looked around. They were on a paved square in between the barracks. Spotlights from the prison towers lit up the area. Dirk spied a hand pump in the middle of the square. Bram saw him eyeing the pump. He whispered, "Dirk, don't even think about it. Good way to get a beating or be put in the Rose Garden."

"What's the Rose Garden?"

Bram pointed toward the other side of the barracks and explained, "If you cross Kotella, the head of the camp, he'll punish you by making you stand in a small area between barbed wire, which he named the Rose Garden. Some are there for days, come rain or shine. Now go find your group so the guards can get a count. At lunch, you will get soup."

Dirk's eyes drifted one more time from the water pump to the Rose Garden. *Not worth it,* he thought.

He spotted his uncle Hans on the other side of the square and took his father by the arm. "Come, Father. I think we should be over there."

They made their way over to the group from Putten, but the guard would not let them go to where Hans was. They were told to get in line at the end. Once all the prisoners were present on the square, the guards began their count.

The prisoners were left standing on the square for about three hours. Talking was not allowed, they learned. That, too, could earn them a beating. Dirk noticed that the temperature had dropped considerably right before sunup. He shivered. His jacket wasn't warm enough. He wished he had worn his winter overcoat when they had left the house on Sunday. Once it was light, Dirk looked around for possible escape routes. He could not see any.

Dutch-speaking SS guards finally came out and shouted that the prisoners were dismissed to begin their work. The newcomers from Putten were told to remain in the square, so they could be given work duties. The guard asked what their jobs at home were, and work in the camp was assigned accordingly.

Dirk, who had worked for a tailor in Putten, was sent to the room where the camp guards' clothes were repaired and patches were sewn on to the prisoners' clothing.

Johan got potato duty. He was sent out with other prisoners to dig up potatoes in a neighboring field. They were guarded by armed SS soldiers while outside the fence of the camp. Dirk found out later that Uncle Hans was assigned to maintenance of the buildings.

At lunch, everyone was paraded through the kitchen to receive their daily bowl of thin, bland potato soup and a piece of white bread before going back to work. Evenings were spent in the barracks talking, telling stories, playing cards, and writing letters.

Day and night, the distant sound of rumbling anti-aircraft guns and canons could be heard. Friday brought a huge surprise for the prisoners. All new arrivals received a Red Cross food parcel. Dirk could not believe his eyes when he opened the packet. "Father, look," he exclaimed as he went through the parcel piece by piece, "there is cheese, butter, crackers, raisins, herring, salmon, luncheon meat, biscuits, jam, coffee, tea, sugar, and chocolates. And what's this? Oh, soap and cigarettes."

He danced around in the aisle in front of their bunk. He had displayed the canned and boxed goodies on their bed. Johan left his goodies in the box.

"Bram, did you see this. Did you get one, too?"

Bram peeked his head over the edge of the upper bunk. "Not today. I got one last week. Enjoy it, young man. Don't eat it all at once, or you'll get sick. Trade the things you don't want with others. You don't smoke, do you? I can take the cigarettes off your hands, if you're willing to trade them for a deck of cards?"

"I do smoke, but you can have one of the packs."

Dirk tossed the cigarettes up to Bram's bunk, who handed Dirk a well-used deck of cards.

"Those are my lucky cards. They have won me many cigarettes. Take good care of them, okay?"

"Thanks, Bram. Will you teach us how to play?"

"You bet I will. We'll start tomorrow. I want to finish my book tonight before the lights go out."

Johan was curious now. "Where did you get the book, Bram?"

"Also won it in a card game. It'll get me into the next card game. I'll probably be able to trade it for another deck of cards."

Johan looked at Dirk. "Sounds like we need to learn how to play, son. Could come in very handy down the line."

During the next few days, lots of trades were made among the prisoners. Things were even traded with some of the guards.

* * *

A week had passed since their arrival. The Red Cross parcel had been the main excitement. On Wednesday, October eleventh, something changed. The prisoners were left standing in the square all day. There was no dismissal to go to work. No food or anything to drink all day. The rumbling noises in the distance seemed to have subsided. The guards seemed nervous.

"What do you think is up? Do you think the war is over?" whispered Dirk to his father.

Johan looked around to make sure no guards were near and whispered back, "One can only hope, son. Rumor is that the Germans are losing the fight. One of the guards in the potato field told me that the Allied troops have advanced into Germany from France and Belgium."

Later in the afternoon, rumors surged through the lines that they would be transported. At sunset, additional guards came into the square and divided the waiting men into groups of one hundred. The rumors apparently were correct.

Curious, Dirk asked his father, "There is no way they can move us by train, is there? I heard in the workshop that the Allied planes have bombed huge holes in the rails everywhere."

"That might be true," Johan responded, "but the Germans patch them up as quickly as they are damaged. When I was working in Putten on one of the farms close to the railway, I barely escaped a roundup of men needed to fix the railroad. It had been bombed the night before. The Germans desperately need the rail system to conduct their war, and the Allies know it, so they keep bombing it. I assume that we will be left standing here today to wait until the rail is fixed so they can move us."

Dirk admired his father's wisdom but grumbled, "I guess we shouldn't lose hope. Maybe one of us can escape from the train."

Johan had an opportunity to escape when he had been sent out to harvest potatoes from the fields outside the camp, but he did not act on it because he did not want to leave Dirk behind. They had talked about it and had made a pact. If any opportunity presented itself again, they would take advantage of it, even if it meant leaving the other behind. They agreed that it would be well worth it if, at least, one of them was able to make it home to the women.

* * *

It was nighttime before the men were ordered to start moving out the gate. This time, the heavily guarded procession did not go through the city streets of Amersfoort; instead, they marched in total darkness on roads around the city. Near the train station, all roads had been blocked off, so the townspeople would not witness this major departure.

Approximately two thousand men were lined up on the train station platforms, including the six hundred from Putten. The rumor mill had it that they were going to German work camps. This actually gave a number of the men waiting to board the train some hope; they had been to Germany earlier during the war and had worked in the factories. They said that, at least then, they were housed and adequately fed. During the early years of the *Arbeitseinsatz*, men working in the German factories were allowed short leaves to go home to visit their families. When too many went into hiding and did not return to Germany, that privilege was taken away. Instead of laborers, they were then considered prisoners.

At the train station, German SS soldiers were everywhere, armed with loaded guns. Dirk realized that trying to escape here would mean a certain death.

The SS soldiers pushed the prisoners into the awaiting train, yelling their usual, "*Los! Los! Schnell! Schnell!*"

The train seemed to move for days. No drink or food was provided to the prisoners. They had to look on as the guarding SS soldiers ate and drank their rations. The toilets in the trains had been locked and only could be used by the guards. Bathroom breaks for the prisoners happened when the train was stopped. Five men at the time would have to relieve themselves next to the train with several guards pointing guns at them.

On Friday morning, the train came to a stop in the middle of farm country, right before the border into Germany would be crossed. They were held up there the whole day until a bombed-out rail line had been repaired.

Allied planes were circling overhead. In fear that the waiting train would be shelled or bombed, the SS soldiers exited the train and took cover on either side of it, pointing their machine guns back at the train, in case anyone attempted to flee.

The prisoners were fearful. They were tired, thirsty, and absolutely famished. Johan nudged Dirk. "Look. Turnips are growing in the field out there. We could eat those if we could get to them."

Dirk's eyes lit up. "Oh, boy! You're sure? I am going to ask the SS soldiers if they will let us go into the field to pull some. Maybe we can get one for each man on the train."

The guards agreed and sent an armed soldier to accompany Dirk and Johan into the field. They were so busy that thoughts of escaping did not even occur to Dirk. The turnips were received gratefully by the famished prisoners on the train. One of the German soldiers, who seemed to have a conscience, talked a nearby farmer into bringing buckets of water to the train. It was barely enough for a few sips for each of the men, but they were immensely thankful. A few of the prisoners managed to pass notes to the farmer, which he promised to send home for them.

* * *

Saturday night, the train reached its final destination: Kamp Neuengamme, near Hamburg, Germany.

Chapter Seven

. . . .

PUTTEN AFTER THE RAID

THE BRUTAL NAZI RETALIATION HAD DRASTICALLY changed the lives of the people in Putten. Until this horrific event, even with war raging in the countries south and west of the Netherlands and in spite of the Nazi occupation, their existence had been relatively calm and peaceful. Now, sorrow and pain had replaced this feeling of calm. Women and children had not only lost their husbands, sons, and fathers, but many had also lost their homes and all their belongings. Putten was in a state of utter confusion, disorder, and fear.

To get back to some kind of normalcy, the mayor of Putten convened what was left of the village council to grapple with the daunting responsibility and work of rebuilding the infrastructure.

Teachers and administrators were attempting to get the schools back up and running. It was a difficult task at best because a good number of teachers were among the unfortunate men hauled off by the Germans. At least, the schools had not been torched.

During the day, women and children could be seen in the village, rummaging through the rubble of their burned homes, looking for personal possessions that might have survived the fires. Businesses were trying to reopen.

Many had lost their shopkeepers and owners, again leaving the women and children to clean up the debris and repair the damage caused by the fires and by the looting of the German soldiers during that frightful night, ten days ago.

Janneke had been back and forth into the village a couple of times to see if she was needed at work. The doctor, who also was a member of the village council, had decided to temporarily close the medical practice and only take care of emergencies, for which he would have his wife help him. He had assumed that Janneke's help might be needed at her home on the farm.

Janneke's home had become a very crowded place. The farmhouse was now shared by Janneke, her parents, her older brother, Aunt Ellie with her two teenage daughters, and three evacuated families. In total, there were eighteen mouths to feed.

After the German soldiers had left the area, Papa, Henk, and the male evacuees had come out of their hiding place and resumed all the farm duties. The evacuee-moms and their children were staying in the attic rooms left vacant by Janneke's brothers Willem and Gerrit. Aunt Ellie and the two girls were bunking with Janneke in her room. Janneke's mother and father remained in their room, and her brother and the rest of the men slept on the floor of a small efficiency summer apartment, just next to the main farmhouse.

Aunt Ellie, an accomplished seamstress, was frantically making mattresses. She sewed sheets together and stuffed them with straw. As long as there was daylight, the rhythmic ticking of her sewing machine could be heard in the main house. All blankets, including horse blankets, had been aired out and cleaned for use. Winter coats served as additional blankets. Everyone seemed to cooperate to make it work. The children were happy not to have to go to school. They saw it all as an unexpected vacation.

As soon as someone mentioned school, Janneke remembered the envelope the headmaster of one of the schools had stuffed into her bag during the raid. She rushed to her room to make sure it was still in her bag. When Janneke entered the room, she found Ria and Hennie lying on her bed, reading her books. Ria was wearing her favorite shirt. Until now, Janneke had not realized what an intrusion this would be. She felt like addressing it, but then remembered that these girls had lost everything they owned; instead, she said, "Hey, girls, let's go up to the attic. There is a trunk full of clothes that don't fit me anymore. They will probably be perfect for you."

Ria's and Hennie's faces lit up. They jumped up off the bed and followed Janneke to the attic.

It had been a while since the trunk had been opened. A strong odor rose from it when she lifted the lid. Ria held her nose. "Phew, Janneke, what smells?"

"It's only mothballs, dear. They keep the bugs out, so they won't eat holes in the clothes. Look through these, girls. Pick the things you want. I will make room in my closet and empty a drawer in my dresser for each of you."

"Thanks, Janneke. Oh, these are great." Hennie had pulled out a pair of riding pants. "Since we are on a farm now, we should dress the part, right? If these fit me, may I have them?"

"Sure. They're yours," Janneke replied as Hennie put them on.

"Yeah, they fit. All that's missing now is a horse. Will you teach me how to ride?"

Janneke smiled and answered, "Yes, I can do that but only if you help me with my chores."

Ria tuned in, "Me, too! Me, too, please! When can we start?"

Janneke, enjoying their enthusiasm, replied, "Right now, the horse stalls need to be cleaned."

The girls looked at each other, wrinkling their noses. "Oh, yuck! We don't have to shovel horse poop, do we?"

"Well, yes, that is part of owning horses. Pick some clothes from the trunk that you don't mind getting dirty and come join me in the stable. I will find you some rubber boots to wear. The horses also need to be brushed, and I'll show you how that's done."

When Janneke started down the stairs, she overheard the girls arguing about who would do the shoveling and who would do the brushing. She returned to her room and found that the envelope the schoolmaster had given her was still in her bag. She decided to ask Pieter to drop it off at the school the next time he went into town.

Before going to the stable, Janneke sat down with the women in the kitchen to have a cup of tea. Mama poured her a cup and gave her a hug. "It's so good to have you home, Janneke. I need your help setting up a schedule for kitchen duty. We actually have way too many cooks in the kitchen."

Aunt Ellie laughed. "Yes, literally! Way too many. I'm staying out of the kitchen, even though I'd love to teach the girls how to cook, but that would mean even more cooks in the kitchen." And then she added, "Besides, I have too much sewing to do."

Janneke responded, "There are plenty of things to do around the farm, besides cooking. I don't believe that anyone has to be bored around here. In fact, Aunt Ellie, in a while, your girls are going to help me clean the horse stalls. I promised to give them riding lessons if they help me with my chores."

"That is wonderful, so glad you got them off their duffs. Thank you, Janneke!"

One of the evacuee-women chimed in, "Could the smaller children also be given light chores? I think it would help their dispositions. They could be put in charge of fetching eggs, maybe even feed the chickens, or fetch potatoes from the root cellar, things like that."

Mama responded, "That could be good for them, yes, but my son Henk thinks that the children aren't even aware of the war or why they are here. They seem to be very happy with their extended vacation and are busy exploring the farm, already making up their own games. Henk gave them some ropes and lumber, and the boys are building a tree house and a swing to go with it. I saw the girls jump rope and play hopscotch and hide and seek. Maybe we should just let them play."

Janneke agreed, "Indeed, young children should play. It is good for their development. When it is too cold to play outside, there are several trunks in the attic with our old toys." She stood up from the table and announced, "I'd better get out to the barn. There isn't a lot of daylight left."

In the hall, she hollered up the staircase for the girls to hurry up. They came barreling down the stairs, still arguing over who would do what. Janneke smiled. Seeing them in her old clothes was sort of endearing.

While walking to the stable, Hennie asked, "Janneke, why don't we have lights anymore at night? I don't like it when we have to go to bed so early. Mama says to blame the Germans. She says they have cut off our lights. I that true?"

Janneke wondered how much the girls knew about what led up to the events of the past few weeks, so she asked, "Do you know what Mad Tuesday was?"

"Yes, I do," Ria eagerly responded. "Remember, Hennie, that was the day we wore orange bandanas and went to the highway to party because Mom and Pop thought the war had ended. Remember? People were yelling and spitting at the people that walked by on the highway. Why did they do that, Janneke?"

Janneke handed each of the girls a pair of rubber boots and a shovel and said, "I'll tell you while we shovel. We'll start on the stalls that were left empty by Willem's and Gerrit's horses."

Janneke fetched a large wheelbarrow and started scooping. "Come on, girls. Just watch me and do what I do. Now, to answer your question, the people who were being spat at while walking on that highway were German-friendly traitors. They, too, thought the Allied troops would be here any moment to free us. They were afraid of retaliation by their own people for helping the Germans, so they scampered for the German border."

Janneke went on to tell them about some of the things she had read in the underground papers, which she had carried for the resistance in her medical bag. She told them about D-Day, when the Allied troops landed in France, and the many lives that were lost by those courageous soldiers from America, England, Canada, and other countries while they were fighting the Germans in order to free Europe. She told them about Operation Market Garden, the failed attempt by the Allies to conquer the bridges around Arnhem.

"Had the Allies been successful in capturing all the bridges around Arnhem," she continued, "we would probably be free now, but unfortunately they did not, so the war did not end. Since Putten is north of Arnhem, we continue to be occupied by the Germans. The fighting between the Germans and the Allies is very heavy around Arnhem, so all the people of Arnhem were forced to leave. Because we live not too far north of their city, many of them came to this area. To sabotage communications between this area and the Allied troops, the Nazis have destroyed the power lines that bring electricity to us. They also keep cutting the telephone lines. So, Hennie, your mother was right about the Germans. They are indeed to blame for our not having lights at night."

"That is not fair. It's so mean. We did not do anything to them, did we? Why are they doing these things?"

"That's war," sighed Janneke. "When there is a war, the people suffer."

"Like the people that stopped by today begging for food?" asked Ria.

Her question surprised Janneke. "I did not know we had food seekers stop by today. But, yes, like them. The Germans have also taken over all our trains to move their troops and supplies to the front. The result is that the food grown around here and up north cannot get to the people in the big cities to the west. There are millions of starving people in Amsterdam, Rotterdam, The Hague, and other cities. We are very fortunate to live here on the farm, to have food and shelter. Please remember to be nice to those poor starving people when they come by the farm, begging for food. We share with them as much as we can. With winter approaching, we may also have to give them shelter from time to time."

The girls had been doing their fair share of mucking while listening intently to Janneke's stories. Four wheelbarrows of horse manure had already been hauled off and dumped. The horse poop did not seem to bother the girls any longer. For a while they silently continued mucking, and then Hennie asked, "Aren't the evacuee-families who are staying with us on the farm from Arnhem?"

Janneke, sort of surprised that Hennie had grasped what she had told them, answered, "Yes, two of the families are from Arnhem. They came here a few weeks ago after being chased out of their homes by the German soldiers. The other family is from The Hague. They have been here much longer. Earlier, during the war, their house was requisitioned by the Germans, to make way for a German defense barrier at the North Sea."

"So they're like us...with no house to go back to?" Hennie inquired.

"Indeed," is all that Janneke could think to say. She looked at Hennie and realized that these girls were struggling with a whole lot more than just losing their clothes.

While she hugged them, Hennie continued, "They are lucky, though; at least they still have their fathers with them."

Ria chimed in, "Papa and Dirk are coming back soon, right, Janneke?"

"We hope so, Ria. Until then, we have each other, right?"

"Yeah, I am so glad you are our cousin."

As the sun started to set, they walked, arm in arm, back to the house to clean up. In the washroom, Janneke showed them how to scrub up. Refreshed and full of stories, they showed up for dinner.

* * *

Seating eighteen people was not easy, but Mama proclaimed that, in the past few weeks, life had been in enough upheaval, so she wanted everyone to eat together, including the children. The table and chairs from the summer quarters had been added to the dining room. A fire was burning in the fireplace. Lanterns had been placed on the tables and on the large sideboard. It reminded Janneke of the huge dinners they used to have for birthdays and special holidays.

Janneke sat next to her father and noticed that he wasn't participating in any of the conversations. The children were chattering away. Hennie and Ria were sharing their newly learned information with Henk and the evacuee-men. Mama, Aunt Ellie, and the evacuee-women were running around, getting the food on the table. But Papa sat silently next to Janneke, seemingly in deep thought. She nudged him and softly asked, "Papa, is something bothering you?"

He shrugged his shoulders and whispered back, "I don't want to alarm your mother. I'll tell you later."

When everyone was seated, Papa stood up to say the meal's prayer. He reflected on the sadness that war had brought to Putten and on the men that had been taken from the town, as well as from the family gathered around the table, and he gave thanks for the bounty on the table in front of them. Except for his voice, the room had been quiet momentarily. As soon as the children heard the word "Amen," they continued their chattering, and the girls continued with their stories.

After dinner, Janneke followed her father outside. Papa asked her to come with him to go talk to Pieter. The waning moon dimly lit the path to Pieter's house. They walked in silence. Papa was a man of few words, and Janneke realized that, whatever it was that was bothering him, he wanted to discuss with both of them, together.

Pieter's dogs were outside and came running to greet Janneke and her father. Their barking alerted Pieter, and he came out to see who the unexpected visitors were.

"Good evening, love," Janneke called out. "Papa and I came to see if you had the coffee on."

"Of course, of course, come in! What a nice surprise!" Pieter apologized for the messy kitchen. "I shot a buck today, and I just finished dressing him out. In fact, I was going to stop by in the morning and offer the meat to your extended family."

Papa looked at Janneke and uttered, "We will gladly accept the meat. That will be a big help in feeding so many mouths, won't it, Janneke?"

Janneke walked over to Pieter, who was at the sink washing his hands. She planted a big kiss on his cheek and added, "Yes, indeed, thank you so much. Right now, though, could you take a short break from this bloody job? Papa is worried about something, and he wants to discuss it with you."

"Sure, sure, please go into the living room, and I'll be there as soon as I clean up a bit."

Pieter handed Janneke one of the lanterns, and she took her father into the living room. She loved this room. It was so representative of who Pieter was. A huge stone fireplace surrounded by comfortable dark brown leather chairs on one side of the room. Pieter's hunting trophies were displayed on the wall around the fireplace. Huge bookcases, loaded with books and family photos in tarnished silver frames, adorned another wall, and through a huge picture window, you could see into the front yard and the forest behind it. A heavy carved desk sat in a corner with more pictures on it, including some of Janneke. His diplomas and certificates were displayed on the wall above the desk. The aroma of a recent wood fire still lingered in the air.

Pieter entered the room carrying a tray with three mugs of piping-hot coffee, sugar and cream. He announced, "If you are cold, I can start a fire." Both Janneke and Papa shook their heads. The temperature in the room was quite comfortable. "Well, all right then. Please sit down and tell me what is on your mind."

Papa took a deep breath and started, "I am worried about my two youngest sons, Willem and Gerrit. As you know, a few weeks ago, I sent them away to go stay with my wife's family, believing it would be safer for them up north. Today, I received word that they have been seen not very far from here in the township of Drie. They were spotted at the house of Forester Schenk. Do you know him, Pieter? Is that something you could check on for me?"

Janneke was glad that the lantern threw off little light, so Papa could not see the horror on her face. She had been at Forester Schenk's house a few times to pick up messages for the underground resistance. That had to mean that Willem and Gerrit had joined the resistance. She had to stop herself from saying that out loud. For some time now, she had wished that her father knew about her and Pieter's role in the resistance. But even as minor as these roles were, she and Pieter had vowed to each other not to let anyone know. Not many people in Putten were aware of the resistance activities in and around their village. If they were to find out that the botched attack that led to the raid had been the work of the resistance, they would have never understood and would have looked down on anyone associated with the resistance.

Before Janneke could say anything, Pieter calmly answered, "I understand your worry. The good thing is that the boys weren't in Putten during the raid."

"True," Papa replied. "But what could they be doing in Drie? Did they find work there?"

"That's entirely possible," answered Pieter. "I do know Forester Schenk well. It may take me a few days, since the phones are not working right now, but I will check it out for you."

Papa stood up while Janneke stayed seated. "Thank you, Pieter. I'll be on my way then."

Pieter jumped up to see him out and asked, "Is it okay with you if Janneke stays for a while? I will walk her home later."

"Of course, it is. You two don't get to spend nearly enough time together with this war continuing on. Enjoy the evening." After a wave to his daughter, he went outside and disappeared into the dark evening.

While Pieter scurried around to start a fire, Janneke's mind was racing. She could not help but feel responsible and wondered, What have I done? If the boys have joined the resistance, it is my fault. I talked Father into sending them away. How am I going to fix this? What if something happens to them? Papa will never forgive me.

"What is going on in that pretty little head of yours?" inquired Pieter while cuddling up to her in the big chair she was sitting in. He produced a handkerchief from his pocket and gently dabbed away some of the tears that rolled down Janneke's cheeks. "How can I make it all better for you?"

"Can you please make the war go away, so we can all go on with our lives? The end seems so close, and then things like this happen."

"This, being your brothers' joining the resistance?"

"Yes! So you think that, too?" Janneke sobbed.

"Indeed, I do. Why else would they be in Drie? And they may be your younger brothers, but they are grownups. You are not responsible for their decisions or their actions."

Pieter took his fiancée in his strong arms and let her weep. His loving embrace felt so wonderful that it took her only a few minutes to relax and focus her full attention on just him.

"I am so fortunate to have you in my life. I love you so much. I feel safe with you. I want to be held by you forever."

Thoughts were racing through her head again. Was this a next step in their relationship? She had never uttered such intimate words before, and she started to doubt that she should have, until Pieter picked her up and carried her to his bedroom, speaking to her in a gentle, loving tone of voice.

Chapter Eight

KAMP NEUENGAMME, GERMANY

RIGHT AROUND MIDNIGHT, IN PITCH-BLACK DARKNESS, Dirk, Johan, and the rest of the two thousand Dutch prisoners left the train they had traveled on for the past five days. SS soldiers led them deeper into the camp. Hungry, thirsty, and exhausted, they entered a huge cellar below what appeared to be the main building of Kamp Neuengamme.

Hopes for some sort of humane treatment in this new place quickly vanished. In the first locale, their heads were shaved bald. Afterward, they were directed to lineup in an area close to where they had entered. There seemed to be only one door in and out of this place.

Dirk joked with his father and others around them about not having realized before how ugly they were without hair. Someone produced a small mirror. It was passed around, and most didn't even recognize themselves. They nervously laughed and made fun of each other.

An SS guard rudely put a stop to their playfulness; he pointed his gun at the prisoners and ordered silence: "*Ruhe. Schweigen.*"

At the start of the line, several prisoners received blows from the butts of the guards' weapons. The shaving of the heads continued in near silence, except for the shouts of the guards. Dirk and Johan feared that this could very well be the last time they had a chance to laugh with their friends and neighbors from Putten.

More beatings were dealt out to some unfortunate men who were so nervous they weren't able to stand still. Dirk could barely contain his anger. There had been moments at Kamp Amersfoort when he had wanted to take on some of these guards, and he feared that he might not be able to contain himself here for very long, especially if this kind of treatment was the norm.

"Son," whispered Johan when he noticed Dirk's fists. "Don't get us into trouble."

After a long wait, the door opened. In groups of one hundred, the prisoners were moved to another building to hand over all their personal possessions: wallets, watches, combs, notebooks, rings, photos, playing cards, cigarettes, pipes, and any other objects they had managed to keep with them until now. Each prisoner was handed a numbered patch, and their personal items were registered under that number. Dirk's number was 58939, his father's 58940, making them wonder if 58,938 people before them had received this same treatment.

The next stop was an outside bathhouse. The men stripped naked and turned in their clothing and shoes. They stood shivering in the chill of the mid-October night. Cold and humiliated, most men crossed their hands in front of their private parts.

Further down the line, SS guards stood ready to give the naked men a very rough soap-down with a nasty-smelling substance. The line moved slowly as the prisoners were ordered to lie down on wooden benches to be shaved—more like scraped—so that all body hair was removed.

These sadists obviously had zero respect for humanity as they pointed their weapons directly at the defenseless, scared men while making fun of them. The humiliation was hard to take. Dirk had never felt so helpless. His father's words kept playing through his head: "Blend in with the group. Don't try to be a hero. Our revenge will come, but only if we stay alive."

If anyone showed his anger, he was scraped even rougher. Blood was dripping from the cuts of several men around Dirk and Johan. After a five-minute shower, and still dripping wet, they were pushed into yet another lineup for the next area. One pair of underwear, a striped pair of pants, and a jacket were thrown at them. Additionally, they received a filthy old cap or hat and some dirty shoes or clogs. It did not matter if things fit or not. Again, Dirk wondered, how many men before him had worn these things and what had happened to them?

"At least, now we look like real prisoners," someone quipped, and a deep grumble moved through the crowd. The thin clothes were not enough to keep them shielded from the humid cold night air.

Once more, in groups of one hundred, they were taken to the barracks where they were housed with other prisoners already there. The thought of being able to lie down and finally get some rest gave them a short-lived feeling of relief. They were soon disappointed, once again, when they found out that there weren't enough beds for everyone there either. Wooden single bunk beds, three-high, had to be shared by two and, sometimes, three men. An order was shouted to undress—only an undershirt was permitted. And a thin cotton blanket was the only thing to keep them warm.

By now, Dirk and Johan were used to bunking together, so, at least, they could keep each other warm. They were so utterly tired that they quickly fell asleep.

* * *

Not even an hour later, the lights flicked back on, and the prisoners were rudely awakened by what looked like other prisoners, except these men were armed with wooden bats, which they beat against the wooden bunk frames while repeatedly screaming in German, "Wake up, beasts! Fast! Fast!"

Dirk and Johan jumped from their bunk so fast that Johan stumbled, and if Dirk had not been there to catch him, he would have fallen flat on his face. Still half-asleep and disoriented, Johan uttered, "What now? What is happening?"

"That's our wake-up call, Father. We had better get dressed."

They unrolled the clothes and shoes they had used for pillows and put them on. Out of habit, Johan looked at his left wrist. "Oh, I forgot. No watch."

"I would think it's around four-thirty in the morning," answered Dirk.

"Son, it's easy to lose track of time in a place like this. I will state every morning what day and date it is. If you then repeat it, we should be able to remember it. Today is Sunday, the fifteenth of October."

"That is a good idea, Father. It is Sunday, October fifteenth," repeated Dirk.

Farther down in the barracks, someone wailed in Dutch, "My shoes! Where are my shoes? My shoes are gone!"

One of the guards rushed over to the wailing man, threatening him with a beating if he didn't stay quiet: "*Schweigen mann, oder ich mochte dich schlagen.*"

"But someone stole my—"

Before he could finish his sentence, the bat had landed on the side of his head. The poor man toppled over, blood coming from his mouth. The guard laughed and continued on his way. Everyone else stood frozen.

Dirk ran over to the poor man. He was a fellow Puttener. Another young man came running from the other side of the barracks. Together, they helped the old man up. Dirk looked at the tall, skinny kid who had come to help and extended his hand to him and said, "Hi. I'm Dirk." He figured that the kid was probably even younger than himself.

"Hello. I'm Nickolas. Everyone calls me Nick. Do you speak English, Dirk? Or better yet, French?"

"My English is better than my French," Dirk replied. "I also speak some German."

"Great. We will speak in English. Most of these kapos don't speak English. Do you know this old man?"

"Yes, he's from the same town I'm from."

"Where is that?" Nick inquired.

"Putten, in the Netherlands."

"Would you explain to this poor man that they will not give him another pair of shoes? He will have to steal someone else's."

Dirk told the bleeding man what Nick had said.

"Stealing is a sin," lisped the old man, spitting out a couple of teeth. Dirk was not at all surprised by the answer of the old man from his very religious hometown. He tried to point out the man's misplaced righteousness, telling him, "In this godforsaken place, it's every man for himself. Anyone around you could be a thief, so keep what little you own on your body at all times."

"God will help us and also forgive them," the old man uttered.

Dirk told Nick that the old man had not grasped the evil of this place yet. Then, very curious about those brutes with bats, he asked Nick, "You called the guy who hit this poor man a 'kapo.' Is that his name?"

"No, kapo is short for Kamp Police," answered Nick. "They are convicted German criminals who were brought here by the SS to police other camp prisoners. You'll be able to recognize them by a band around their upper arm, and they usually carry wooden bats or rubber clubs. All of them are thugs without any kind of conscience. They are happy to comply with the SS's cruel treatment of prisoners in return for better treatment for themselves. The kapo you saw hitting the old man calls himself Brutus."

"Thanks, Nick. I hope to see you later."

"You will. I will look you up after the count."

Dirk returned to his father who eagerly asked, "The man who was beaten looks familiar. Is he okay?"

"I hope so, Father. He is also from Putten. I wish we could do more for him. He seems like a good man. He believes that God is going to come to his rescue, but I think we had better take faith in our own hands in this place, don't you, Father?"

"Not sure, son, but you are probably right," answered Johan, still stunned by what had just happened. "Who are those guys with the bats? Aren't they prisoners themselves?"

"Indeed, they are, Father." Dirk, then, recounted Nick's explanation for his father.

Afterward, Johan frowned and uttered, "Best not to anger them."

The kapos came back through the barracks, shouting at the men to get out quickly, *"Heraus. Draussen. Schnell. Schnell."*

Like in Amersfoort, the prisoners were handed a piece of bread on the way out of the barracks, but with just one difference—this bread was black. Dirk smelled the bread, broke off a piece, and tasted it. He said, "It tastes okay, Father. This must be how they bake bread in Germany."

Outside it was still dark, and a drizzling rain was coming down. All prisoners had lined up in front of their barracks to be counted. After the count, they were left standing there until well after it became light. It did not take long before they were all completely drenched.

At the first sign of light, Dirk looked for a possible escape route. To his great disappointment, there were huge barbed-wire electric fences surrounding the barracks and the plaza they were standing on. Guards with bloodhounds were patrolling the outside perimeters of the fence.

Finally, after hours of standing in the rain, the guards shouted something, and the prisoners dispersed. No one was allowed back inside the barracks. Some left to go to work.

Nick went over to Dirk. While pulling Dirk by the arm, Nick urged, "Come with me. I work in the kitchen. I'll see if they will let you work there as well."

Dirk explained to Johan what Nick had said. He hesitated to leave his father by himself, but Johan spurred him on, "Go, son. You may be able to get a few extra bites that way. I'll be right here. Go!"

On his way across the square, Dirk looked for Uncle Hans, but he could not spot him among the thousands of bald men in striped pajamas.

Dirk waited outside while Nick disappeared into the office that belonged to the SS officer in charge of the camp kitchen. When the door opened again, Nick stuck out his head and gestured for Dirk to come in. He led Dirk to a desk in the back of the room.

The German officer behind the desk took off his reading glasses and looked Dirk over. He nodded at him and spoke in German; his voice was sympathetic but business-like. "Nick tells me you want to work in the kitchen. How old are you, son?"

"I am eighteen, sir."

"Do you know how to cook?"

"Yes," was Dirk's firm answer while he stood, rigid, in front of the German. He wasn't used to lying, but how hard could it be? Besides, Nick could teach him.

"Well then, we are very short-handed in the kitchen. You can start working with Nick immediately. I just need your first name and prisoner number."

"Dirk, number 58939, sir."

"My name is *Hauptsturmführer* von Schilling. If you witness any improper use of food in the kitchen, you will report it to me. Understood?"

"Yes, Sir *Hauptsturmführer*." Dirk noticed a slight smile on von Schilling's face when he dismissed the two boys. It gave Dirk the impression that he might not be as evil as most of the SS personnel he had encountered so far. Dirk followed Nick out of the office.

As soon as the door closed behind them, Nick elbowed Dirk. "You did well, my friend," he said. "Now we get to work together."

Dirk lightly punched Nick back and confessed, "Yeah, but I have never cooked anything in my life, so you'll have to teach me."

"Nothing to it, my friend. It's pretty easy when the cook only has potatoes, cabbage, turnips, and carrots to work with. Every day we make *steckrueben* soup with those ingredients, and today, because it is Sunday, everyone receives an extra portion of boiled potatoes. Tonight, an extra piece of bread is served with black coffee. That's about it."

"But how can we survive on that?"

"We can't, and that is intentional. The SS motto is 'extermination through work.' They feel that we are expendable because we are enemies of Hitler and Germany. They believe this gives them the right to exploit us by using us as slave labor and for various experiments."

"Experiments?" gasped Dirk. "What kind of experiments?"

"Prisoners are injected with arsenic, so they die. This is done to teach the experimenters to practice autopsies. Others are injected with the tuberculosis bacterium into their lungs, so they can experiment with vaccines to find a cure when there is an outbreak among the German soldiers. See that brick building on the other side of the electric fence?" After Dirk nodded his head, Nick continued, "That's where they do those experiments."

Dirk looked at Nick in awe. "How do you know so much?"

"My father is a medical doctor. He is here, too. They have him working in the infirmary almost day and night. When I see him, he tells me things."

"Does he have to help with the experiments?"

"No, thank God. He is a prisoner, just like the rest of us. They keep him in the infirmary where he tries to help as many sick prisoners as he can. A hopeless job, he tells me, because of the total lack of cleanliness, shortness of bandages and supplies, and practically no medicine available."

"We seem to have some things in common," Dirk observed. "How did you and your father end up here together?"

"My father was a surgeon at a hospital in Paris. For several years during the occupation, we were able to hide downed Allied pilots at the hospital. They were brought there by the resistance. We would arrange false papers for them and smuggle them out of France. Early this past summer, the Germans found out and arrested us. My father and I were brought here. My mother was taken elsewhere. We don't know where she is."

"I am so sorry, buddy. I guess I am fortunate that my mother and two sisters weren't deported. We don't know, though, what has become of them since the village was burned down."

Nick sighed. "You may be worse off than we are. At least, we hope to have a home to go back to. You know, a few years ago, I thought it was all a game. I liked the excitement of doing secret things. I did not realize what the consequences might be. I am sure my father and mother did, but I wanted to help. As a young boy, I could go places undetected, where they could not."

"So are you French?" inquired Dirk.

"Well, sort of. My father is American. My mother is Swiss, and I was born in France. At home, we speak English, but everywhere else, we speak French. I am so glad you speak English. Where did you learn it?"

"In high school. We had to take English, French, and German classes. I have always struggled with French. English comes easy, though. My father and most of the men from Putten only speak Dutch."

"You can translate for them then, right?" inquired Nick.

"Yeah, I suppose," answered Dirk vaguely while looking around the camp's kitchen.

"Great," answered Nick. "And one more thing before we start cooking. I heard you tell von Schilling that you are eighteen. I am only sixteen," said Nick.

"A very wise sixteen-year-old, but don't let that go to your head," quipped Dirk.

While they carried the kettles of hot soup to the square to be served to the prisoners, Nick asked, "Do you play soccer?"

"Yes," answered Dirk, thinking that seemed like an odd question to ask here in this camp.

Nick caught Dirk's inquisitive look and explained, "Every Sunday afternoon, the kapos set up a soccer match in the square. Men from different countries have to play against each other. Since your group just arrived here, they'll certainly want a Dutch team to play. The winners of the first match play the kapos. The kapos always win. They are mean and don't play by the rules."

"What happens if they lose?" asked Dirk.

"Nobody wants to find out, so if they pick you to play, make sure you lose. There is more—"

A kapo interrupted the boys' conversation and ordered them to immediately get in line where they belonged. Dirk went looking for his father while wondering what else Nick had wanted to tell him. He found his father in the food line in front of their barracks. "Father, there will be a soccer match this afternoon on this square. Nick said that, since we are new arrivals, they may choose us to play. My years with the soccer club in Putten may yet pay off."

He omitted telling Johan what Nick had said about playing the kapos. He secretly hoped that Brutus would play, so he could sneak in a couple of crippling ankle kicks to pay him back for beating the old man that morning.

The food lineup was different from the one at Kamp Amersfoort. There were no bowls here or mugs for the potatoes. Every fifth man had to step forward and receive a portion of potatoes in his hat to share with the other four in line. Dirk had seen other prisoners in the kitchen cook the potatoes in kettles similar to the ones he and Nick used for the soup, but he had not paid much attention to how they cooked them. It was now obvious to him that the potatoes had been thrown in the pots dirty and with the peels still on, even the rotten ones had been used.

After receiving their portion, Dirk and Johan tried to take out the rotten potatoes and attempted to peel the rest. The prisoners around them eagerly took their scraps and ate them.

"Have you ever been so hungry as to eat rotten potatoes, Father?"

"No, son, I haven't, but these poor souls have been here a while, and they don't seem to care. I guess we will have to get used to this."

Next came the soup. A bowl was filled with the watery broth. It was slurped up eagerly by five prisoners, the last one licking the bowl before it was filled again for the next five.

"This is what Nick and I had to cook, Father. I am afraid there isn't much nourishment in it."

Johan, trying to make light of the situation, said, "Tastes like cabbage water, son. You have a lot to learn to be a chef."

"No joke, Father. It worries me. I don't know how we will survive on this stuff."

After the kettles had been cleared out, the prisoners were ordered to gather around the square, leaving a large open space in the middle. Dirk was almost excited. "I guess the soccer match is next, Father."

"Not so sure, Son. What they are wheeling onto the square doesn't look like a soccer goal to me."

"Father, you're right. That looks like a gallows. I have seen pictures of them in books. Do you think that's what that is?"

"Nothing surprises me anymore, son," Johan responded solemnly.

They watched as the structure was secured to the ground in the middle of the square. Dirk wondered if this was what Nick had wanted to tell him.

A shackled prisoner appeared on the square. He was flanked by two kapos who led him up the makeshift podium and placed him in the middle. A third kapo climbed the podium and swung a rope over the beam above them.

In a panic, Dirk grabbed Johan's arm. "Father, they aren't really going to hang this poor man, are they?"

"Ouch, son. You're hurting me."

Dirk let go. "They can't do this. We've got to do something."

Just then, Nick came squeezing through the tightly packed crowd. "Dirk, I am glad I found you. I want to take you and your father to the infirmary to meet my father. This is a good time because the kapos will be busy with the hangings."

"So they are going to hang this poor man? Why?" uttered Dirk.

"Come quick. I'll explain later," urged Nick.

While Dirk and Johan followed Nick to the infirmary, a bellowing voice called out over the square, "*Heil Hitler!*"

A "*Heil Hitler*" could be heard in response but only from the kapos and the SS camp guards watching the spectacle. The bulk of the prisoners refused to answer the greeting.

The voice continued, "This man in front of you has committed a crime against Germany and our führer. He broke into the camp's main kitchen and stole food. Those who think he should be punished say 'aye.'"

"Aye" could be heard from the same men who had responded to the earlier greeting.

"Well then, this thief is sentenced to death by hanging."

Dirk stopped and turned around before groaning, "No! They can't do that. The poor man was just hungry. He should not have to die for that."

Nick pulled Dirk along by his arm. "Come on, Dirk. Let's go and meet my father."

Dirk hesitated. He still could not believe they were actually going to hang this poor man. Nick kept pulling his arm. "You really don't want to see the actual hanging, do you? Every time a large group arrives, they perform this spectacle on the following Sunday afternoon, right before the soccer match. They want to scare the newcomers into following the camp rules. You'll get plenty of chances to see a hanging."

"Oh, yes, the soccer match. Don't I need to go back, so I can be ready for the match? I don't want to miss that."

"Dirk, if you want to play, you still have plenty of time before the match. They usually hang two or three prisoners, and then they still have to set up the square for the match. Let's go in."

"Let's go in, Dirk," echoed Johan.

Just then, the door to the infirmary swung open, and a tall, lanky man dressed in a green doctor's coat gestured for them to come in.

"Good afternoon. I thought I heard voices out here. I am Dr. Jack, Nick's father. Please come into my makeshift hospital."

"Father, this is Dirk and his father, Johan."

"I figured as much." Doctor Jack chuckled, while he hugged Nick. "Nick has been excited all morning. He has not talked about anything else but meeting a Dutchman, nearly his own age. I am so happy he has found a friend, and I am pleased to meet you and your father." He shook their hands and continued, "Dirk, Nick told me that your English is very good. During the night, a number of patients from your transport were brought in here who don't speak English. Could you help me by translating some questions I have for them?"

"I will be happy to," answered Dirk.

"Well then, follow me."

Dr. Jack led them further into the barracks. Nick whispered, "My father tries to take very good care of all these patients, in spite of the German orders to let them die. Some have actually recovered and walked out of here, only to be returned to the hell out there. He, sometimes, wonders what the point is, but he is a doctor, after all."

As they walked past the beds, a raspy weak voice called out, "Johan. Dirk. Over here. It's Hans."

Dirk continued on with Dr. Jack, while Johan returned to where he had heard Hans call out.

When the doctor and Dirk made it back to Johan, Hans had dozed off, tightly holding on to Johan's hand.

Dr. Jack bent over Hans to feel his forehead and his pulse. He asked, "You two know this man?"

"He is my uncle," answered Dirk. "What is wrong with him?"

"He is very sick. He has pneumonia and dysentery, which has left him severely dehydrated. It does not look good."

"Can we stay with him?" inquired Johan.

"Just until the soccer match is over," Dr. Jack replied. "The kapos will come through here shortly after that."

* * *

Dirk and Johan left the infirmary when darkness started to set in. Prisoners were scurrying back to their barracks, receiving their pieces of Sunday bread and coffee on their way inside. Even though Dirk and Johan had not participated in the activities on the square, they were still exhausted from not having had much sleep the night before, so they turned in early, but a restful night's sleep was not to be had. Several times during the night, the sirens blared, announcing a possible air raid. All prisoners dressed as quickly as they could while being spurred on by the bats of the kapos. They were herded down to the bomb shelter, the same huge cellar where they began their time in Neuengamme.

At the only entrance, the SS soldiers hollered and screamed, "*Schnell! Schnell! Herein! Herein,*" while pushing the prisoners into the shelter, sometimes causing a stampede. Several prisoners were trampled to death at each of the sirens. No one seemed to care.

Johan and Dirk, exhausted, discouraged, disappointed in humanity, and homesick, talked about what it would be like when they returned to Putten. Where were Ellie, Hennie, and Ria? Were they okay? If only there were some way to get word from them.

Chapter Nine

. . . .

FIRE AT ENNY'S ESTATE

AUNT ELLIE, KEENLY AWARE OF THE fact that Janneke knew some of the soldiers at the checkpoints and could move around Putten without much trouble, begged Janneke to take her and her two daughters to their burned home. She was sure that there was food that could be recovered and wanted to search through the rubble.

Janneke thought she could be right and went looking for her father to discuss it. She found him in the barn, cleaning milk cans. "Hey, Papa! Need any help?"

"I'm nearly done, my dear. Something on your mind?"

"Yes, Papa. I want to take Aunt Ellie and the girls into Putten to help them search through the burned rubble of their home. Aunt Ellie told me that, before the raid, the canning of all the vegetables and meat for the winter had been finished. It's all stored in the concrete cellar beneath the kitchen floor. If the cellar is still intact and the jars are unbroken, we can bring them all here. Mama would be very pleased. She worries about feeding so many mouths."

"I know she does," replied Papa. "So do I. No telling how long it will be before the Allies are able to cross those rivers and free us. I think that's a good idea, but even if the cellar is still intact, how do you plan to transport the jars?"

"Well, that is what I came to ask you. Could we retrieve the carriage from under the hay in the haystack?"

Papa looked surprised. "Can't you take the hay wagon? We have managed to hang on to that carriage this long. I'd hate to have the Germans take it now."

"Papa, the hay wagon is huge. We would attract much more attention with it than with the carriage. Besides, if it comes right down to it, we could do without the carriage on the farm, but we've got to have the hay wagon. Don't you agree?"

"Hmmm, even if I do agree, I worry about four women going into Putten by themselves."

"Papa, I really think it is safe for us to go. When I was in the village last, I did not see any German soldiers, not even the ones at the normal checkpoints. There was German military traffic on the highway, though, but we could take back roads."

Papa smiled. "Like always, you've already planned every detail, and it makes a lot of sense. Will you, at least, allow me to ask Pieter to escort the carriage and its precious cargo?"

"You mean the food we are going to find?" Janneke did not get her father to chuckle very often.

"Yes, the food, of course," he quipped back while putting away the last milk can he had so diligently been cleaning.

"Let's go find Henk to help us uncover that carriage," she said with a hint of excitement. "He knows exactly where it is and how to get it out."

And, of course, when asked, Pieter said he was more than happy to accompany the women because he also had business in the village himself.

* * *

Early the following morning, Papa surprised Janneke by having the carriage parked in front and all ready to go when she came down for breakfast. The horses were snorting and whinnying, seemingly excited to get out.

"Papa, thank you so much, but shouldn't you be out there milking the cows?"

Papa took Janneke's arm to walk her toward the kitchen and responded, "Actually, Henk and our male guests are doing so well with the farm work. They don't need me anymore. I can retire now and enjoy breakfast with my family."

Everyone was surprised to see Papa at breakfast. Pieter also showed up in time for a bite to eat.

As soon as breakfast was over, the four women climbed into the carriage and took off, accompanied by Pieter on his stately Oldenburg mare.

Ria and Hennie felt important. They had never before been in a horse-drawn carriage, especially not in one that was accompanied by a uniformed gentleman on a horse. They pretended to be princesses going for a ride with their governesses.

Aunt Ellie and Janneke gladly played along. It made the thought of their task at hand much easier to bear.

Suddenly, Pieter motioned to stop the carriage.

"Whoooaaa," Janneke called out and pulled in the reigns.

Pieter stopped his horse. He was holding his index finger to his lips.

"What's the matter?" whispered Hennie.

"Ssshhh," whispered Janneke, looking at Pieter who was scanning the forest ahead of them. "Pieter must have heard something."

"I smell smoke," whispered Aunt Ellie.

"Yeah, me, too," said Ria. "Is the forest on fire?"

Pieter answered, "Something is happening up there, for sure. I hear voices. I will check it out. Stay here, but turn the carriage around, just in case. Wait for me to come back." He clicked his tongue twice, and his horse took off.

Janneke turned the carriage around, and they waited. Every minute that went by seemed like an eternity. The girls were getting scared. As a distraction, Aunt Ellie told them to be on the lookout for Pieter; whoever saw him first would win.

After a while, Ria called out and pointed, "Here he comes. I win."

Pieter stopped his horse next to the carriage and said, "We will have to try this again some other day. The main house of Enny's Estate is on fire, and there are German soldiers everywhere up ahead. We have to turn back."

"Oh, my God," uttered Janneke, fighting back her tears.

"What is Enny's Estate?" inquired Hennie.

On the way back to the farm, Janneke told the girls about Mr. and Mrs. Pouw, their breeding dachshunds, and about working for them in the dog kennels during the summer when she was their age.

"Eww! Are those the funny-looking dogs with short legs? I think they are also called wiener dogs, yes?" asked Hennie, with her nose in a wrinkle.

"Yes, that's them," answered Janneke with a smile.

"Why would anyone want to breed those? What good are they?"

"Well, Hennie, the hunters use them to flush out rabbits, and they are also useful on farms to find badgers. They make really sweet pets, too."

Ria, who had been quiet while Janneke told her story, started sobbing. She snuggled up to her mother. "Will we ever see our dog Peppi again, Mama?"

"We'll look for him when we get to the house, I promise." Aunt Ellie pulled Ria against her and let her cry.

Janneke sensed that Pieter wanted to go back and check things out further, so when they were near the farm, she told Pieter that they could make it safely home from there and that he should feel free to go check on Enny's Estate.

Neither of them could voice their thoughts in front of Aunt Ellie and the girls, but both were thinking the same things: How did the Germans find Enny's Estate? And what happened to Tex and the German housekeeper who had stayed behind to take care of the dogs?

"But I promised your father that I'd deliver you back safely," sputtered Pieter.

"I know. I will explain this to him. Please be safe."

Uncertain but agreeable to her request, he blew her a kiss, waved to the rest of the women, and rode off.

Janneke smiled. Pieter had never been so comfortable and open about their relationship before. Their lovemaking several nights ago had put a spell on him. Aunt Ellie had noticed it, too, and winked at Janneke.

* * *

Janneke was anxious for Pieter to return. To pass the time, she spent the afternoon giving Ria and Hennie their first horseback riding lesson. It was hard for her to concentrate on the girls. She kept thinking about Enny's Estate. How much of the country estate did the Germans destroy? Are the dogs okay? Was Tex able to get away?

"Hey, Janneke. How many more circles do we have to walk beside the horses before you will show us how to get on them?"

Ria's voice brought Janneke back to the task at hand—teaching the girls how to bridle, saddle, and mount a horse.

"Oh, sorry, girls. I'm a bit distracted today."

"Yeah, we noticed." Hennie giggled. "We figure you're missing your boyfriend."

"He is not just my boyfriend. Pieter and I are engaged to be married."

"Really? When? Can we be bridesmaids or maybe flower girls?" Ria gave her reigns to Hennie to hold while she danced around and hummed a melody Janneke did not recognize.

"Ria, stop that. You're making the horses nervous," Janneke requested. "Hennie, give her back the reigns. And, by the way, there won't be any wedding until this stupid war is over. Right now, it's time to learn how to mount your horses. I will mount and dismount my horse. I want you to pay close attention to all my moves. Then I will help each of you to get onto yours. It isn't hard when you do it right."

By the time Janneke had dismounted, Ria was already in the saddle.

"Come on, Hennie," she called out to her sister. "It isn't hard at all."

Janneke had noticed Hennie's apprehension about being so close to these gentle giants. She walked over to Hennie and told her to gently stroke the mare's neck and talk to her. Janneke produced some dried apple pieces from her pocket and gave them to Hennie. "Here. Let her eat these out of your hand."

"She won't bite?" asked Hennie, still worried.

"No, she will pick them up with her lips. She likes treats. After she eats them, nuzzle her and let her say hello to you."

That seemed to help Hennie get over her fear. Janneke held the mare while Hennie mounted.

"Now, girls, today we are just going to walk the horses, so you get a feel of the saddle and how the horse moves. All that is needed is a gentle squeeze with your knees and a slight tightening of the reigns. Follow me."

After going around a few times, Ria yelled, "Hey! I see Pieter. I win again." She was pointing at the farmhouse.

Janneke told the girls, "Keep walking around until I get back." She spurred her horse and galloped off to meet Pieter.

As she sped off, she heard Ria call out, "Yes! That's how I want to be able to ride a horse. You will show me, right?"

Janneke was already too far away to answer her but figured it wouldn't take Ria very long to be able to ride like her. When Janneke reached Pieter, they stopped their horses next to each other. "What did you find out? Are the dogs okay? Was Tex still there?"

Pieter reached over and planted a kiss on Janneke's cheek. "Hello, beautiful. Sorry it took so long. I only have a few minutes, but I wanted to let you know that I believe all will be okay. Tex is at my house for the night. Tomorrow, I will take him to a farm in Barneveld. He heard that a resistance group is held up there that is hiding other downed Allied pilots and paratroopers. Apparently, they are helping the resistance to communicate with the Allied troops south of the rivers around Arnhem, and he wants to join them."

"Oh, good." Janneke sighed. "He'll be safe with you. But why did the Germans set Enny's Estate on fire in the first place? How did they find it?"

"I spoke with the German soldiers when they stopped me because I was getting too close to Enny's Estate. They again mistook me for Dutch police and told me that a German officer had been held there several weeks ago."

"Lieutenant Eggert," gasped Janneke. "He talked?"

"Yes. After his return, the German command interrogated him. One of the questions was if he had heard or seen anything unusual. Since he had been kept in blindfolds most of the time, he could not tell them where he had been. He did, however, say that he had heard a lot of dogs barking while he was there. This sent the Germans on a search in and around Putten for dog breeders. Since there were no other breeders in Putten, it led them directly to Enny's Estate."

"Oh, my God," uttered Janneke. "Mrs. Pouw said that it would only be a matter of time before they would find out. She was right. I just never expected the dogs to give the place away. So where was Tex when the house was on fire?"

"Tex spent some pretty frightful moments in the cellar. The house burned down right above him. After the German soldiers left the area, I went in and searched the grounds. When I came to the house, I found him."

"The dogs?" inquired Janneke.

"So terribly sorry to have to tell you this, but they perished in the fire." Pieter pulled out his handkerchief and made an attempt to dry the tears that were trickling down Janneke's cheeks.

"Thank you, darling. I appreciate you coming out here to let me know. I worried all afternoon. Is there anything you need me to do?"

"Yes, there is. Please tell your father that I will stop by Forester Schenk's house tomorrow afternoon to check on the boys. I will do that after I drop off Tex."

"Please let me come with you," begged Janneke.

"It's too dangerous. Tex will be carrying weapons that were left at Enny's Estate by the resistance. If, and it truly is a big if, we get stopped, he wants me to act as if I caught him and am taking him in. He said he'll handle the rest."

"I understand. May God be with you on your journey," Janneke said, trying to convey more confidence than she felt. "Will we see you tomorrow evening?"

"Absolutely. I will need you to get your father away from everyone. If the boys indeed joined the resistance, he has a right to know. And how do you feel about letting him know about our involvement?"

"I would really like that," agreed Janneke. She had come so close to telling him several times that it would be a relief for him to finally know. "How about if we wait for you at your house at dusk?"

"Great. I should be home close to then. How are the girls doing? Are they catching on?"

"Yes. Especially Ria. She'll be riding like you and I ride in no time. Hennie is still a bit afraid, but she made great progress today."

"Wonderful! Tell them that, after tomorrow, we will attempt to make the trip into Putten again."

Pieter bent toward Janneke again and kissed her. "I love you. You'll be with me in spirit during my journey tomorrow."

"I love you, too. Have a safe journey."

With a heavy heart, Janneke watched her fiancée gallop off. When Janneke got back to the girls, Ria was bouncing in the saddle while her horse was going around in a full-blown trot. Hennie was standing next to her horse in the middle of the corral. Ria called out, "Look at me, Janneke. My horse just did not want to walk anymore. My butt hurts. Am I doing something wrong?"

Janneke pulled up next to Ria and said, "You are in a trot, and you have to move with the horse by posting. Watch me and feel the movement of the horse. Hold on with your knees. You will know you are doing it right when you go with the movement of the horse. That's it. Feels better, right?" She turned to Ria's sister and instructed, "Okay, Hennie. Get back on your horse and walk with me. I'll show you how to trot, as well."

* * *

At dinner that evening, Ria could not stop talking about riding and how she wanted to be able to ride like Janneke and Pieter.

While clearing the dishes, Aunt Ellie thanked Janneke for giving the girls so much to be excited about and for taking their minds off their father and brother and the loss of all their possessions.

"Aunt Ellie, I know you want to be strong for the girls, but how are you holding up?"

"I am okay," she responded. "I still have trouble understanding why this had to happen to us. I miss my Johan and my Dirk very much. A house and everything in it can be replaced, but why did those Nazis have to take my husband and son?" She wiped away her tears.

"I am so sorry this has happened to you," Janneke said while hugging her. "All we can hope for is that this war will be over soon and that they will be returned to you safely."

Chapter Ten

. . . .

DIGGING THE FRIESENWALL TANK TRAPS

ON THEIR THIRD DAY IN NEUENGAMME, a large group of prisoners, including some one hundred men from Putten, were taken into to Hamburg to clean up the rubble in the city after the nightly bombings. Dirk heard that most of them were tradesmen like carpenters and bricklayers. He figured that Uncle Hans would have been a part of this group had he still been alive.

Before Hans died, Dirk and Johan had tried several times to visit him, but the kapos had not allowed them into the infirmary. Nick had brought them a message from his father about Hans's passing.

* * *

On October twentieth, another large group of prisoners, including Dirk, Johan, and most of the remaining men from Putten, were put on a train and transported to Camp Husum-Schwesing, one of many subcamps of Neuengamme. The subcamps were referred to by the prisoners as death camps because so many had already perished there.

Dirk and Johan soon discovered that the Nazi slogan "death by labor" should have included "as well as by torture and starvation."

With nearly one hundred men packed shoulder to shoulder in each freight car, there was no opportunity to sit or lie down. They traveled all day without food or water. When the train reached its destination late in the afternoon, they were unloaded, divided into groups, and assigned to various barracks.

Here, too, they had to share a single bunk with one or two other prisoners, but, at least, they had straw mattresses. Dirk's hopes of things being better in this camp were quickly crushed after hearing the stories from the prisoners who had already been there for a few weeks.

The veterans spent the evening telling the newcomers what was in store for them. Part of what Dirk discovered was that the barracks were so cramped because they were housed with well over two thousand prisoners in a camp that had been built to accommodate—at the most—four hundred people. It sounded like the food situation was similar to that in Neuengamme: a daily bowl of *steckrueben* soup and a piece of dry bread.

The veterans warned that the toilet facilities were broken and so filthy that many just went outside, behind the barracks. Dirk's biggest disappointment: no infirmary. They said that, if you could not work, you were left to die. Dirk worried about his father. Apparently, the kapos here were even meaner than in Neuengamme.

The work to be done was digging tank traps, and the kapos were in charge. Dirk learned from Dr. Jack that Hitler had ordered the construction of the tank traps called *Friesenwall* along the northwestern border, in case the Allies chose to attack from there. That was why the men were brought to Camp Husum-Schwesing.

Dirk was totally discouraged after what he had heard that night. Thoughts of escaping were occupying his mind again before he fell asleep.

* * *

The morning started very early. Still in the dark, after the usual rude wake-up call by the kapos, Dirk and Johan found themselves lined up outside the barracks.

Under the watchful eyes of the SS soldiers, the daily count took place. Ice-cold rain was soaking the prisoners to the core. The usual piece of dry bread had been handed to them on the way out of the barracks. Having been told by their fellow prisoners that this would be the only thing they would get to eat all day, Dirk and Johan each broke off half of his piece and put it in their pocket for later.

They stood in front of the barracks until it was light. Finally, a German officer flanked by several underlings paraded into the plaza and stopped in front of the lineup. Dirk noticed the man's face was almost purple and his hands were trembling.

The officer cleared his throat and shouted, "I am *Untersturmfuehrer* Hans Griem, the head of Camp Husum-Schwesing. You are here to work and follow the rules. The guards have orders to bring me anyone who isn't able to do either of those things, so they can be executed."

He grabbed his pistol from its holster and wildly shot into the air. Dirk whispered to his father that he would not be surprised if this crazy man actually took pleasure in killing prisoners.

Orders were shouted, and in groups of one hundred, the prisoners were moved to the rail cars which were parked just outside the camp. Because of the lack of footboards or steps to get into the freight cars, the prisoners had to jump up and pull themselves in. Those who jumped in first were fortunate because, at the back of the line, the kapos were beating on the prisoners to speed up the process. The first ones in pulled up the others, but it was never fast enough for the kapos.

The train traveled for about forty-five minutes before it came to a stop. After jumping out, there was another lineup and additional beatings for those who fell or didn't get in line fast enough.

The digging site was yet another mile and a half away. To get there, they marched through soggy pastures. Water soaked their shoes with every step they took, as they jumped over the many ditches that separated the pastures.

The kapos were present at each ditch and clubbed anyone who hesitated. The more who fell into the water, the better the kapos liked it. Many of the men were already sick, and for those who fell in, it chilled them even more. This was only the first day, and before arriving at the digging site, some sixty prisoners had lost their place in the lineup because of missing jumps over the ditches.

Dirk and Johan were some of the fortunate men who kept their spots in line. They looked on as the sixty who weren't so fortunate were ordered to sprint back and forth from one end of the pasture to the other while the kapos shouted obscenities at them and clubbed them at each end. The accompanying armed SS-soldiers did not lift a finger to end the spectacle. This went on for more than ten minutes.

Finally, shovels were distributed, and the digging started. Many prisoners had never used a shovel before. Dirk had found out the night before from the stories of his fellow prisoners that there were few farmworkers among them. Most were lawyers, pastors, ministers, policemen, artists, store owners, or office workers who weren't used to such physical work. This was very hard physical labor. The soil was wet clay, which was very heavy and impossible to throw since it stuck to the shovels. As the trench got deeper, the soil had to be thrown up over the side. Water started seeping into the trench. By the end of the morning, the prisoners were digging in frigid water up to their knees.

After hours of digging, Johan stopped for a moment. He needed to straighten his back, and his stomach was hurting. A kapo came toward him and lifted his bat, yelling, *"Los! Los! Schnell. Schnell!"* Johan quickly resumed digging.

Dirk, realizing that his father was trying to do his very best with the task at hand, whispered to him, "Father, slow down. What are we digging these for anyway? Certainly, our lives don't depend on them. Just act like you're working hard. Don't exert yourself too much, and hopefully, we'll make it through this nightmare."

The yelling didn't stop all day. Also, others were digging as if their lives depended on it. Some were like Dirk, doing the minimum to stay beneath the radar of the vicious brutes who felt important because they were in charge.

The kapos were watched by a handful SS soldiers who did nothing to stop—and probably implicitly encouraged—their brutal beatings of the defenseless prisoners.

In the afternoon, a couple of kettles with coffee were delivered, but the prisoners weren't allowed to stop working. The SS soldiers and the kapos drank their share, and the rest was poured out in the pasture.

To return to the camp at the end of the day, the prisoners were subjected to the same drill as in the morning—jumping the ditches, jumping into the train, and then jumping out of the train to be back at the camp where each received their bowl of the watery soup.

Dead tired, hungry, hurting everywhere, and still in their wet clothes with no heat in the barracks, the prisoners tried to sleep in those single bunks shared by two or three men. This was the drill every day for several weeks. Day and night, they were surrounded by armed SS soldiers who would shoot at anything they considered or perceived to be a threat.

The camp was surrounded by electric barbed-wire fences and constantly patrolled by SS soldiers with their bloodhounds. The thought of escaping had long left Dirk. Additionally, every corner of the camp had huge spotlights and machine guns. There really was no way out of this godforsaken place.

No news from outside came into the camp, so pretty soon, most prisoners lost all sense of time and date, except for Johan and Dirk. They continued their ritual of saying the date and the day of the week every morning.

Come rain, hail, snow, fog, or ice, they had to dig. Johan's health was deteriorating rapidly. His stomach could not tolerate the watery cabbage soup. Dysentery was running rampant among the prisoners. Without an infirmary in this camp, some just succumbed to their misery and died, while others were clubbed to death by the kapos because they were so weak and could no longer lift the heavy shovels.

Daily, well after dark, the train arrived back at the camp, depositing its cargo of worn-out, emaciated workers who would receive their daily ration of *steckrueben* soup on the way to their barracks.

The dead were offloaded and tossed onto a heap right outside the entrance of the camp. Dirk wondered what happened to these bodies because they would always be gone the next morning.

* * *

According to Johan's daily account, it was Friday, November 3, 1944. During the usual morning lineup, rumors were whispered that the prisoners would be transported again. No one knew anything specific. But the count was taking longer than usual, and they were left standing in line for most of the day.

Dirk whispered, "Father, something is up. Maybe they'll take us back to Neuengamme. I'll get you to Dr. Jack as soon as we get there."

Johan was barely able to keep it together at this point. "Son, that would be great. Thank you for taking care of me."

The train arrived, and the prisoners were loaded into the freight cars. There was one startling difference today: the kapos and their usual yelling and beatings were absent. In fact, the kapos were part of the lineup, without their bats. They were spurred on by the SS soldiers to jump into the freight cars with the rest of the prisoners. One of the kapos told Dirk that the train was not going to Neuengamme but to a different camp. He did not know the name of the camp.

Chapter Eleven

· ·

RESISTANCE

AFTER SUNDAY DINNER, JANNEKE ASKED PAPA to go with her to Pieter's house. The two walked arm in arm on the familiar path. The beauty of late fall was all around them. Yellow and orange leaves on the canopy above them were glistening in the late afternoon sun, some of them gliding down toward them as if they were early snowflakes. The oak brush that lined their path showed off its deep red and brown leaves.

Janneke took a few deep breaths to take in the smell of fall. She loved this time of year. She sighed. It was so hard to imagine that, not far from this peaceful scene, people were fighting a war. She wondered if indeed her brothers had joined that fight. "Papa," she started, "Pieter went to Forester Schenk's house today to check on Willem and Gerrit. He will let us know tonight what he found out about the boys."

"Oh, good. I still think it is very curious that they did not make it any farther than Drie. I hope they did not get themselves in trouble."

"We'll soon find out, Papa."

"I reckon. And another thing I am curious about is why you did not make it into Putten yesterday. What happened?"

"Papa, remember Enny's Estate where I used to work summers when I was a teenager?"

"Sure. The Pouws' place—nice people. I heard that they have been very kind to many Jewish families hiding from the Germans during this everlasting war. Were they found out?"

"Well, we don't exactly know what happened," she answered, not wanting to give him too much detail, "but when we were close by yesterday, we could see that the main house was on fire and there were German soldiers searching the woods. Pieter thought it wise to turn around and try again in a few days."

"That was a good decision," he agreed. "I am glad he was with you."

"Me, too," Janneke responded.

When they started up the driveway, Pieter's dogs came running to greet them. Janneke let out a sigh of relief, since that meant he was home. All day long her head had been filled with what-ifs.

When they arrived at the back door, they found Pieter's horse tied up next to the door, dripping wet, with Pieter's saddle still on. Janneke wondered what his hurry was to get inside the house. It was unlike him not to tend to his horse first thing upon returning home. She handed her father a bucket she'd found by the back door and asked, "Papa, would you please pump some water for the horse? I'll go find Pieter."

She entered the back door of the house and called for him. She noticed a trail of blood on the floor. Finally, he answered her, "Could you come into the bathroom? I need your help."

Janneke hurried to him, finding first a bloody shirt on the floor outside the bathroom door. A feeling of horror overcame her. When she entered, she found Pieter leaning over the sink, attempting to rinse his arm under running water. She gasped, "Oh, my God, Pieter! What happened? How did you get hurt?"

"I was shot in my arm," he replied. "I think I have stopped the bleeding, but I need your help cleaning and bandaging it. There is a first-aid kit on the shelf above the sink in the kitchen. Would you please get it and see if you can find the things we need?"

Janneke immediately switched into nursing mode. She worried that Pieter might have lost too much blood. This would have caused him to go into shock. She had him sit down on the commode, lean against the vanity, and hold his arm—wrapped in a towel—above his head.

She ran to the kitchen and called out to her father, "Papa, Pieter is hurt and cannot tend to his horse. Would you take his horse to the barn and put him up for the night? Do you need a lantern?"

"I think it's still light enough to see where everything is. If I need one, I'll come get it. I'll see you inside as soon as I'm done in the barn."

"Thanks, Papa."

She grabbed the kit from the shelf and started back to the bathroom. Realizing she needed more light to examine the wound and bandage Pieter's arm, she went back to the kitchen and lit two lanterns. She left one in the kitchen for Papa and took the other into the bathroom.

Pieter was still holding his arm above his head while pressing the towel on the wound. She placed the lantern on the vanity and checked him over. "You are lucky, dear. The bullet entered and left your upper arm. Just a flesh wound, I think. The bone doesn't seem to have been hit." She carefully cleaned the wound while, at the same time, keeping an eye on Pieter's pale face. While bandaging his arm, she asked softly, "Did this happen while you were with Tex, or did it happen in Drie?"

"In Drie," he answered. "When your father comes in, I will tell you both about my visit there. It's not good news, I am afraid."

"Were you shot by the Germans?"

"Yes."

"Could they have followed you here?"

"No, they were too busy rounding up people at Forester Schenk's house."

"Oh, no! Now you have me really worried."

She helped Pieter stand up and, with him heavily leaning on her, they walked to the living room.

Pieter started to tremble. Janneke situated him in his easy chair and pulled out an ottoman to elevate his legs. She fetched a couple of pillows and a blanket from his bedroom and propped up his arm on one of the pillows before covering him.

While she was lighting a fire in the fireplace, Papa entered the room.

Concerned, he asked, "Is Pieter okay? I noticed a lot of blood on the saddle and the neck of his horse."

"Pieter took a gunshot in his arm, Papa. He is going to tell us shortly what happened, but first I'm going to get him something to eat and drink."

"Gunshot? Do we need to get him to a hospital?" asked Papa.

"No, I can't go there with a gunshot wound," interjected Pieter.

"It's a flesh wound, Papa. The bullet went in and out through the muscle of his arm and nicked a blood vessel. We stopped the bleeding, and I have cleaned and bandaged the wound. He did lose quite a bit of blood, so while I go to the kitchen to fetch him some nourishment, could you keep an eye on him to make sure he does not pass out?"

"Of course, dear. I am so glad you know what to do."

Janneke returned with a tray holding a glass of water, a cheese sandwich, some warm milk, and two cups of coffee. She handed one coffee to Papa and put the other down for herself, then turned to Pieter, and said, "Try to drink this glass of water. We need to re-hydrate you and get your blood pressure back up."

Pieter took a few big gulps and started coughing. Once he quieted his cough, he sheepishly looked at Papa and uttered, "So sorry I don't feel very well."

"I can see that, son," answered Papa. "You probably are lucky to be alive."

"I know. I want to tell you why all this happened, but I don't know where to start…your boys…I need to tell you about your boys."

"Pieter," interjected Janneke, "you need to eat this first." She took the empty water glass from him and handed him the sandwich.

"I'm really not hungry," rebutted Pieter.

"I don't imagine you are, dear, but we need to get some food in you, or you will collapse."

"Yes, of course. I'll try." Pieter stopped trembling after drinking the water, but his face was still as white as a sheet, and his eyes weren't quite right.

After he finished with the sandwich, Janneke handed him the cup of warm milk and warned, "This will taste strange, Pieter. I have added honey and applesauce to the milk to get some nutrients back into your body. They were the only things I could find in your kitchen besides the cheese and bread."

Pieter wrinkled his nose in response but accepted the cup. After he drank it down, he uttered, "Thank you, love, but that made me a bit queasy. Good thing is that I don't feel like I am going to pass out anymore."

"Great. That's progress," Janneke responded.

She appreciated the fact that Papa was such a patient man. She knew he desperately wanted to find out about the whereabouts of Willem and Gerrit, but the first priority was to attend to her fiancée. "Pieter," she told him, "take a couple of very deep breaths and let me know if the nausea is going away."

Pieter closed his eyes and did what she asked. After a few minutes of deep breathing, he opened his eyes and said, "That helped. I feel better. I think I can tell my story now. Is there more coffee? I would like some."

"Of course, but don't start until I am back in the room." Janneke rushed out and came back with the pot of coffee she had brewed earlier and a cup for Pieter, which she filled and handed to him.

Pieter gratefully took a few sips and then began, "Well then, I'll start with my initial visit to Forester Schenk. I arrived at his house right before lunch. Since it was Sunday, they had family visiting, and Mrs. Schenk was in the kitchen, fixing a meal for all of them. She insisted that I stay to eat with them. Before lunch, Forester Schenk showed me to a bench in the garden and indicated that he was pleasantly surprised with my visit and wanted to know how people in Putten were coping after the raid. I told him that the real purpose of my visit was to find out if two boys from Putten named Willem and Gerrit were staying at his house."

While Pieter clumsily reached for his coffee cup again, Janneke interrupted, "So Willem and Gerrit weren't there? You would have seen them, right?"

"They weren't there at that moment," he answered her, "but Forester Schenk told me that the boys were indeed staying with him. They were helping his son keep the radio communications equipment running in a bunker in the woods close by. Without electricity, the equipment had to run on batteries, which needed to be charged continually. A charger powered by a bicycle had been rigged up, and the boys' help with that was much welcomed."

Papa cleared his throat. "That bunker is one of the places the resistance holds up, right?"

"Yes, they receive messages from England to be promulgated to the resistance," answered Pieter.

"But how did the boys get there?" inquired Papa. "They were supposed to be on their way to spend the winter up north in Friesland."

Pieter looked at Janneke, who nodded at him as if to say "Go ahead and tell him." So he continued, "Forester Schenk told me that they were brought there by Piet of the Veluwe, one of the heads of the resistance in the area."

"I have heard of him," responded Papa. "I did not realize that the boys knew him."

"I don't believe they did. Apparently, the boys were angry about being sent away. After they left the farm, they asked around about who they should talk to about joining the resistance. They ended up in Ermelo with Piet, the head of the resistance in Ermelo, who in turn took them to Forester Schenk's house in Drie. The boys did not want you or Janneke to know where they were."

Janneke grabbed her father's hands. "Papa, I had no idea. I just wanted them out of harm's way. I am so sorry."

Papa freed one hand and patted hers. "You did not send them there dear," he reassured her. "They made that decision…to be defiant. I am worried about them, of course, but at the same time, I am proud of them for wanting to fight for our freedom. But that's not the whole story, is it, Pieter?"

"No, it isn't. I left after lunch, but before going home, I decided to try to find the bunker. I wanted to talk to the boys. When I reached the area where Forester Schenk had said the bunker was, I heard several shots ring out, then shouting in German, then more shots. I turned around and went back to warn Forester Schenk of trouble at the bunker. When I got to his house, there was a car parked in his driveway. German soldiers were hauling people out of the house at gunpoint. I could be wrong, but I believe I saw Piet, the head of the resistance in Ermelo, in the backseat of that car. I turned around and left as fast as I could, but one of the German soldiers came running down the driveway and fired at me, hitting me in the arm."

"So, at this time, we don't know if the boys are okay?" questioned Papa.

"No, we don't. I will contact the Dutch police in the area to see what I can find out. Something else to worry about is, if the Germans have Piet of the Veluwe, they may have the names and addresses of many people involved in the resistance. If that's the case, they will likely start rounding them up, one by one."

Janneke had quietly listened to Pieter's account. Tears were rolling down her cheeks. Between sobs, she confessed, "Papa, Pieter and I could possibly be on that list of names. We have not been involved with the resistance on a daily basis, but we have aided them from time to time."

"I already suspected that, my dear daughter. You had knowledge that others didn't."

"But, Papa, why didn't you say something?"

"Some things are better left unspoken," he replied simply. "Pieter, do you think they could have your names?"

"It's possible but unlikely," answered Pieter. "We used code names. The only place they knew us by our real names was at Enny's Estate, and there is no one left there. The Pouws are in hiding with their family in Amsterdam, and this morning, I took Tex to a farm in Barneveld, a brand new address not recorded anywhere in the resistance records."

"Who is Tex?" inquired Papa.

Pieter realized he had probably said too much but felt that his future father-in-law could be trusted and should know the truth. He continued, "Tex is a British soldier who escaped from the Germans by jumping from a train close by. I found him walking in the woods about a month ago and took him to Enny's Estate to hide."

"Was he at Enny's Estate when they set it on fire?"

"Yes, he was," answered Pieter. "He was hiding in the concrete cellar while the house burned above him. After the fire, I went through the rubble and heard banging under the floor. A beam had fallen down and obstructed access to the cellar. After I was able to remove it, I opened the floor hatch, and he came up the stairs pointing a gun at me. When he realized it was me, he put it away and gave me a bear hug. He mumbled something like, 'Thank God, it's you.' And then, 'Sorry about the gun, my friend. I did not know who would find me.' He thought he must be a cat with nine lives and this was his seventh. Eventually, I brought him here for the night and took him to Barneveld early this morning. After that, I went to Drie to talk to Forester Schenk."

Papa sighed deeply and uttered, "So what now?"

Janneke pulled herself together, relieved that she could now discuss more things with her father. She answered his question. "I believe I should stay here to care for Pieter, Papa. When Pieter has regained his strength, we should make a plan to go into Putten again to Aunt Ellie's house to try to retrieve the canned goods."

Pieter agreed, "It would be great if Janneke could stay here. Is that okay with you?"

Papa nodded in agreement. "Of course it is."

Pieter continued, "Regarding going into Putten, I will accompany Janneke and stop by the police station to inquire about what happened in Drie."

Ready to leave, Papa rose from his chair and said, "Actually, I want to go into Putten as well. I need to check on my sister Gerrie and her family."

Janneke walked Papa to the kitchen before giving him a big hug and saying, "Thank you, Papa, for understanding the situation. Please tell Mama that I will be there in the morning to pick up some food. Pieter does not have much in his cupboards. I guess he survives on just coffee, cheese, and applesauce."

Papa, not used to hugs, hesitated at first but then returned her hug and spoke words that were like music to Janneke's ears, "Indeed, he needs you here, not only now, but all the time. I hope that will happen soon for you two."

Chapter Twelve

· · · · · · · · · · · · · · · · · · · ·

RETRIEVING FOOD IN PUTTEN

THE JOURNEY INTO PUTTEN WENT WELL this time. Papa was at the reigns of the open carriage with Janneke right next to him. The rest of the seats were occupied by Aunt Ellie and her two daughters. Pieter accompanied them again on his own horse.

No German soldiers were encountered on the way, and even the weather was cooperating. When they arrived in Putten, Pieter went his separate way, to the police station. He would go to Aunt Ellie's house after his visit to the station.

Papa silently handed the reins to Janneke. She took them, assuming that he wanted to look around, as he had not yet seen the damage caused by the raid. They had taken the back roads and entered the village on the side where many houses had burned. Families were searching through the rubble of the destroyed homes.

Papa sighed. "So unbelievable to see this damage. I wasn't quite ready for it."

* * *

When the carriage stopped in front of the ruins of Aunt Ellie's house, Ria and Hennie quickly jumped off and started calling for their dog Peppi. Papa jumped down and extended his hand to help Janneke and his sister-in-law Ellie down from the carriage.

Janneke was worried about her aunt. She had lashed out and had been so angry when Janneke found her the day after the German SS soldiers had their bonfires in Putten. No telling how she would react this time to seeing the ruins of what was once her home.

Papa climbed back onto the carriage. "My dear ladies, I am off to see my sister Gerrie. I should be back in a few hours."

"Okay, Papa. Please give my love to Aunt Gerrie and the children."

Janneke turned around to Aunt Ellie. She stood frozen on the sidewalk, staring at the burned house. Janneke gently took her aunt by the arm and guided her to where the front door once was.

The brick walls were still standing, but the tile roof had collapsed inside them. Everything else had turned to black and gray ash. Metal skeletons of lamps and other objects were sticking up from the ash. Clay tiles from the collapsed roof were scattered everywhere.

In the kitchen, pots, pans, and broken dishes covered the floor. The granite kitchen counter had collapsed onto the floor with the sink eerily sticking up, still connected to the plumbing.

Janneke was relieved that Aunt Ellie seemed to be focused and concentrating on the task at hand—retrieving the canned food from the cellar.

"Janneke, here is the hatch that leads to the cellar. Help me clear the floor, would you?" her aunt asked of her.

Just then, Ria and Hennie appeared in the kitchen. They were coming from the backyard. "We found him! We found Peppi!"

Peppi came running toward Aunt Ellie and jumped up to lick her face. Janneke could not tell what kind of dog he was, but he was jumping around, happy to see everyone. He was covered in soot, and very soon so was Aunt Ellie. The girls also had black streaks all over their clothes, arms, and faces from their own Peppi greetings.

Janneke was glad to see Aunt Ellie smile during the rambunctious reunion with Peppi. Aunt Ellie tenderly stroked Peppi and uttered, "So glad you hung around, old boy. You must be hungry. Girls, take Peppi to the backyard. It looks like the shed did not burn, so his dog food is probably okay. And, Janneke, as soon as your father returns, we should give Peppi some of the water that your mother packed with the sandwiches."

While running out with Peppi, Ria remarked, "Okay. We'll feed him. Then we'll wait up front for the carriage to come back."

"Oh, no, you won't," responded Aunt Ellie. "I need your help right here to move this rubble from the hatch and get the canned goods out of the cellar."

Pretty soon everyone was covered with soot. Together they managed to lift the hatch. Aunt Ellie went down and shouted, "It's all good. It's pretty dark down here, but I believe that all the jars are still closed. Okay, girls, let's form a chain to get the jars up. Hennie, please come two-thirds down the stairs. I'll hand the jars to you. Ria, come down just enough so you can get the jars from Hennie and hand them to Janneke."

Janneke stacked them outside by the front door. When Pieter showed up, he helped as much as he could with his one arm in a sling. He joined in the chain, cutting Janneke's distance of carrying the jars in half. Janneke inquired, "Any news about the boys?"

Pieter shook his head. "The police in Putten have not heard anything about a roundup in Drie, but they told me that they will inquire for us."

When Papa arrived with the carriage, all the jars were out of the cellar and ready to be loaded onto the carriage. He joked when he saw his family all covered in soot, "When you are finished with this job, you all can hire out to be Saint Nicholas' black helpers. December fifth is just around the corner."

Aunt Ellie chimed in, "Yeah, and I suppose you'd like to be Saint Nick?"

"But I am Saint Nick. I come laden with gifts," Papa quipped as he brought out two baskets and a blanket. "Who is hungry?" He spread the blanket on the front lawn, opened both baskets, and explained, "Aunt Gerrie also put a basket of goodies together for us." Janneke reached out to help her father, but he stopped her. "No touching the food, dear. I am the only one with clean hands." He threw her the towel that had covered one of the baskets. "Try to, at least, get some of the soot off."

Janneke smiled. "You're right, Papa. Thank you for serving us. How is

Aunt Gerrie? And the children? Are they okay?"

While taking the food out of the baskets, he answered, "They seem to be managing. Gerrie has taken in boarders, Hans's family. They had to leave Amsterdam because there was no food. They told me how thousands of people are literally starving to death in Amsterdam because the Germans have taken over all the trains and cut off all food and supplies to them. Hans's sister, her husband, and their three young children walked for five days to reach Putten. During their journey, they knocked on many doors, begging for a bite to eat. Some sent them away, but others shared their food with them and allowed them to spend the night in their barns or haystacks. They finally made it to Putten. Turns out that they are a huge help to Gerrie. I won't be so worried about her now."

Janneke started to ask, "How is Aunt Gerrie coping with..." But she stopped mid-sentence. Aunt Ellie and the girls were within hearing distance. She realized that talking about Gerrie's loss would only bring more sadness for them.

Papa understood and focused everyone's attention on the food.

"Let's eat. Gerrie baked us some tasty bread and gave us a jar of her home-made mulberry jam. Mama fixed cheese sandwiches. Who wants what?"

Ria popped up, "I want bread and jam. But first, could I please have some water for Peppi?"

The dog heard his name and came running up.

Papa distributed the sandwiches and poured some water in the container that had held the sandwiches. Peppi eagerly drank it. No telling when he had last had a drink of water.

Pieter checked the dog over and asked, "Peppi is a bird dog, yes? Does he know how to hunt?"

Aunt Ellie, holding Peppi back from jumping onto the blanket, answered, "Yes, he does. Johan would take him bird hunting. He is trained quite well. He is also a great companion to the girls."

"That's good. Peppi can stay with my dogs if you like. The girls can come visit him any time."

After finishing their food and loading the canned goods, they started the journey back with a fully loaded carriage. Aunt Ellie joined Janneke and Papa up front, and the girls rode in the back with Peppi and all the food. Janneke held the reigns. Pieter followed the carriage on his horse.

As they rode out of town, they encountered a curious procession of people pushing carts, transport bicycles, wheelbarrows, and even baby carriages loaded with firewood. A white cloth, serving as a flag, was attached to each transport vehicle.

Aunt Ellie called out, "Janneke, stop the carriage. There is one of my neighbors."

Aunt Ellie jumped off and went over to a woman hanging on to two young children while also pushing a cart. From the carriage, Janneke and Papa watched as the two women hugged and talked for a while.

Aunt Ellie returned visibly upset. "That was my neighbor Lottie. Her husband was taken in the raid as well. She and the children are living in their shed. Her house burned, too, but the shed did not, just like ours."

Janneke hugged Aunt Ellie. As she helped her back into the carriage, she offered, "I feel so sad about your losses. Should we invite her and the children to come to the farm?"

"I mentioned it to her, but she wants to be at the house in case her husband returns. It made me think that maybe the girls and I should live in our shed in case Johan and Dirk show up."

Ria and Hennie overheard what their mother said and begged her to let them stay at the farm.

Janneke asked, "Aunt Ellie, what do you want to do?" She gestured to her father for his input.

He chimed in, "What's going on with the firewood? Where did they get it? Does your neighbor have a wood stove in her shed to stay warm and cook?"

"She does. Before the raid, Lottie used that stove to heat water for the laundry, and she also used it to do her canning. She now has wood to keep them warm for a couple of months."

"Where did she get the wood?" asked Papa.

"Apparently, the town council met with the people who own the forests around Putten and asked them to make wood available for the people of Putten at a reasonable price because there is no coal to heat their homes. So yesterday and today, people could go to designated places in the woods to buy a load of wood. When she told them that one load would only hold her over for a couple of months, they said that, if it's a cold winter, they will make more wood available after the first of the year."

"Ellie, is there a stove in your shed?" inquired Papa.

Aunt Ellie sighed deeply. "No, there isn't. Forget it. We couldn't stay there. It was only a thought. Let's go."

"Oh, good, let's go home to the farm," answered the girls, almost in tandem.

Ria continued, "I am sure that Father and Dirk will be able to find us when they get back, right, Janneke?"

"We hope so, sweetie. We hope so," answered Janneke, surprised that the girls had made the farm their home in such a short time. She clicked her tongue and flicked the reigns to journey home.

Chapter Thirteen

Kamp Ladelund - Germany

Bundesarchiv, Bild 183-61059-0001
Foto: o.Ang. | 1938/1944 ca.

Loud screeching from the train's brakes awakened Dirk from a dream about teasing and chasing his sisters on a beach somewhere. Oh, how he missed them. He had dozed off and was leaning against his father's bony shoulder. The foul smell in the closed freight car immediately brought him back to reality.

It was worse every time they were put on transport. The bucket in the corner had been filled to overflowing, and some were too weak to even go there. Dysentery was now plaguing many of the prisoners.

"What day is this?" asked Dirk.

"It is Saturday, November 4, 1944," answered Johan without hesitation. "Saturday, the fourth of November," repeated Dirk.

"Father, tomorrow is your birthday."

"I won't have a birthday this year, son. I actually want to die right now." Johan was bent over, holding his belly. He added, "Just let me die right here."

"Hang in, Father. Maybe this camp will have an infirmary."

"Son, look around you. Many of these men are in worse shape than I am. Besides, we were sent here to work, not to be in the sick bay."

"But, Father, maybe they can give you medicine. I wished we still were in Neuengamme. Dr. Jack would have you back to normal in no time."

The side doors to the freight car flew open, followed by the usual shouting, "*Heraus! Schnell! Schnell!*"

After their eyes adjusted to the light that poured in through the open doors, they could see that there was no platform or train station where the train had stopped. Dirk helped his father up and told him to put his arm around his shoulder. Together, they hobbled to the exit. They were stiff from sitting the whole day.

"Sit here on the edge, Father, and wait until I tell you to jump."

Dirk jumped onto the tracks, then told Johan to jump. When he caught him in his arms, he realized how frail his father's body had become. Since Johan could not keep the *steckrueben* soup down, the only thing that had kept him alive was the daily bread. In Neuengamme, Dirk had been able to bring Johan potatoes or extra bread from the kitchen. In this last camp, though, he only could give his father half of his own piece of bread.

Dirk worried about what the food situation would be like in this camp. He hoped this camp would be larger and that he could work in the kitchen and, again, get some extra nourishment to his father.

While the SS guards were busy lining up the prisoners and doing their count, Dirk scanned the area. They were surrounded by dormant farmland. Here, too, the ground was soggy and too cold to be walking around in their flimsy prisoner garb and what was left of their decrepit footwear. He could feel his father shivering next to him. In Neuengamme and then in Camp Husum-Schwesing, they had been hardened by the cold, but this cold seemed even more penetrating. Patches of ground fog hung above the fields. In the distance, Dirk could see the outline of a church steeple—the procession of about one-thousand prisoners, guarded by the SS soldiers, started moving toward that sole sign of civilization. Where the muddy dirt roads turned into cobblestone roads, they passed a sign that read:

Ladelund
Schleswig-Holstein

Dirk whispered to his father, "Do you have any idea where Ladelund is?"

"I don't know exactly, but if my recollection of geography is right,

Schleswig-Holstein is a province of Germany, way up north at Denmark's border," answered Johan.

"Denmark?" gasped Dirk. "Then we must be close to Sweden. Dr. Jack told me that, if we could make it to Sweden, we would be safe."

Johan looked at his son, still so inexplicably full of optimism, while he shook his head and asked him, "Haven't given up on the thought of escaping, have you?"

"Nope. When an opportunity presents itself, I want us to be ready."

"Now remember, son, we talked about this before, if that opportunity comes and it does not include me, you take it, you hear?"

"I remember, Father, but wouldn't it be great if we both returned home? Once we make it to Sweden, we can stay there until the war is over."

"Home," repeated Johan longingly.

Dirk had noticed that his father's depression deepened every time they talked about home. They often talked about what might have become of his mother and sisters. Were they safe? Were they even alive? If they were, did they have a place to live? The last time they were together was at the train station in Putten. The image of his mother—being held back behind the fence by the SS soldiers, holding up coats and a bag, shouting that all houses in Putten would be burned—would never leave him. He grabbed his father's arm and squeezed it. "At least, we still have each other."

A painful smile was all Johan could manage in response.

* * *

The village of Ladelund did not appear to be very large. As the procession passed through, some people stopped at the side of the road and watched the strange parade with wonder on their faces.

The procession passed the church with the steeple that had been their beacon during the earlier walk from the train. Dirk read the sign at front of the church and ribbed Johan, "Father, this is a Lutheran church. Wasn't the Dutch Reformed Church established by Martin Luther?"

"Indeed, it was," answered Johan, curious about his son's sudden interest in the church.

"Well then, we must belong to the same religion. Maybe we can get the minister of this church to contact our church in Putten and let them know where we are."

"Son, as far as we know, our home church was burned down with the rest of Putten. Besides, how would we get word to this minister?"

"We'll see. If they let me work in the kitchen, I may be able to talk to the head of this camp and ask him to let the pastor come out to pray with us. Look around, Father. Many of the men on this transport are from Putten."

"I don't know anymore. All these men look alike to me. But you may be right. In the train, I heard some of them speaking our dialect."

The procession took a right turn into a fenced area. SS soldiers opened a makeshift gate for the prisoners to walk through. The sign on one of the buildings read: *Reich Arbeitsdienst.*

Dirk whispered, "Father, this is not good. This camp looks way too small for all of us. I doubt there is an infirmary or a kitchen here."

"You're right," answered Johan. "I counted only a handful of small buildings."

The new arrivals were split up into groups of two hundred. The groups were distributed over the five small buildings. When Dirk and Johan entered their assigned building, they were astounded.

"Father, this is crazy. Look at how many men are already here, and they are sitting on the ground. There are no bunks. You don't suppose we have to sleep on the dirt floor?"

The only bunks Dirk could see were near the exit, and they were occupied. He led his father to an open floor space in the middle of the room, and they sat down. Tired and cold, they took things in around them. There was no heat source in the building. Straw had been tossed on the floors, but the prisoners who were already there had gathered all the straw around them, leaving only the bare dirt floor for the arriving prisoners.

Dirk felt numb and defeated. His hopes of the war ending and of being free again were now fading. It was incomprehensible to him how their lives had been reduced to being worth nothing, less than animals' lives. The German dogs and horses lived in luxury compared to them.

Dirk asked the men around them where they were from. Many were from the Netherlands or Belgium. Johan could speak Dutch with them. Others were from Poland, Norway, Denmark, or Russia. Dirk inquired, "How long have you been here?"

A man, about the age of his father, answered, "We arrived here two days ago."

"What are we here for?" continued Dirk.

"To dig tank traps along the Danish border," he replied.

"Did you all have to get started with that or were they waiting for us to arrive?"

"We dug today. It's bad here, the worst we've experienced."

"Do you know who heads up this camp?"

The man shook his head and pointed to the kapos by the entrance. "Maybe they can tell you. Be careful, though. They are mean."

"Is there a doctor or an infirmary here where I can get some medicine for my father?" The prisoners overhearing Dirk's question smirked. One of them spoke up, "A doctor? We barely have toilets here. The whole camp has about ten. There is no running water. These barracks were built to hold, at the most, seventy people each, and I bet there are more than four hundred of us just in this one. And you are asking about a doctor?"

But Dirk wasn't giving up. "Is there a kitchen?"

After more smirking, the same man continued, "Unfortunately, no kitchen. They brought in watery soup from somewhere. That's the only fluid we have had—the only food at all, for that matter."

Dirk turned to his father. "We're not giving up, Father. Tomorrow, I will see if I can talk to the head of the camp."

There was no response. Johan had fallen asleep leaning against Dirk's shoulder. The lights were turned off. Dirk was able to lower his father to the dirt floor without waking him up. He then laid down with his arms around his father's frail body to keep him warm.

* * *

Right before dawn, the kapos' rude wake-up call came. It was different here from the other camps because of the lack of bunks. The kapos walked through the mass of prisoners, kicking and clubbing them while screaming their mantra, "*Aufwachen! Heraus! Schnell! Schnell!*"

The prisoners scrambled to their feet. While Dirk bent down to help his father up, a kapo punched him in the ribs with his wooden bat, yelling, "*Aufstehen!*"

Dirk could barely contain himself. As Dirk readied his fist to strike, Johan grabbed Dirk's arm and used it to pull himself up. Johan made sure to hold on to his son's clenched hand as he mumbled, "Son, remember we need to stay alive to get our revenge."

Outside, the usual lineup took place. There was no bread like in the other camps. After the count, the head of the camp appeared to address the prisoners.

Dirk gasped, "Father, that is Griem, the same guy that was the head of Camp Husum-Schwesing. This is not good. He is the man who let the kapos run amuck."

Others were whispering about him, too.

A red-faced Griem stumbled in front of the prisoners. While swaying his pistol back and forth and aiming it at the prisoners, he slurred, "*Ruhe, oder ich schiesse.*"

"Father, he is drunk," whispered Dirk.

Griem shouted an introduction similar to one they had heard in Husum-Schwesing, and here, too, he shot wildly in the air with his pistol. One of the bullets whistled over the heads of the prisoners and hit the roof of the barracks. The prisoners ducked, which gave Griem much pleasure. He laughed out loud and shot over their heads again, this time even lower, shattering one of the barracks' windows. He then shouted the command for the prisoners to go to work.

The SS soldiers led the procession out of the gate and onto the streets of Ladelund, where the kapos took over, urging the prisoners on. Daily, the people of Ladelund saw this procession of undernourished men in striped rags leave their village and then return at sunset, carrying their dead. Some villagers would leave baked goods by the side of the road on the prisoners' route. If caught, they could be punished for their acts of kindness by the German regime, even though, unfortunately, the food only benefited the kapos. They picked it up and divided it among themselves. None of it was shared with the rest of the prisoners.

* * *

A week after the prisoners arrived, Pastor Meyer of the Lutheran church made a visit to the camp while the prisoners were out working. He was shocked by what he saw. Dead bodies were stacked up by the gate. Feces dotted the ground around the barracks. He went to find the head of the camp to tell him how distressed he was about the treatment of these prisoners.

The pastor was able to get *Untersturmfuehrer* Hans Griem to oblige his request to allow a horse-drawn cart to pick up the bodies and bury them in the churchyard. After being further pressed, Griem also agreed to give the pastor the names of the men to be buried and to let him come back daily to pick up the dead. Additionally, Griem agreed to send two prisoners back with the cart daily to dig the graves; they would, of course, be accompanied by an SS soldier.

* * *

By mid-November, Johan's condition had worsened dramatically. He remembered what Dirk had told him in Kamp Hussum-Schwesing: to just make it look like he was working and not strain himself. But the trek back and forth to where they were digging was becoming more difficult for him every day. Dirk had to support his father more and more to keep him from falling. When they arrived at the site and the shovels were distributed, Dirk asked, "Father, what day is today?"

"Today is…uh…I can't remember, son. I am too tired."

That morning, Dirk had asked the SS soldiers to allow his father to stay in the barracks. They denied his request. The only way he could have stayed behind was if both arms or legs were broken or if he had collapsed and were dying. "Today is Sunday, November nineteenth, Father."

"That's nice," was Johan's answer, conveying to Dirk that his father really did not care anymore.

After digging for about an hour, Johan sat down in the mud. "I am done for, son. I cannot move my arms or my legs. Please make sure you make it home to Ellie and the girls. Take good care of them, son."

"Of course, I will. But, Father, stay with me." Dirk pleaded. He tried to pull Johan up on his feet.

A kapo noticed the commotion, came over, and pointed his bat at Johan. "*Aufstehen,*" he shouted.

Johan attempted to stand up, but his legs would not hold him.

"*Aufstehen,*" repeated the kapo.

When Johan did not stand, the kapo lifted his bat, and before Dirk could stop him, he hit Johan in the neck. He fell over. There was no movement in his body. Dirk assumed that his neck was broken by the blow. Engulfed by fury, Dirk jumped on the kapo's back and started to choke him. Another kapo pulled Dirk off and started beating him. After the first blow, Dirk ducked to avoid the next one. He tried to swing at the kapo, but his arm wasn't working. He felt a sharp pain in his shoulder before he was knocked out by repeated blows of the bat.

* * *

When Dirk came to, he was on the ground in a field next to the lifeless body of his father. The kapos must have dragged them there. He had seen them do that many times before, pulling the bodies of the dead and the collapsed prisoners from the trench, leaving them in the field until the digging was done for the day. Other prisoners would have to carry them back to the camp.

Dirk moved his legs. They seemed fine, as did his left arm, but he could not move his right arm. He tried to sit up, but the throbbing in his head was so severe that he had to lay back down. His right eye felt swollen, and he felt some substantial bumps on his head. Dirk was determined to carry his father back to the camp though, so he decided to rest as long as he could. He hoped that his headache would go away. He looked over at his father and felt deep sorrow. It had not yet sunk in that he would have to go forward without him.

Dirk was excused from digging the next day. His arm was useless, and he faked a broken leg. An SS soldier looked at Dirk's limp arm and his bloody, swollen face and agreed that he wasn't able to dig that day. In spite of his injuries from the beatings, Dirk had somehow found the strength to carry his father's body back to the camp the night before. It had been heart-wrenching for Dirk to leave his body by the gate.

Dirk knew that the dead were picked up daily, but he did not know by whom or where they were taken. He explained to the SS soldier who had agreed to let him stay behind that day that one of the bodies by the gate was his deceased father. To his complete surprise, the soldier answered, "So sorry for your loss. If you can hobble along, you can go with today's cart. You may have to do some digging, but it won't be anything like digging the tank traps." Dirk wanted to ask him many more questions, but the soldier left before he could.

As soon as the prisoners were out of the camp, Dirk went to the gate area. He counted thirteen bodies, including his father's, discarded by the Germans like trash. His anger from the day before had turned into utter anguish. How could this be real? he wondered. Who are the monsters that are doing these things? He wondered about the soldier who had given him permission to accompany his father. He seemed to have a heart, and Dirk couldn't help but wonder, Why is he here? Why is he a soldier for these monsters? Does he not have a choice?

Dirk knelt next to his father's lifeless body and wept. His grief temporarily took his mind off his physical pain. His head was still throbbing, and his shoulder and arm were so painful that it made him nauseous.

The click/clacking of horse hooves on the cobblestones made Dirk look up. A middle-aged man steered a horse-drawn cart through the camp's open gate. After stopping the cart, the driver threw a bundle of large paper bags down to the ground.

Another prisoner and a soldier joined him, and together they wrapped the bodies in the bags and loaded them onto the cart. Dirk helped as much as he could with one arm. He made sure he knew which bag contained the remains of his father.

Dirk asked, "Where are we going?"

The soldier silenced him. There was no talking allowed. The driver of the cart climbed aboard and took his seat, and the two prisoners walked behind the cart with the soldier following them. This must have become a familiar sight to the people of Ladelund because several times a greeting was called out to the driver, to which he responded as if on a leisurely drive.

After a long walk the Lutheran church came into view. In spite of all his pain, Dirk could not help but feel excited. Maybe this would be his chance to talk to the minister of the church.

The cart indeed turned into the churchyard and stopped. Dirk saw many new graves. He felt a small sense of peace, knowing that this was where his father would be buried. He made a silent promise to himself that he would bring his mother and sisters here after the war.

The driver of the cart showed the soldier where the prisoners were to dig. Dirk overheard him say that there had been too many to bury individually, so the prisoners were to dig one grave for all thirteen remains.

Shovels were handed to the two prisoners, and the work began. Dirk found out quickly that shoveling with one arm did not work very well. He asked for a smaller garden shovel which worked much better. The driver disappeared into the church, and the soldier just stood around and smoked cigarettes.

After digging for quite a while, a different man came outside and talked to the soldier, while pointing at the two prisoners. The soldier told Dirk to go into the church with the pastor. The other prisoner had to keep digging.

Once inside, the pastor asked, "Do you speak German?"

"Yes," answered Dirk.

"I asked the soldier to let you come with me to pray. My name is Pastor Meyer. Who are you, and where are you from, son?"

"My name is Dirk, and I am from Putten."

"Ah, yes, Putten," repeated Meyer. "We have buried many men from Putten in our churchyard already."

Dirk cried, "My father's remains are in one of the bags we brought. Can I go back out to make sure he is buried properly?"

"I am so sad to hear about the loss of your father, my boy. But since the soldier has allowed you to be in here, I would like to give you some bread and water. I wish I could give you more food, but your system won't tolerate that. Also, I would like to look at your arm. We can tie a sling for you."

146

The pastor led Dirk to the back of the church where he had set out some bread, a pitcher of water, and a mug on the seat of a pew. He had Dirk sit down and told him to eat. He went into a side room of the church and came back with a shallow bowl of water and two towels. He used one towel to gently wash the blood off Dirk's face. He examined his head and told Dirk, "There are several cuts, but they have closed. Your eye is swollen. Can you see okay?"

Dirk nodded affirmatively. He couldn't talk because his mouth was full of bread, which he was quickly devouring.

Pastor Meyer then folded the other towel and tied it around Dirk's neck to make a sling. He very gently bent Dirk's arm to put it in the sling. It hurt so bad, Dirk wanted to scream; instead, he grimaced and moaned a bit.

"I think you have a broken shoulder, son. If you keep it in the sling, it may heal."

"Pastor Meyer," Dirk began, "I believe we are of the same faith. Could you let our minister in Putten know where we are?"

"I am working on that, Dirk. I have convinced the head of the camp to give me the names and origins of the deceased men we pick up, and I am registering them in the church diary. Maybe you can tell me why so many of the prisoners in this camp are from your village?"

Dirk told him about the attack and the roundup. He tried to impress upon the pastor that they were all innocent.

As Dirk and pastor Meyer finished their conversation, the church door opened, and the soldier summoned Dirk back outside.

Pastor Meyer walked out with Dirk and whispered, "I will say a prayer for your father tonight. You do the same, okay?"

Dirk went back to work, and pastor Meyer took the second prisoner inside.

* * *

Dirk was excused from digging the tank traps for one week. He then had to join the others again. Following his own advice—to just act like he was working—he was able to make it until mid-December. At that time, the camp was dismantled, and the remaining prisoners were transported back to Neuengamme.

During the time Dirk was there, almost half of the camp's prisoners perished.

Chapter Fourteen

PUTTEN—DECEMBER 5, 1944

DAYLIGHT HAD BECOME PRECIOUS NOW THAT the nights were long and cold. At four-thirty in the afternoon, it was dark, and the sky would not show a sign of light again until eight-thirty in the morning. Electricity in and around Putten still had not been restored.

Fortunately, Janneke and Pieter had been able to barter lamp oil for milk and eggs with a policeman in Putten. If used sparingly, there would be enough oil to keep the lights on at the farm, as well as at Pieter's house, throughout the winter.

In the fall, several oak trees had been cut down on the farm to provide fuel for heating and cooking during the winter. Janneke and Pieter had pitched in with the cutting and splitting of the wood in return for their share of the firewood.

Janneke had moved in with Pieter. They had discussed it with Papa, who had implicitly already given his blessing when Pieter was wounded. Mama had agreed as well, although with some reservation.

Janneke and Pieter talked about getting married at the town hall, but Mama insisted that it should be a traditional church wedding, which, in her mind, would not be completely appropriate until Janneke's brothers were home and the men of Putten had returned.

Ria's and Hennie's horseback riding lessons had paid off. Janneke was proud of the girls. They had become very proficient equestrians. It had been a great diversion for them, taking their minds off the absence of their father and brother and the loss of their home. Almost daily, they came by Pieter's house on horseback to see Janneke and to play with their dog Peppi.

Today was a special day, the annual celebration of the birthday of Saint Nicholas.

"Hello, Janneke. We brought you something," announced Ria as the girls walked into the kitchen.

"I'll be right there," Janneke replied from the living room. She put down her mending and went to greet the girls in the kitchen, where a plate of traditional round ginger cookies, the size of nuts, were sitting on the kitchen table. These were truly some of Janneke's favorite treats.

Hennie pushed the plate toward Janneke. "Your mother baked these this morning, and she wanted you to have some. You and Pieter are coming tonight when the children open their presents, right?"

Janneke popped a cookie into her mouth and replied, "Of course, we are. It will be fun to see the surprised faces of the kids."

Mama had shared that, in order to do something nice for the young children that were staying at the farm, she wanted to celebrate Saint Nicholas Eve like they did when Janneke and her brothers were children. She and Aunt Ellie had been busy knitting mittens and scarfs. Ria and Hennie made cloth dolls for the little girls. Papa and Henk had used the best pieces of the felled oak trees to craft toys for the kids. They had also made a table shuffleboard, a game the whole family could play.

"I'll make some tea," offered Janneke.

The girls shook their heads. "No, thanks, Janneke. It'll be dark soon. We'd better get back."

Shortly after their departure, Pieter came home from another trip into Putten to inquire about Janneke's brothers. When Pieter entered the kitchen, he took a whiff and remarked, "Something smells really good in here." A rabbit stew had been simmering most of the afternoon on the cooking stove.

And then he noticed the treats on the table. "Oh, yum, ginger cookies. Did you bake these?"

"No, Mama did. The girls brought them. What did you find out about Gerrit and Willem?"

"They were able to confirm that the head of the resistance has been apprehended by the Germans, but they still couldn't tell me anything about Forester Schenk or the boys," Pieter answered while he walked toward her. He took her in his arms and whispered in her ear, "I missed you today. I love you so much. Not only are you beautiful, but you also take such good care of me. Our children will be very fortunate with you as their mother."

Janneke was surprised but savored the moment. This was the first time Pieter had mentioned starting a family. She pulled away, still slightly stunned by what Pieter had just said, and replied, "Children?"

"Yes, I want, at least, four, two boys and two girls. You think you can manage that?" He smiled and playfully pulled her back into his arms.

"When can we—"

The back door flew open. Two German soldiers, pistols drawn, grabbed Pieter and ordered him to come with them.

Janneke yelled in German, "No! Stop! What are you doing?"

One of the soldiers pointed his weapon at her and yelled back, "Who are you?"

"My name is Janneke. I am a nurse, and this man is in my care."

The soldier grabbed her by the arm. "Aha, Nurse Janneke, you are on our list as well. You are both enemies of Germany."

"What are we being accused of?" she inquired while struggling to shake off his grip.

The German soldier looked at her in disbelief, as Pieter had already been taken outside, and he wasn't sure why she was stalling. He grew impatient with her. "You know what you did. You aided the resistance in this area. Your names are on the list of *partizanen*. Now come with me."

"But we haven't done anything wrong."

"That will be determined by our superior who ordered to have you picked up."

"And who might that be?"

"*Obersturmfuehrer* Raschke. Now hurry up and come with me."

"I have met him," Janneke exclaimed.

"Sure, you have."

As the soldier pushed her toward the door, another soldier came in and asked, "What's the holdup?"

Janneke wasn't giving up. "I have met him. I have met *Obersturmfuehrer* Raschke. He was at the square in Putten during the raid."

"So?" asked the newcomer while he poked his gun in Janneke's back.

He ordered, "Outside!"

"But I need to feed the dogs," Janneke cried.

"What dogs? Where are they?"

"In the barn. I need to stay here and take care of them."

The soldier removed his gun from Janneke's back and left for the barn. After he reached the barn, three shots were fired. When he walked back into the house, he pointed the gun at Janneke and sternly said, "Now you don't have to feed them. You're coming with us. *Schnell!*"

Janneke's stomach tightened. She felt like she wanted to throw up. She was trying her best not to cry, but as she grabbed her coat, tears were streaming down her cheeks.

A covered military truck was parked at the end of the driveway. The soldier who had walked out with Pieter extended his hand and pulled Janneke up into the dark truck. The two soldiers with her were pulled up into the truck as well.

When Janneke's eyes had adjusted to the darkness inside the truck, she could see that Pieter's hands had been tied behind his back and his ankles were tied together. They, however, did not restrain her.

Pieter whispered, "I am so relieved to see you. I heard shots. Are you okay?"

Janneke tried to sit down next to Pieter but was told to sit across from him, far enough away so that she could not touch him. She panicked and started sobbing. "No, I'm not okay. These brutes shot the dogs. Oh, Pieter, it's my fault. To stall them, I told them that I had to feed the dogs. I was hoping that, somehow, they would leave me here to take care of them. I am so terribly sorry."

"Quiet! No talking," yelled one of the soldiers.

"Bastards," she exclaimed under her breath. It was drowned out by the sound of the engine of the truck, as were her soft sobbing noises. She was crying because she felt like she had let Pieter down. She also felt angry about not being able to control the situation.

* * *

The ride seemed to take forever. When the truck finally stopped, they heard the driver say, "Reporting to *Obersturmfuehrer* Raschke. Got some *partizanen*."

"Go through," came the answer.

Next, the truck stopped in front of a dimly lit brick building. The soldiers untied Pieter's wrists and ankles and told him to jump down from the truck.

Pieter turned around to help Janneke down but received a blow to the ribs and was told to move on. They pushed him toward the entrance of the building. By the time Janneke entered the building, Pieter had disappeared into the darkness. She could hear voices down the hall but could not make out where exactly they were coming from.

The soldier leading her began to pull her in the opposite direction from where the voices came from. She panicked and, while trying to free herself, screamed, "Let go of me! Where is Pieter? I want you to take me to him."

The soldier paid her no mind. He intensified his grip on her arm and kept moving. He opened a door and pushed her through. Before he left, he said, "Get some sleep. Someone will come and get you in the morning."

Panic, once more, engulfed her. She cried, "Where am I? What is this place? Don't leave me here. Where is Pieter?"

The soldier left without answering. She heard him lock the door and walk away.

Janneke looked around the small, dimly lit room. The room was cold. The cement floor and the naked walls seemed to want to steal her body heat. She shivered. There was a folding table attached to the back wall of the room, next to it, a wooden chair. There was a bed, also folded to the wall. She pulled down the bed. It had a straw mattress, a sheet, and two wool blankets, but there was no pillow. In one of the corners at the front of the room, she noticed a corner cabinet with a tin plate, cup, and wooden utensils. A stone jug with water had been placed on top of the cabinet. In the opposite corner stood a covered bucket with a toilet paper holder next to it. A small window up high had steel bars on it.

Janneke sat down on the cot. Never before had she felt so utterly alone and sad. She longed for her family with whom she should be at that very moment, eating ginger cookies and drinking chocolate milk while celebrating Saint Nicholas's birthday. They had to be worried about her and Pieter, as they should have been at the celebration by now. She wondered if they had gone to the house to check on them and if they had found the dogs. She reflected on the events that had caused her to be here and tried to imagine what might happen next. The emotions of the last couple of hours poured out. She cried herself to sleep.

* * *

Early in the morning, a different soldier opened the door to her cell. Janneke hoped that he would answer when she asked, "Where am I? And what is going to happen to me? Take me to Pieter. He was brought here last night with me."

All this soldier said was, "You are to come with me."

She followed him down the hall to a large room. A soldier, gun at the ready, was guarding the door. Once inside the room, Janneke was told to take a seat at a large table in the middle of the room and to be quiet, no talking was allowed. Three soldiers were standing at a wall in the room and a handful of women were already seated at the table. Most of them were older than she was. She was terribly disappointed that Pieter was not in the room.

A German officer entered. He greeted the soldiers with a "*Heil Hitler*." The soldiers repeated what he had said and saluted.

Janneke recognized him as the officer from the square during the raid. He looked around and seemed to nod at her as if he recognized her as well.

Next he addressed the women at the table. "You are all here because you are *partizanen* and have committed crimes against Germany. Your men are being interrogated separately and will be executed tomorrow, unless they give us information as to the whereabouts of other *partizanen*. You women can also save yourselves by giving us the names of other *partizanen*. If you choose not to, you will be sent to a holding camp in Westerbork until you change your mind. Who wants to go first?"

He paused and looked at each of the women individually for a moment. No one spoke up.

Janneke's mind was racing. He said that they were going to execute the men tomorrow. Had he said that purely to scare them, or was he serious? She wanted to ask questions, but he had been such a bully during the raid. Would she only make things worse if she said something? She, of course, knew of many more names, but divulging them would probably not get her or Pieter released. She ultimately decided that she could not aid the Germans in their brutal treatment of innocent people who were trying to do something for their country, so she stayed quiet as well.

The officer jumped to his feet and impatiently shouted, "That's it! You will be transported to Westerbork immediately."

He abruptly left the room. One of the soldiers who were present told the women to line up, two to each row, and follow him. Another soldier joined at the end of the line. A truck, similar to the one she had arrived in the night before, was waiting outside.

Daylight was just setting in. Janneke frantically looked around to see if she could spot Pieter anywhere but to no avail. It was apparent that they were at some sort of military base. There were many German soldiers moving around, and trucks were parked in front of red brick buildings.

The two soldiers who had walked them out also accompanied them into the back of the truck, and Janneke took a seat next to the younger of the two. He had stared at her several times and blushed when she returned his gaze. He was in his early twenties like her, possibly even younger. Once the truck was moving, she asked him in German, "Where in Germany are you from?"

He shyly looked at her and answered, "From Stuttgart. Are you German?"

Janneke thought she'd pry a bit more, since, at least, he had answered her. "No, I am from here, but I would love to go to Stuttgart someday. Does your family live there?"

"They did, but they are all dead now." He brushed away a tear.

"What happened?"

"My father was killed several years ago while fighting in Poland, and my mother and two sisters died when Stuttgart was bombed by the Brits last month."

Tears were streaming freely now. For a moment, Janneke forgot that he was the enemy. She grabbed his hand. "I am so sorry. What is your name?"

"Heinrich," he answered, quickly pulling away his hand and seemingly embarrassed about his breakdown.

Janneke wanted to console him. "I truly feel bad for you, Heinrich. This war has taken many innocent people, and for what?"

"Have you lost people, too?" Heinrich asked.

He seemed genuinely interested, so Janneke answered, "Most of the men in my town, my brothers, and now most likely my fiancé, who was picked up last night with me. Do you know what is going to happen to the men they are holding? By the way, where were we? Where did we just come from?"

Heinrich looked at Janneke and, with sad eyes, said, "I am sorry for your losses, too. You spent the night at a base called the Willem III Kazerne in Apeldoorn."

"Have you been stationed there long?"

"I arrived in Apeldoorn a week ago."

Emboldened by his openness, she pressed on, "What is the purpose of Camp Willem III Kazerne. What is going to happen to my fiancé?"

"*Partizanen* are held there. He will be interrogated to give up the names of other *partizanen*."

"Does this interrogation include torture?"

Heinrich looked away and only said, "If he does not cooperate, he will be shot."

"But will they torture him?" she pressed.

Heinrich's eyes turned cold. The second soldier in the truck shouted, "No more talking!"

For the rest of the journey, they traveled in silence. Janneke tried one more time to make conversation with Heinrich but was told again to be quiet.

After about an hour and a half, the truck reached its destination.

Chapter Fifteen

· ·

KAMP WESTERBORK, THE NETHERLANDS

THE TRUCK STOPPED WITH ITS MOTOR still running. Janneke overheard someone ask the driver for orders. She tried to peek through the split in the heavy green cloth that covered the rear of the military truck. A woman behind her asked, "Where do you think we are?"

"I don't know," answered Janneke. "It is very foggy out there."

The woman then tried to move to the back of the truck but was stopped by one of the soldiers. "Stay seated!" he ordered.

The truck started moving again but only for a few minutes. This time, it stopped, and the engine was turned off. The two soldiers who had been riding in the back with the women jumped down and ordered the women to get out of the truck. They climbed down. Janneke was the first one out. She turned and extended her hand to the rest to help them down.

It was misting and cold outside. Janneke shivered. She looked around and thought, "This must be Kamp Westerbork that Obersturmfuehrer Raschke spoke of. I sure hope we can get something to eat here. I am starving."

Because of the fog, she could not make out exactly what this camp looked like. When she looked back, she saw the outline of a crossing gate where the truck had entered. In front of her was a yellow brick building.

The soldiers guided the women inside the yellow brick building and into a room that had the word *Registration* on the door. The women were instructed to sit down on the wooden benches in the back of the room and wait until they were called.

Janneke hung her head as reality set in. She was no longer free. What was to become of her? In her underground papers, she had read that Westerbork used to be a holding camp for Jewish people before they were sent to Poland. She thought about her mother and father. Surely, they had found out by now that she and Pieter were missing. She wished Pieter was there with her. Seeing him would make things much better. She looked up in time to see the two soldiers hand their paperwork over to the clerk. They then started to leave. The young man she had conversed with in the truck gave her a nod on his way out.

The clerk at the desk was an older Dutch-speaking man. A yellow star was attached to his clothing. When called, Janneke sat down in front of him and asked, "What is going to happen to me? Will I be sent to Poland?"

He shook his head and replied, "No, fortunately for you and me both, the transports to Poland have stopped. The last train to Poland left several months ago."

"Then where will they take me?"

"If you follow all the rules of this camp and work hard, they may not send you anywhere," he responded.

"Who are the people held here?"

"There are Jewish families. Some were here before the transports to Poland stopped; others were brought here after that. Newcomers are mostly women who assisted the underground resistance. I have to assume that's why you're here. Now let's get you registered. First name?"

"Janneke."

"Last name?"

She hesitated while recalling that she had been picked up in such a hurry back at Pieter's house that she did not get her ID. She did not want to get her father in trouble, and they already had Pieter…

"You do have a last name, don't you?"

"De Groot," she said, giving him Pieter's last name and address. She added that she was married to Pieter and that she was a nurse.

"That's nice," answered the clerk, "but for women, we don't ask for occupation. Did you bring any personal belongings?"

"No, they certainly did not give me a whole lot of time to pack a suitcase," Janneke answered, somewhat agitated by the man's lack of concern.

While he was writing, he mumbled, "I'd be careful if I were you. Smart alecks don't do so well here." He handed her a slip and explained, "On the top are your barracks and bunk number. Take this to the clerk at the next desk, and she'll get you some clothes and other things you will need. Then wait outside that door over there to be taken to your barracks." He halfway smiled at her. "This afternoon, report to workshop number three."

Janneke's stomach reminded her again that she had not eaten for well over twenty-four hours. "Where can I go to eat?" she asked.

"Just follow the crowd in about an hour" was his response.

Janneke was so concerned about food that she forgot to ask what kind of work he was talking about. He waved his arm for her to move on and called out, "Next!"

Janneke wondered what his story was, but she wasn't given an opportunity to ask.

* * *

It was still misting. Wind now made the mist feel even colder as Janneke joined the other women from her transport. They were standing around in a group, trying to figure out where they needed to go. No one had come to take them to their barracks. They all found it very strange that no one was watching them or pointing a gun at them. It was obvious that they were imprisoned, though. They were surrounded by barbed-wire fences. There was a wide ditch around the camp, and through the fog, they could see the outline of several watchtowers.

Guards were walking along the fence with dogs by their sides. Janneke approached one of them to ask for directions to their assigned barracks. "Pardon me. We just arrived here and wonder if you could steer us in the direction of our barracks," she said to the guard in German.

He answered her in Dutch, "You can speak Dutch. All of the guards here are Dutch. There are very few Germans in this camp. Let me see what barracks you have been assigned to."

Janneke's arms were full of the things she had just been given. Overalls, a shirt, socks and boots, some undergarments, a small towel and soap. She dropped some things as she clumsily tried to produce the slip of paper with the barracks number on it. When the guard bent down to pick up her things, a gust of wind blew off his hat. Janneke reacted by stepping on it, so it would not blow away. She brought her hand to her mouth in fear of his anger, but he laughed instead. Janneke was relieved and apologized for stepping on his hat and thanked him for picking up her things. She was acutely aware of how much this guard looked like Pieter: same build, same height, a full head of wavy dark brown hair, and steel blue eyes that peered at her from under a lock of hair covering half of his forehead.

The guard looked at her paper and continued, "Follow this road. Your barracks is the fourth building on the left."

"I appreciate it. Thanks," answered Janneke.

The rest of the women followed her. They all were assigned to the same barracks.

* * *

Inside the barracks, Janneke found her bunk number. The wooden bunks were three-high, hers was in the middle. A sheet, a flat pillow, and a blanket were stacked on a thin straw mattress. Wash lines had been strung between the bunks with clothing hanging on them to dry. The barracks was empty except for a few women with very small children huddled around a wood stove in the corner. Janneke put down her things on the bed and approached the women by the stove.

"Hi. My name is Janneke. I just arrived and am wondering where everyone is."

"Working," one of the women answered, "and the children are in school."

Janneke was surprised that there was a school in the camp. She continued, "Who is in charge of this barracks, and where can I find this person?"

"Mrs. Becker, and she is working with everyone else."

The loud rumbling of Janneke's stomach brought forth the next question. "Can you tell me where I need to go to get something to eat?"

She followed the women to a locale in a different building, next to the camp's kitchen. The food was not too bad. Potatoes cooked with carrots and onions. Janneke believed that she even tasted a morsel of ham in it. As hungry as she was, though, she gobbled it up without caring too much about what was in it.

Next was finding the workshop she had been assigned to. After finding the building, she entered it, and the sound of loud hammering greeted her, intermingled with the voices of women who were trying to be heard over the hammering. Clouds of black dust floated in the air, making it difficult for Janneke to breathe. She found a handkerchief in her coat pocket and held it in front of her nose and mouth. A short, chubby woman came walking toward her. "Hello. I am Mrs. Becker. What can I do for you?" She pulled down the red handkerchief she was wearing over her mouth and nose. Then, she smiled. Janneke guessed that she was in her forties.

"Mrs. Becker, my name is Janneke. I just arrived and am reporting for work."

"Ah, yes, I was told this morning to expect a new group. Where are the others?"

"I assume they will be here shortly. They were still eating when I left."

"Okay then. Follow me. Keep your coat with you. There is a hook under the table to hang it."

"What will I be doing?" Janneke asked.

"We recycle batteries," Mrs. Becker told her as she handed Janneke a hammer, a screwdriver, and a chisel. She then took her to a table in the back of the room and yelled, "Ladies, this is Janneke. She will be joining you at this table."

The conversation briefly stopped. Someone shouted, "Welcome, Janneke!"

Mrs. Becker showed Janneke where the coat hook was and advised her to use the handkerchief she was holding and tie it so her nose and mouth would be covered. Some of the women at the table wore handkerchiefs on their faces as well. All of them were covered in the black dust. Every time someone opened a battery, black dust filled the air around them. Some of the women were coughing. Janneke thought about what an unhealthy environment this was. She made up her mind to talk to Mrs. Becker about everyone wearing medical masks when she had a chance.

The women next to Janneke showed her how to bust open a battery and separate the parts. Tar was thrown in one basket, metal caps were removed and put in another basket, and the carbon bars were tossed in yet another. It did not take Janneke very long to become just as dirty as the women around her. The great thing was that they could talk while they worked.

As soon as Janneke had the hang of the work, she took up conversation with the women around her. Most had been in the camp for a while. They shared with her that it wasn't so bad. Of course, they were being held against their will and working for free, but their daily needs were met. Apparently, Camp Commander Gemmeker believed in treating the prisoners as human beings. The women told Janneke that there was a hospital and a theater in the camp and that their children were able to go to school within the camp. They said that she could attend Dutch Reformed or Catholic church services if she wished. None of them could say that anyone had been terribly mistreated.

Janneke asked what other services, besides recycling batteries, the camp provided for the Germans. Apparently, many other things were recycled at Westerbork to capture the metals and minerals needed by the Germans to continue their war effort. There also were workshops producing toys and furniture. Janneke wondered if Commandant Gemmeker treated his prisoners well simply to have a large pool of free labor. She continued to pry and found out that some of the women ended up here when it was discovered that they were Jewish. Others were women like herself, picked up because they had aided the Dutch resistance. The women who were here with family members talked about how they were separated from their husbands and sons, who were housed in separate barracks. The younger children were all housed with their mothers.

Janneke asked if they knew what was going to happen to them. They said that, until a few months ago, a train would leave the camp every Tuesday to transport prisoners to Poland—to a camp called Auschwitz. They couldn't tell her why but said that those transports had stopped last September. Janneke remembered that the man who had checked her in had said the same thing. She wondered if Poland had been freed. From the underground newspapers, she knew that, by the end of the summer, Russian troops were marching toward Germany from the east. Meanwhile the Allies were coming in from the southwest. One could only hope that meant that the end of the war was near.

* * *

For several months, the daily routine was the same: perform the filthy work, bathe in the bathing facilities at one end of each barracks, handwash clothes, eat, and go to sleep. The only exceptions were Sundays, which were spent playing ball outside but only if the weather was nice. When there was bad weather, they spent their Sundays inside. Books were traded back and forth. Janneke learned how to play cards and chess.

If anyone came into the camp with money, they could buy things. But Janneke had no money when she arrived nor things to trade. It did not take very long though, before word got out that she was a nurse. In payment for medical advice or minor treatment of the women and children, her co-prisoners started giving her books, games, notebooks, and soaps.

When the camp manager heard about Janneke's nursing skills, he had her moved to the clinic, which was an extension of the hospital. Yet another surprise for Janneke, the camp had its own clinic. She now had much better accommodations, food, and clothing. She even got to wear a nurse's uniform again. Most importantly, she could send and receive correspondence. Janneke immediately penned a letter to her family:

January 15, 1945

Dearest Father, Mother, Brother, Aunt, and Cousins,

This, being the first opportunity to let you know that I am alive, will be brief. I am not sure who reads the incoming mail here, so please, when you write back, be careful how you answer some of my questions. Papa knows why Pieter and I were picked up.

I am in Kamp Westerbork, a holding camp, and I do not know what has happened to Pieter. Last I saw him was in Apeldoorn, where we became separated. Have you heard anything from him?

The treatment here is tolerable. Camp management has recently put me to work in their medical clinic, and they are keeping me very busy. I am in good health and will write more about me very soon.

I desperately want to know how all of you are faring during this bitterly cold winter. You are always on my mind. I miss you so much. I need to know about the status of Pieter's house. Have the horses been tended to? I am sure you found the dogs.

Ria and Hennie - I am so terribly sorry about Peppi. He was one of dogs they shot. I truly am sorry you had to lose him once more. Please write me to let me know how you are doing.

Papa - The boys? What have you found out about them? Where are they?

Aunt Ellie - Is there any news from Uncle Johan and cousin Dirk?

Mama - I worry about you most. I wish I could be there to help you with the care of all the people you and Papa have taken in on the farm. I hope things are manageable and that you are taking good care of yourself.

I so look forward to hearing from you all.

With much love and anticipation,
Janneke

P.S. I had to borrow a stamp from one of the nurses. Would you please include some stamps in your letters so I can keep writing you?

Every day during her lunch break, Janneke stopped by the mail room, hoping there would be a letter from home. It took almost a month for the first letter to arrive. Instead of going to the dining hall, Janneke retreated to a quiet place she had found under a huge oak tree near the outside perimeter of the camp. Even though there was a high fence between her and the landscape, it felt peaceful to sit here. It reminded her a lot of home. Freshly turned farm fields stretched out in front of her. The windows of a distant farmhouse glowed in the sun. A farmer spurred-on his horse to pull a plow, too far away to see him clearly. Pollard willow trees lined the ditches around some of the plots of land. To Janneke, those trees looked like old men with wild, windblown hair, hurrying against the wind. She sat down under the tree and pulled her coat around her legs. It was still cold, even though it was a rare sunny day. She took the letter from her pocket. It was from Ria—several postage stamps fell out when she unfolded it.

February 10, 1945

Dearest Cousin,

When you suddenly disappeared, we were so afraid that we would never see you again. When your letter came, Hennie and I danced a happy dance. We even asked Henk and your father to join in on our happy dance. And you know what? They did, hesitantly at first, but pretty soon, all of us were dancing around the table. We now know that you'll come back to us. Please tell us more about what it is like where you are. Do you think we may be able to visit you? Henk said that, by horse and carriage, Westerbork is probably about four hours from Putten.

Whenever we could, Hennie and I went by Pieter's house, hoping that you and Pieter would be back. We knew things were bad when we found the dogs. Hennie and I cried so hard while we buried them behind the barn. Pieter's horses are here on the farm until he gets back. We ride and groom them when we have time.

Our mother has found us jobs in Putten. Hennie works for Mrs. van Gulden, the wife of the doctor you worked for before the raid. By the way, Mrs. van Gulden was very happy to hear of the arrival of your letter. Hennie helps her with the children, while Mrs. van Gulden works with her husband in the medical practice.

Yours truly now works as a housekeeper for Mrs. Schouten of the bookstore. I never knew that taking care of a home was so much work. I am learning fast, and I might even learn how to cook. So far, I have not had to cook, but Mrs. Schouten wants me to learn.

Janneke, I am going to tell you a huge secret. You have to promise not to tell anyone, not even Hennie. Please, promise! I have met a boy. His name is Dietrich. I like him very much, and I know that he likes me a lot, too. We meet up several times a week when I go riding by myself. Hennie often has to stay at the doctor's house overnight and on weekends. You can't tell anyone, okay, Janneke? I know how everyone feels about the Germans, but Dietrich is different. He is nice to me and very good looking, too. I know you would like him. We met when your bicycle broke down on the way home from work. (I hope you don't mind that I am using your bicycle.) I had a flat tire, and Dietrich fixed it for me. I know you are the only one who would understand. I had to tell somebody.

I miss our chats. I so hope you come back soon.

Please write me back forthwith.

Your cousin,

Ria

Janneke stared at the letter. She felt sorry for Ria. Her first love, a forbidden soldier. She thought about how Ria was so much like herself: independent, adventurous, and willing to take a risk. Janneke could only hope that their attraction would wane because the family would never accept a German suitor for Ria. How could they, after all that had transpired?

She sat a while longer, reminiscing about the first time she had met Pieter. What a crush she'd had on him. She had known from the beginning that she would marry him. Oh, how she missed his steady and solid companionship, his wisdom, and his strong embrace. She could not give up hope that he might still be alive.

The camp clock chimed once. She hurried back to the clinic's usual hustle and bustle of sick people in need of care.

* * *

Two letters arrived a few days later. As soon as Janneke could, she escaped to her quiet spot under the oak tree. One letter was from Papa, and the other was from Aunt Ellie. She opened Papa's letter first.

February 12, 1945

Dear Daughter,

You made your mother very happy with your letter. Since your disappearance she has prayed to God every day, asking him to send you back to her. Now she has hope that God is hearing her prayers. Life has been difficult for her. She is, of course, mourning the boys. They indeed died in Drie, on the same day Pieter witnessed his friend's family being taken away. Truly a sad day when we received word. The boys were laid to rest in Ermelo. We don't know exactly where or by whom. When we find out, I will take your mother there to say goodbye.

We have no word from Pieter. Henk and I have winterized his house, and the horses are here on the farm with us.

We have had to slaughter two of our milk cows. As you know, the Germans demand about half of everything we produce or slaughter for their military. Food is scarce, but we feel very fortunate to have enough and to be able to share with the food-seekers who stop by the farm on a daily basis now. In the big cities, thousands and thousands are dying because all supplies were cut off. The winter has been much colder than normal. The food-seekers told us that people in Amsterdam were pulling up the tram rails to use the ties as fuel to stay warm.

We pray that God will have mercy on us and free us soon and that he will continue to watch over you and send you back to us soon.
May God bless you and keep you safe,
Papa

Janneke refolded her father's letter, held it against her heart. Then, she brought it to her lips to plant a kiss on it. She felt a deep love for her parents, now more than ever. She thought about how cruel war was and wondered how things could ever go back to normal. Furthermore, after five years of war, she had forgotten what normal really was.

Next, she opened Aunt Ellie's letter.

February 12, 1945

Dear Janneke,

You probably can imagine how happy we were to receive your letter. So much has happened since you were so rudely taken out of our midst. I am so glad to know you are alive and well. I hope you are being treated with the respect you deserve. What kind of camp is this? You wrote that you were working in the medical clinic. Are you taking care of the prisoners in the camp? Are you a prisoner as well? Are they forcing you to do this? Where do you live? Are they feeding you adequately? I wish I could look in on you.

Janneke, you know that I am not a God-fearing woman, but every Sunday I have been going to church with your parents. A bit of news has been trickling in from Germany about some of our men, and this news is announced during the Sunday church services. There isn't news every Sunday, but when the minister announces the names of our men who allegedly have died in the German camps, the whole congregation weeps. Your uncle Johan was on a list of names they read last month. I haven't had the courage to tell my daughters. I keep hoping that, somehow, they made a mistake because there is no word about Dirk, and I am sure they would have tried to stay together. Most announcements have come from the pastor of a town named Ladelund. The German pastor said that the conditions in the Ladelund camp were dire and that he felt ashamed that such atrocities could occur in his home country. He did not give any other details. I feel in my heart that Dirk is alive, so I can't give up hope that Johan might be alive as well. Of course, we are also mourning the loss of your two brothers. I believe your father wrote to you about them. My deepest condolences for your loss, Janneke. Such a sad loss.

Ria told me she wrote to you about her and Hennie getting jobs. I ran into Mrs. van Gulden during the Christmas church service. She was perplexed by your disappearance and asked how she could help. I told her that I was looking for employment for Ria and Hennie, and she said she'd like to employ one of my daughters to help her with the children. Hennie is the one who wanted to go to work with the children. Mrs. van Gulden then told Hennie that Mrs. Schouten of the bookstore was looking for a housekeeper. So they both work in town now.

Life around here isn't the same without you. I try to cheer up your mother, but I haven't been able to lift her spirit. I hear her weep at night. My own loss doesn't seem so important compared to hers. To lose your children has to be the worst ever. Your letter helped somewhat. When your father read it to the whole family, I saw your mother smile, the first time in a very long time. I have been sewing clothes for her. I bartered some milk and cheese for black and gray cloth. She has gone into deep mourning over the loss of the boys.

Otherwise, all is as well as can be expected. Please let us know how you are being treated. And since we can send letters, do you think I could send you a package? If so, let me know what you would like for me to send you.

With love,
Your Aunt Ellie

P.S. Your brother, Henk, asked me to send you his love. He is not much of a writer, he said.

Janneke sat for a while, staring into the distance, thinking about the things she just had read, and longing for her family. Something rolled in her view, a ball, and then a dog appeared, a huge German Shepard like she had seen with the guards when she entered the camp. The dog came toward her and sat down in front of her. She reached to pet him but froze when the dog growled and showed his teeth. Janneke heard a man call out behind her, outside her field of vision because of the tree. Once he came around the tree, she recognized him as the young man who had given her directions when she arrived at the camp. He recognized her as well. He gave a command to the dog, who ran off to retrieve his ball. The young man sat down next to Janneke, his blue eyes sizing her up. She had to look away from his gaze. He again reminded her too much of Pieter. He obviously wanted to make conversation, but a sudden sadness overwhelmed her.

He inquired, "Nice to see you again. What are you doing here?"

"I am reading letters which I received from home. What are you doing here?"

"Giving my dog some playtime," he answered.

"He doesn't seem to be playing," Janneke responded. "He growled at me."

"That is how he is trained," answered the guard in the dog's defense. "He is trained to let me know when a stranger is trying to befriend him. He is only loyal to me, so if I give him the command that all is well, he'll relax around you." He called the dog and gave him a command, then said, "It's okay to pet him now."

Janneke had the urge to befriend this young man and to pet the dog. She wanted to ask him about what was happening outside this fenced-in area. She felt out of the loop and desperately wanted to know what was going on with the war. Instead, she stood up and uttered, "I have to get back to the clinic. Have a good day." She quickly walked around the huge tree trunk and started toward the clinic. To her great relief, the guard did not follow her or call her back.

* * *

On Sunday, Janneke stayed in her barracks to answer the letters she had received. She decided to write a generic letter to everyone but to answer Ria separately.

February 18, 1945

Dearest Father, Mother, Brother, Aunt, and Cousins,

Thank you so much for your letters. They brightened my days and gave me the courage to keep going.

Mama – my thoughts are with you every day. I understand how sad you must be. I truly wish I were there to help you through these terrible times. I know Papa and Aunt Ellie will do anything to help ease your loss. Please let them into your heart to help you cope.

Papa – I am so terribly sad to hear about the boys. We will find out where they have been buried, and when I get back, we will all go visit their resting place.

Aunt Ellie – Thank you for your thoughtful letter and your update on my uncle and cousins. I am sure that Mama appreciates the clothes you made for her. You asked if a package would make it to me, and I really don't know. If you wanted to try it, I could use a warm scarf and some socks. To answer your questions about the clinic, it is attached to a big hospital. I assist a doctor who himself is a prisoner. The clinic treats prisoners, as well as soldiers and guards. I don't feel like a prisoner and am not treated as such; however, I, of course, cannot leave.

Ria and Hennie – Welcome to the working world. It sounds like you have great jobs. I don't know Mrs. Schouten, but Mrs. van Gulden is a dear. You will be treated very well by her. Please give her and the doctor my regards. And Ria, visiting this camp, I am afraid, is not possible. I truly feel fortunate to be able to send and receive letters, but I don't have visitation rights.

Henk – I know you love me. No need to put it on paper, and please know that I love you, too.

With all my love,
Janneke

Next, Janneke wrote a letter to Ria, letting her know how happy she was for her to have met a boy she liked. At the same time, Janneke felt she had to caution her about how the family would react if they found out.

Aunt Ellie and Janneke exchanged several more letters. Aunt Ellie's letters were always positive and full of hope. At the beginning of April, Janneke received a package from her. To Janneke's surprise, it had not been opened by the Germans to check its content. Aunt Ellie had sent her a red, white, and blue striped scarf—the colors of the Dutch flag—and orange socks, in honor of the exiled Queen Wilhelmina of the House of Orange. Janneke smiled at her aunt's hidden message. She was looking forward to the day that she could wear them because that would mean the war was over.

Chapter Sixteen

. . . .

THE DEATH SHIPS

SINCE THE DEATH OF HIS FATHER, it had been difficult for Dirk to keep track of the days and dates. He had tried to continue Johan's morning habit of repeating the day of the week and the date, but the last date he remembered with certainty was Christmas when he heard the guards of Kamp Neuengamme celebrating and singing Christmas songs. After that, it all had become a blur.

Dirk had been transported from camp to camp to dig Hitler's pointless tank traps alongside Germany's border. When a job was finished, he was transported back to Neuengamme, the central camp, where he would again meet up with Nick. Every time he returned to Neuengamme, he would look for the others whom he had arrived with originally, but it had become impossible to recognize anyone. All the prisoners looked like walking skeletons, with filthy, flimsy rags—a poor excuse for clothing—hanging off their bones. Dirk's shoes were held together and tied to his feet with rags he had found in the kitchen trash. It seemed fewer and fewer of his countrymen remained. It had to be spring because the days were getting longer and the cold had diminished somewhat. Most days were still damp, but the nights were bearable now. The trees were starting to bud.

This time, Dirk had returned to Neuengamme from a sub-camp named Meppen-Versen. He felt almost happy to be back. He looked forward to seeing his buddy Nick and hoped to regain some strength if he could visit the kitchen.

First, he needed to visit the bathhouse. Most sub-camps did not have working bathing facilities, and if they did, they were filthy and overflowing with sewage. The facilities at Neuengamme were by no means clean, but at least, they were somewhat functional. The showers had broken long ago, but the washbasins still had running water.

After washing up, Dirk set out to see Nick in the camp's kitchen. He wasn't there. In a panic, Dirk knocked on the door of the office in charge of the kitchen.

"*Herein*!" sounded through the door.

Dirk hesitated. If *Hauptsturmführer* von Schilling was not there, the kapos would punish him. He slowly pushed the door open and scanned the room. The chair at the desk, where von Schilling normally sat, was empty. Dirk started to turn around and leave, but the need to find Nick was stronger than his fear, so he stepped into the room. A kapo came toward him and, bouncing his bat in his hand, asked, "*Was machst du hier? Heraus!*"

"Nick is not in the kitchen. Where is he?" cried Dirk.

"*Machs niks, heraus.*" The kapo lifted his bat but was stopped by von Schilling who had entered the room from the back.

He nodded at Dirk in recognition.

"We are shorthanded in the kitchen. I need you to go there and start working immediately."

"I was just there looking for Nick," responded Dirk nervously. "But he wasn't there. I was hoping you could tell me where he is."

Dirk knew that *Hauptsturmführer* von Schilling had taken a liking to him and to Nick. He had sons approximately their same age. If anyone could tell him what had happened to Nick, it would be him.

"Ah, yes, your friend Nick. He is in the infirmary under the care of his father."

"The infirmary? Is he ill?" Dirk's panic intensified.

"No, he is not ill, but he is hurt. He dropped a kettle of hot soup on his feet and has broken toes. His legs and feet also have third-degree burns. That is the reason we are extremely shorthanded in the kitchen. You know how the camp kitchen runs, so I want you to take his place until he gets well enough to return to his duties."

"Oh, no! Is he going to be okay? And yes, of course, sir, I will go there at once."

Von Schilling looked at Dirk as if he wanted to say something else. Instead, he gestured for Dirk to leave, but Dirk had one more pressing thing he wanted to know. "What day and date is it today, sir?"

Von Schilling gave him a curious look but answered anyway, "Today is Wednesday, April eighteenth."

"Wednesday, April eighteenth," repeated Dirk. "Thank you, sir."

Dirk was torn. He wanted to go to the infirmary to see how his best friend Nick was doing, but von Schilling wanted him in the kitchen. He decided he'd better go to the kitchen first and see Nick after he was done there.

While he went through the familiar motions in the kitchen, his thoughts drifted to his mother and sisters. He wondered if he would find them alive when he returned. His mother's birthday was in the spring, but he could not remember the exact date. As a birthday present, he and his younger sisters would help her plant her garden. Of course, his sisters would often goof off, leaving him to pick up their slack. He used to hate them for that, but at this moment, all he could feel was love for them. How much he would give to work that garden again.

He had promised his father that he would do his best to make it back to them to let them know what had happened to him. Dirk knew that he had to stay under the radar and do what he was told.

As soon as his kitchen duties for the day were over, Dirk headed to the infirmary to see Nick. He was surprised to see Brutus guarding the door. He had not seen Brutus since the first few days he spent in Neuengamme. This did not bode well. After the kapo who killed his father, this guy was the next meanest kapo he had encountered in all the camps. Dirk had witnessed how Brutus seemed to get great satisfaction from beating his fellow prisoners for practically no reason at all, without stopping until he saw blood.

Dirk decided to avoid what would certainly be an unpleasant encounter and try to see Nick another day. He walked away feeling great disappointment and helplessness. Was he letting his best buddy down by letting this kapo scare him off? He kept walking, reminding himself of the promise to his father.

Dirk entered the assigned barracks and found his bunk. At least, he had a bunk all to himself this time, which, relatively speaking, felt like a luxury. Even though the straw was matted down and filthy, it beat having to sleep on the bare dirt floor or on hard wooden boards, packed in with so many other men that you could not even move.

Dirk fell asleep, thinking about the promise he had made to his father to do his best to stay alive and make it home to his mother and sisters.

* * *

Well after midnight, Dirk woke up from a restless sleep. He realized that there had not been any air raids so far that night. It was eerily quiet, no droning sound of airplanes followed by blaring alarms, kapos shouting and clubbing to herd the prisoners into the bomb shelter.

He wondered if he could make it to the infirmary without being seen. His current barracks was located just across the square from the infirmary, and the bath house was in between. He decided that he would fake sleep-walking if he were caught.

He laid awake for a while. He had to see Nick. He was sure he could make it, as long as the dogs did not hear him. He had seen the bodies of several prisoners in the past, lying in the square, ripped apart by the dogs. After surviving everything else, this was not how he wanted to meet his death. If he didn't try to see Nick, his only friend in this godforsaken place, he would feel like a coward, but at the same time, he wanted to live, so he could see his mother and sisters again.

Just before morning light, he got up and quietly slipped out of the barracks. Once outside, he stood by the door for a while and listened intently. No sound of guards or guard dogs. The lights from the prison towers darted back and forth across the square. He estimated that he could make it to the bathhouse if he timed the lights right. Then he could continue on in the shadow of the bathhouse to the infirmary.

He got up the courage to make his attempt and, with his heart racing, made it successfully to the infirmary. A sigh of relief escaped him when he arrived and discovered Brutus was not guarding the entrance.

While standing to the side, he pushed the door open, just enough so he could see inside through the crack. It was pitch black inside. When it remained quiet for a moment or two, he entered and felt around for the green doctor's coats he had seen hanging beside the door whenever he had visited Dr. Jack to get medicine for his father. They were there. Putting on one of the coats made him feel a little safer.

He, then, walked, slowly, into the pitch-black barracks while whispering Nick's name. After a few minutes, going from bunk to bunk, the answer came, "Over here. Papa?"

"No, it's me. Dirk."

Once Dirk reached Nick, the two embraced and softly cried in each others arms like long-lost brothers. Nick was the first to whisper, "I am so glad you found me here. When did you get back?"

"Yesterday. Von Schilling told me what happened to you and that you were here."

"Yes, I have been here for several days. This might sound strange, but I actually feel fortunate that the accident happened. Now I get to spend time with my father."

"How is your father?"

"Extremely tired and totally disillusioned with humanity and the medical field. It is hurting him to the core to know that, if he had medicine and supplies, he could save many of the patients. But he has not received any medicine or supplies for several months now. All he can do is try to comfort people while they are dying. Daily, between ten and twenty bodies are carried out of here and taken to the burn house."

"What has he heard about the war?"

"He heard the guards talking about the Russians getting ready to take Berlin. That's where Hitler is, you know. Also, the British and American forces are advancing further into Germany from the South. He said that the SS soldiers in the camp are nervous. He heard some of them talking about defecting."

"It sounds like the end of the war could be near, which makes me wonder what will happen to all of us," Dirk solemnly replied. "By the way, we haven't had any air raid alarms tonight. Were there any during the past week?"

"Yes, there were, the night before last. They aren't bothering to put us prisoners into the shelter anymore, though, which is fine with me, since I can't walk very well."

"So sorry, buddy. Does it hurt a lot?"

"Yes, it does, but if my legs are up, the pain is less. Papa has taught me some breathing techniques to deal with the pain."

"I wish I could stay here with you, but I'll be missed in the kitchen. I will—"

Before he could finish his sentence, the lights flicked on, and Dr. Jack came toward them. Dirk jumped up. He felt silly in the doctor's coat. How was he going to explain that?

"Papa, look who is here!" Nick cried. "It's Dirk. He's come back again."

Dr. Jack embraced Dirk and smiled. "Good morning, Dr. Dirk. I can certainly use your help right now."

"So good to see you, Dr. Jack. I would love to assist you, but I should make my way to the kitchen."

"I don't believe you are going to be cooking for anyone today. I was just woken up with orders to get all the patients ready for transport."

"Transport?" gasped Nick and Dirk in unison.

"Transport?" repeated the patients around them.

"Yes, the whole camp is going on transport. They are getting the trains ready as we speak."

"But where are we going?" Dirk asked.

"I don't know. All I know is that the camp is to be totally cleared. Will you please help me, Dirk?"

"Of course, I will. Let me know what you need me to do."

"Thank you, Dirk. Go to the kitchen. If today's bread has arrived, take the doctor's coat you are wearing and use it to make a sack. Fill it with as much bread as it will hold and bring it back here. Then, you can help me with transferring the patients to the train."

A camp guard appeared at the door just as Dirk started to leave. Dirk overheard the guard tell the doctor that anyone who wasn't able to walk on his own was to stay in the infirmary. Dirk turned back toward the doctor to protest, but the doctor, knowing Dirk was thinking about Nick, shushed him and calmly said to the guard, "I understand."

He then turned and said, "Go, Dirk, before others take all the bread."

Dirk grabbed another doctor's coat from the infirmary door and ran to the kitchen. The bread had arrived, and no one else had come to the kitchen yet. Dirk tied the two coats into sacks and filled them up.

When he returned with the bread, Dr. Jack had lined up all the patients who were able to walk in front of the barracks that had served as the infirmary all these months. He took the sacks from Dirk and handed them to two prisoners who looked strong enough to carry them to the train.

"Dirk, why don't you wait by the door, and as soon as the order comes to move to the train, you can get Nick and carry him on your back."

"I can get him now, so we'll be ready to go."

"No, I don't want the guards to ask questions until we are moving."

"But, Dr. Jack, how will we get him to the train unnoticed?"

"As a doctor, I have had to give medical care to most of these guards. They owe me. When I tell them that Nick is my son, they will allow me to take him."

* * *

For many days, the prisoners bounced around in the freight cars, exhausted, filthy, and without food or drink. Many were getting sicker by the day. The bread Dirk had been able to bring was long gone. No one had imagined they would be traveling longer than a day, at the most two days, but the grueling journey had continued for the better part of a week now.

Every time the train came to a stop, the prisoners hoped they might be at their final destination, only to be disappointed time and time again. Stops were made at other camps where more prisoners were added to the already overcrowded freight cars. Soon, there wasn't room to sit or lie down. Many prisoners perished around Dirk, Nick, and the doctor. They were either crushed to death or just succumbed to their illness and despair. Dysentery was running rampant. Grief and total helplessness were carved into the prisoners' gaunt faces.

The three had given up talking about anything a few days after the journey began. It was all too painful and incomprehensible.

At each stop, the dead were taken off, and the rail cars, with the prisoners in them, were hosed out. Fresh straw was tossed in. Dirk and Dr. Jack made sure that Nick had enough room around him so that others would not trample his burned legs. During the hose-down, all prisoners rushed toward the doors, to try and catch a few drops of water in their mouths. Dr. Jack would hold up the rags he kept around Nick's burned legs in front of the water stream in order to rinse them out. The prisoners would yell at him because that prevented the water from reaching them.

Finally, the train came to what had to be the final stop. The yelling and clubbing started as soon as the doors flung open. Everyone was ordered to get out of the rail cars. Dr. Jack lifted Nick onto Dirk's back, and while he carried Nick outside, Dirk said, "Today is Tuesday, May first."

Nick repeated after him, "It is Tuesday, May first, today."

Dr. Jack nodded in agreement. He had told Dirk in the train that he appreciated what his father had taught him. It was keeping him in touch with the days as well.

It took a minute before their eyes adjusted to the bright light. They eagerly sucked the fresh air so deeply into their lungs that it hurt. The stench in the freight cars had been so overwhelming that they had barely been able to breathe.

Dirk looked back at the freight cars. Many prisoners had not made it out. Some had tried but were hanging half inside, half outside the cars, and some had fallen onto the tracks and could not get up. The SS soldiers ordered the kapos to toss those bodies back into the freight cars and to close the doors. Soon the train moved away.

The prisoners were ordered to start moving. Thousands of walking skeletons in rags moved through an area with huge warehouses on either side of them. Dirk and Dr. Jack took turns carrying Nick on their backs.

Dirk took several deep breaths through his nose and noted, "Dr. Jack, the air here smells like the sea. Do you smell it? I grew up where there were woods and have gone to the coast on vacation. I know the difference, and this air smells like the coast. Where do you think we might be?"

Dr. Jack took in a deep breath through his nose as well. "You could be right," he answered absentmindedly. He was intently focused on a group of SS soldiers to the side. They had their noses in a newspaper. Dirk followed his gaze, and as they passed the soldiers, they both read the huge headline: Hitler is Dead. The heading above it read: *Lubecker Nachrichten*.

"Nick, Nick, look! Dr. Jack, are you seeing what I'm seeing?" Dirk could not contain his excitement. He whirled around with Nick on his back. Dr. Jack grabbed a hold of Nick who had nearly fallen off during Dirk's sudden move.

"Let's not celebrate too early, Dirk. If it is true, we don't know what that means for us. From the name of the paper, I assume we are in Lubeck, a harbor city on the Baltic Sea."

"I knew I smelled the sea," cried Dirk. "We're going home."

At the end of the warehouse district, the procession turned, and the harbor came into view.

"You see? I was right," Dirk cheered, full of renewed hope.

They came to a halt. Dirk stretched and tried to see what was happening at the beginning of the line. "They are putting us onto a ship," he said.

Nick, who had been very quiet up until now, popped up and said, "Papa, if they are putting us all on the same ship, we aren't going home, are we?"

"I fear that you may be right, son. There are too many nationalities among the prisoners to take us back to our countries. Maybe they'll take us to Sweden on the other side of the Baltic Sea. Sweden has been able to remain neutral. I used to receive medical supplies from the Swedish Red Cross. They tried to help us as much as they could, but for the past two months, I have had no contact with them, so I don't know if they have come for us prisoners."

Dirk's cheer now changed to "Oh, boy. We're going to Sweden. We'll be free in Sweden. They'll take us home from there, right, Dr. Jack?"

"Time will tell, Dirk. Time will tell," said Dr. Jack, smiling at the young man's enthusiasm.

"I got you to smile, Dr. Jack. Does that mean you agree with me?"

"I like your optimism. It gives me hope as well."

The line, still guarded by SS soldiers with their guns drawn, advanced slowly. They passed a huge freighter with *SS Athen* written on the side. It was flying a German flag.

The procession moved past it, though. They were loaded onto some smaller shuttle-type boats that were going back and forth, in and out of the harbor.

It took all afternoon for the line to advance far enough for the threesome to be able to board one of the shuttles. Even though there was only room to stand, it wasn't nearly as crowded as the past twelve days on board the train, and there was fresh air blowing through the open windows of the shuttle.

Dirk put Nick down and asked, "How are you holding up, good buddy?"

Nick looked up at him and started to cry. "I feel like I am a real burden to you. What has happened to your plans to escape? I always thought you would do it somehow, and there probably are some opportunities here."

Dirk sat down next to Nick, gave him a hug, and exclaimed, "No, no, you are my buddy, never a burden. Besides, we are going to Sweden, and all will be well. We're almost there. I feel it in my bones."

Prisoners around them perked up as "Sweden?" rippled through the crowd around them. "We're going to Sweden?"

Dr. Jack put his hand on Dirk's shoulder and advised, "Hold your voice down, Dirk. You are spreading rumors that may not be true."

The shuttle left the waterway they had been following and continued out into more open water, like a huge lake from which they could still see land all around.

"Look over there, Dr. Jack. There are three ships anchored pretty close together. Do you think Sweden has sent them to get us?"

"I see them. They are flying white flags. That is a good sign. Can you read their names?"

"Not yet, but I will as we get closer. Would you please lift Nick on my shoulders, so he can see them, too?"

Nick was the first to be able to read a name. "That huge ship with the three funnels is called the *Cap Arcona*."

Dirk tuned in, "The one with four funnels says *SS Deutchland* on the side. Can you read the name of the smaller ship with one funnel, Nick?"

"Almost... it says... *SS Thielbek*. Which one do you think we will be boarding?"

"I don't care," cheered Dirk. "We're going home."

"Dirk, I hope it is true, but something isn't right. All three are German ships, not Swedish," remarked Doctor Jack. "Granted, they are flying white flags, but there is something not in order. The SS soldiers are still guarding us with their weapons drawn."

While Dirk let Nick down from his shoulders, Nick asked, "Papa, what do the white flags mean?"

"White flags are internationally recognized as a sign of truce or cease-fire. They are carried or flown to show surrender. Anyone carrying a white flag should be unarmed and is not to be fired upon."

Nick turned to Dirk and proudly told him, "Papa fought in World War One. He knows."

"I know. Dr. Jack knows a lot," Dirk responded. He had great respect for Dr. Jack. He went on to say, "He knows even more than my father, and he knew a lot. I wish he could be here with us now that we are going home."

Dirk's mood suddenly changed from excitement to extreme sadness. Dr. Jack, with his arm around Dirk's shoulder, tried to console him, "So sorry about your loss, Dirk, but think of him as being here in spirit. Think of how much he would have wanted you to enjoy this moment of hope."

Dirk was sobbing now. "I miss him so much. Sometimes, I wish I would have died with him." He had cried for the loss of his father at the church in Ladelund, but for the most part had bottled up his grief until now. The suppressed emotions of the past seven months were spilling out all at once. Nick cried softly with him, sympathizing with his friend and expressing his own grief for the death of the man he once knew and respected. Dr. Jack quietly hugged both of them.

The engines of the shuttle boat were silenced. The shuttle was tied up alongside the hull of the *Thielbek*. The freighter rose far above the top of the shuttle, and several rope ladders were lowered down from it. The prisoners started climbing up to the deck. While Dirk carried Nick on his back, Dr. Jack followed them up the ladder. A man just above them did not have the strength to hang on to the ladder. He let out a frightful scream as he fell backward, barely missing Dirk and Nick. He disappeared into the dark green water below them. Dirk saw others fall. Nobody bothered to try and rescue them.

On deck of the *Thielbek*, the prisoners were guided to a large hatch that led down below. SS soldiers, their guns still at the ready, had formed two lines for the prisoners to walk between. Dirk was starting to believe that Dr. Jack was right. If they were to be freed, why were German soldiers still guarding them, ready to shoot, no less? Were they afraid the skeletons walking past them had the strength to revolt and take over the ship?

An iron stairway led down to the cargo hold. It was pitch black down there. A stench, worse than in the freight cars during their journey on the train, rose up from the large opening. Dirk felt Nick's grip around his shoulders tighten. Nick cried, "Oh, no, not again. We won't be able to breathe down there."

The sound of desperate moaning greeted them as they climbed down the stairs. When their eyes had adjusted to the darkness, they could make out the silhouettes of prisoners, many of them, already in the hold. So many, that it seemed impossible to squeeze in even just one more.

"Dr. Jack, this is bad." Dirk had to shout in order for the doctor to hear him. "We have to try and stay close to this stairway when we are down there."

"I agree," Dr. Jack shouted back.

The conditions in the cargo hold were indescribable. Dirk's hopes of going home evaporated into the unbearable stench that rose up through the hatch. The threesome was swallowed up by the moaning crowd in the hold, pushed and shoved forward. Dirk managed to push his way to the left, out of the stream of arriving prisoners. Dr. Jack followed him.

They had to squeeze their way in between other prisoners but found a place to stand. They tried to talk to some of the prisoners around them but could not communicate with them. They tried Dutch, German, English, and French. One of them answered with, "*Jestesmy Polskim.*" Dr. Jack said they were Polish.

Dirk could not put Nick down on the floor to sit. The floor was wet and covered with feces and vomit. Besides, he would be trampled. Dr. Jack lifted Nick onto his back to give Dirk a break. The boy only weighed, at the most, sixty pounds, but Dirk noticed that his own strength was getting worse by the day.

Finally, the stream of prisoners coming down the stairway stopped. The bottom half of the stairway was pulled up, just out of reach of the prisoners. The hatch was left open, but the evening had set in, so no light was visible, even through its opening. The moaning subsided a bit.

Still, screams of despair could be heard intermittently, all through the night. The Polish men around Dirk and Dr. Jack offered to take turns carrying Nick on their backs.

When light could finally be seen through the hatch, Dirk said, "Today is Wednesday, May second."

Nick and the Doctor repeated the date.

A rope was lowered through the hatch. Orders were barked from above to attach the sewer buckets to the rope. Bucket after bucket was pulled up, swinging wildly as they went up, dousing the thousands of people in the hold with the contents.

When the last bucket was lowered back down, the next order was barked through the open hatch to start attaching the dead to the rope. Over thirty bodies were pulled up with the rope with only an arm or leg attached, swinging back and forth above the despondent prisoners in the ship's hold. The noise level increased again as the mass lamented and prayed.

Dirk could feel Nick's grip tighten every time a body was pulled up. Nick bent toward his father and shouted, "Papa, what will happen to the dead? Will they burn them like they did in Neuengamme?"

Dr. Jack shook his head. "I doubt it, son. Ships don't have crematoriums. When someone dies at sea, they are usually buried at sea."

"Do you mean they will just toss them overboard?"

"Sad, but probably true," Dr. Jack replied. Nick shivered.

Dirk chimed in, "They certainly can't fit more prisoners into this ship, so why aren't we sailing yet? How many will have to die before we get to Sweden? We are so close. I hope we start moving soon."

The rest of the day went by with the men standing around, waiting. The night also passed as it did the night before. More prisoners perished.

As soon as light could be seen through the hatch, the same drama from the morning before was repeated.

Still, there was no movement of the ship. Shortly after the last body had been pulled up, a voice bellowed from the hatch opening that French-speaking people should make their way to the stairs.

"Dr. Jack, that includes you and Nick. I speak some French, enough to fool them. Besides, I have to carry Nick."

"That seems perfectly reasonable, Dirk. You are coming with us. Don't worry. I'll do the talking."

The threesome pushed their way to where the stairs would be lowered and gathered there, along with a hundred or so other prisoners. As soon as the stairway began to move downward, other prisoners started to shove and push toward the hatch opening. Prisoners started yelling, and fights broke out.

A shot rang out over their heads. The bellowing voice warned that only French-speaking people could come up. Others would be shot. The crowd backed off. When order was restored, the stairway was lowered all the way. The French-speaking group climbed up.

Even though it was gray and rainy on deck, the sudden light made Dirk squint. As soon as his eyes had adjusted, he looked around for escape routes. He knew they were too far above the water to jump, and, besides, the water would be so cold that he would die quickly from hypothermia. He would have to get on some sort of boat.

His thoughts were interrupted by the voice of a man in a uniform he had not seen before. He definitely wasn't German. His voice was pleasant, speaking calmly in German. What he had to say was translated into French by a person in a similar uniform. Dirk listened as the man spoke, "I am Count Engstrom of the Swedish Red Cross."

Dirk could barely contain his excitement. He elbowed the doctor and shouted, "Yes! Sweden, Dr. Jack."

The doctor urged Dirk to be quiet, but Engstrom had overheard Dirk and came toward them, looking directly at Dr. Jack.

"Are you Dr. Jack Ballard?"

"Indeed, I am, and these are my sons, Nick and Dirk."

Dirk could not believe his ears. Dr. Jack had called him his son. He had a hard time staying quiet but instinctively knew that was what he must do.

Engstrom continued, "Is your wife Swiss?"

Nick, who had been very quiet because of his ever-increasing pain and barely able to hang on to Dirk's back, perked up and shouted, "Yes, Mama is Swiss. Is she alive? Where is she?"

Engstrom nodded at Nick and continued his inquiry with the doctor.

"What is her name, and where was she born?"

"My wife's name is Charlotte Marthaler Ballard, and she was born in Geneva, Switzerland."

"Well then, I have found you and your sons. The Swiss Embassy in Stockholm asked me to look for you. When I was in Neuengamme a few days ago, I asked around for you, and an officer who was just leaving the now-deserted camp—I believe his name was *Hauptsturmführer* von Schilling—told me that there had been a Dr. Jack with a son named Nick at the camp but that you had been transported to Lubeck. Today I had business in Lubeck, which gave me an opportunity to look for you here."

"I don't know how to thank you for all your efforts, Count Engstrom." Dr. Jack was shaking the count's hand, and he did not want to let go.

"Is Charlotte alive?"

"Yes, she is. Charlotte is in a hospital in Sweden. The Swiss Embassy had requested that the Swedish Red Cross look for her, and they found her among the female prisoners at Camp Ravensbruck. I will personally make sure that you and your sons are reunited with Charlotte as soon as possible. Please follow me."

Before they started out, Engstrom spoke briefly, in a low voice, with a man whom Dirk believed to be the captain of the ship. The captain shouted orders to his crew to send the rest of the French-speaking prisoners back below deck.

Dirk watched as Dr. Jack approached the captain and Engstrom and saw him point at the group of men about to be sent back to hell in the ship's hold. The captain seemed to nod in agreement, and the three men came back toward Dirk and Nick.

Engstrom sighed. "Well, I suppose once a doctor, always a doctor. There is room on the ferry. We can take them along."

The captain took the group through the crew's quarters to a port-side landing with a metal stairway down the outside of the ship. The stairway led to an awaiting ferry.

Dirk could not believe there was a stairway on the port side of the ship, while emaciated prisoners were required to climb rope ladders on the starboard side.

The ferry was flying a white flag, as well as a Red Cross flag.

Count Engstrom turned to Dirk, and in his warm pleasant voice he said, "Young man, you must be exhausted. If you like, one of my men can carry your brother down to the ferry."

"No!" insisted Dirk. "I want to carry him." His answer came out much stronger than he intended. "So sorry, sir. Thank you for the offer, but I can carry him."

"All right then, as you wish. You are a good brother."

"Thank you, sir."

Dirk was relieved. He was so close to being free, and he did not want to become separated from Nick and Dr. Jack.

Once on board the ferry, they were greeted by a team of Swedish nurses. Dirk pinched himself to make sure he was on earth and not in heaven. Were these angels or even goddesses? He had not seen any females since he'd left Putten, and suddenly there were so many of them. He could not believe his eyes. The nurses lifted Nick from Dirk's back and laid him onto a stretcher. Immediately, Dr. Jack shifted into the role of doctor. He introduced himself and asked if there was an emergency medical kit on board the ferry. A nurse named Heda came back with a kit. She and the doctor worked on Nick's legs. They cleaned them, dressed the wounds and bandaged Nick's broken toes. Dirk did not leave Nick's side. He held his hand and talked softly to him to take his mind off his pain. "Nick, we're going home. We really are this time."

"I know. I can't wait to see Mama. Last night, I thought I was going to die. Now, there is hope that I will see my mother again. Dirk, I know you will like her. She is kind and very beautiful. When I was young, she doted on me. I never saw her angry. She always had a smile on her face."

Dirk squeezed Nick's hand. "You are still young, good buddy. And if she is anything like you and your father, I know I will like her."

Dirk felt a mild jolt. The ferry started moving.

"Hear the engines, Nick? We are moving. We are going home." There was no answer from Nick. He had fallen asleep. Dirk looked around. He was still too numb to fully comprehend his good fortune.

The nurses gave the freed prisoners bread and water. Heda came over with Red Cross care packages, each one containing a bottle of water, bread, butter, cheese, chocolate and a pack of cigarettes. She gave one to Dr. Jack, and Dirk eagerly accepted the other while he stared at her. Dirk's head was brimming over with feelings of wonder and lust. He would follow Heda to the end of the world if she asked him to. Dr. Jack's voice brought him back to the present: "Now, Dirk, be careful with the food. Just eat some bread and drink water. Your system won't tolerate the other things yet. You will have to start slowly."

"I will," answered Dirk, eagerly devouring a slice of bread. "Dr. Jack, do you know where we are going?" He pointed at the nurses. "Will these angels stay with us?"

"Ah, you mean the nurses?" Dr. Jack smiled. "They'll be with us for a while. And to answer your question about where we are going, Count Engstrom told me that we are going to a Swedish Red Cross ship that is waiting for us in Lubeck's harbor. That ship will take us to Sweden. He also said that the Allies will probably liberate Lubeck today." His last few words were almost lost in the overhead sound of airplanes. Dirk jumped up and ran to a window. They were fighters, flying low toward the ferry.

"Dr. Jack, they are British fighters. They're here. They have come to free the rest of the prisoners."

Everyone who was able to ran to the fore-deck and enthusiastically waved to the planes. Dr. Jack stayed behind with Nick who continued to sleep, in spite of all the noise. Dirk grabbed one of the nurses and danced around with her on the deck. She handed him a white handkerchief, and he waved it at the sky with all his might. The fighters flew over them toward the three anchored ships.

Dirk could not believe the horror that unfolded next, right in front of him. The fighters attacked the ships. Bombs were dropped on the *Cap Arcona*, and soon the ship was on fire. A second wave of fighters appeared, dropping their load on the *Deutchland* and the *Thielbek*. Stunned, Dirk watched as the

Thielbek was aflame and sank in only ten minutes. The other two ships were on fire, listing heavily. Dirk could see people on the sloping decks, trying both to hang on while simultaneously needing to escape the inferno within the ships, and many of them ended up in the frigid water. Another wave of fighters dropped down from the sky and shot at the people in the water.

Dirk ran inside, tears streaming down his face. He spotted Dr. Jack and Count Engstrom by the window and cried, "Mr. Engstrom, make them stop. Please make them stop. Don't they realize that those ships have thousands of innocent prisoners on board? Why are they doing this? We have to turn this ferry around and go help those poor people."

Dr. Jack put his arm around Dirk's shoulder and pulled him toward him. "Sadly, there is not much we can do right now to help them, son. All we can do is be grateful that we were spared and pray for those poor people's souls."

"No! It's not fair." Dirk sobbed. "They were so close to going home. Mr. Engstrom, why didn't they sail the ships to Sweden yesterday? The ships were full and ready to go, weren't they?"

Count Engstrom looked at Dr. Jack, who simply said, "He deserves to know the truth."

Count Engstrom nodded in agreement and put his hand on Dirk's shoulder. "Dirk, those ships were never meant to go to Sweden."

Dirk jumped back. "I can't believe that. Where else would they have been taken?"

"Rumors are that the German command wanted to sink the ships."

"With all the camp prisoners in them?"

"Yes, word is that they wanted to destroy evidence of what happened in the camps. Since the Germans started to empty out the camps, I have been able to negotiate the freedom of several thousand Scandinavians for whom the Swedish Red Cross has sent buses and ships, in order to take them to Sweden. Sweden does not have ships large enough to carry all the camp prisoners. The number was so staggering that we had to choose who we could save."

"But those fighters out there are British, not German," cried Dirk.

"That, my dear boy, is as much of a mystery to me as it is to you. The Swedish Red Cross tried to notify the British government that the ships in the Bay of Neustadt were carrying camp prisoners and not German soldiers, as the Allies suspected. It seems that the message did not get to the pilots of these fighters in time."

"I hate war." Dirk cried on the doctor's shoulder. "Dr. Jack, that would have been us, if Count Engstrom had not come to look for you."

Dr. Jack tried to console the sobbing Dirk.

"We indeed are very fortunate to have escaped this horrific massacre."

"Dr. Jack, why was the Swiss Embassy looking for you. Are you an important figure in Switzerland?"

"No, not me, Dirk. My wife comes from an influential family in Switzerland. They are the ones that put out the search request."

"I owe you my life, Dr. Jack. I can never thank you enough."

"Nonsense. Nick and I would not have made it this far if it weren't for you, so the gratitude is mutual."

The ferry docked on a jetty next to a white ship with red crosses painted on it. White buses were parked on the jetty, also with red crosses painted on them. Count Engstrom shook Dr. Jack's and Dirk's hands and told them, "Well, my friends, here I have to go my separate way. The nurses have instructions to get you situated on the ship next door. It will be leaving for Sweden in just a few days. Good luck to you on your journey home."

Dirk's tears were still flowing freely, as all the recent events slowly began to sink in. He profusely thanked the count for saving his life and turned to the stretcher where Nick was still asleep. Dirk thought that Nick was fortunate not to have witnessed what happened that afternoon. If the doctor agreed, he would never have to know.

* * *

When Dirk woke up the next morning, he had to pinch himself. Had he died and gone to heaven? Was he dreaming? Or were these white sheets that were covering him real. He looked under the sheets and saw he was wearing a white hospital gown. A sudden panic set in, and he sat up. Where was Nick? He scanned the quiet, dimly lit room. Some light was coming in around the closed curtains, and he felt the urge to get up to see what was behind them but did not act on it. Instead, he examined his surroundings closer. There were three long rows of hospital beds. Things from the day before were slowly coming back to him. Oh, good, Nick was still fast asleep in the bed next to him. Dirk was worried about Nick sleeping as much as he did. He had barely been awake long enough to eat a slice of bread and drink some water. Dr. Jack had said that it was better this way. He said that Nick needed the sleep to heal his body. A tube was going from a bottle hanging on a hook at the end of his bed to his arm. Dr. Jack had explained to Dirk that food and medicine were entering Nick's body through this tube. It was all so wondrous to Dirk.

The bed on the other side of Nick was empty. Dr. Jack must have already gotten up to help the nurses. Dirk had never been in a hospital before, much less a floating hospital. First thing, after entering the hospital ship, he had been allowed a hot shower with lye soap. The nurses had taken away his prison garb and given him a white hospital gown to wear. It all seemed so unreal. Sleep had come as soon as he hit the bed…a real bed.

Dirk saw Nurse Heda coming toward his bed. She softly said, "Welcome back to the world, Dirk. I have brought you something to eat and to drink. Today you have some butter and a slice of cheese on your bread, and we will see if your stomach will tolerate it. I also brought you some tea with a touch of honey in it."

All Dirk could manage was a nod while staring at Heda's beautiful face, surrounded by blond wispy curls which were peeking out from under her nurse's cap. He smiled and, somehow, just knew that she would take care of him forever.

Chapter Seventeen

LIBERATION

JANNEKE WALKED TO THE GATE WHERE she had entered Kamp Westerbork four months ago. The memory of that cold and foggy day made this beautiful spring day seem even brighter. A sweet fragrance hung in the air, spread by the blossoming trees along the ditch on the other side of the barbed-wire fence. The birds were chirping and fluttering around while building their nests. Janneke felt a sense of hope.

The clinic had been asked to deliver some medication to Camp Commandant Gemmeker's house for his secretary, Frau Hassel. Because of Janneke's excellent command of the German language, the doctor had asked her to take it there. Janneke had overheard the women in her barracks gossip about Frau Hassel's being Gemmeker's mistress and about her living with him in the large greenhouse, right outside the camp's entrance.

Janneke showed the guard her papers requesting the delivery, and he waved her through. While she crossed the street and walked toward the front door of the greenhouse, it occurred to her that she was outside the camp, in the free world. She knew, though, that she was not free to flee. The doctor at the clinic would be punished if she did not return. He was a prisoner as well, brought there with his family because he was Jewish. Janneke walked up the steps to the front door of the impressive house. Not fair, she thought. They get to live in luxury while we are cramped in crummy barracks just across the street.

She rang the bell, and soon the door swung open. She was first greeted by a waft of fried onions together with another aroma she did not recognize. It came from within the house. Janneke liked the smell. It made her feel hungry. An impeccably dressed German man in uniform greeted her. He looked at Janneke's nurse's uniform and called out over his shoulder, "Elizabeth, your medication is here." He then turned to Janneke. "Hello. I am Commandant Gemmeker, and what is your name?"

"My name is Janneke. I have some instructions for Frau Hassel, regarding this medication."

"Elizabeth," he called out again while smiling at Janneke. "You can call her Elizabeth. Come on in." He led Janneke into a sitting room and left to get Elizabeth. The room felt warm and inviting. A fire was burning in the wood stove. Pictures were displayed on the mantel above the stove. She recognized the commandant and assumed that the woman in the pictures was Elizabeth. Two large chairs had been placed on either side of the stove. She sat down in one of them while waiting. Commandant Gemmeker was not at all what Janneke had encountered before in Nazi officers. He seemed very personable and pleasant. Word had it that he always took good care of the prisoners while they were in the camp. He apparently took pride in treating the prisoners with dignity and respect as long as they were under his command. However, Janneke thought, he may seem nice, but he must have known what was going to happen to the prisoners he had put on all those trains to Poland.

The door to the hall opened. Janneke, expecting Elizabeth to appear, was surprised when a large dog with curly brown hair came in, wagging his tail. He nudged Janneke's arm for attention. She petted him, and soon he jumped into the chair with her. Janneke savored the moment—sitting in this large comfortable chair with the dog's head in her lap. It had been such a long time since she had been this cozy.

After a few moments, Elizabeth entered the room. "Ah, I see you have met our resident watchdog."

Janneke jumped up. "I am so sorry. I did not mean to get so comfortable," she uttered.

"Not to worry," said Elizabeth while she smiled. "I hope our furry friend did not bother you. We don't get many visitors from whom he can demand attention."

Janneke handed Elizabeth the medicine. After instructing her on how to take it, Janneke took a chance and made a personal inquiry, hoping to converse a while longer. "You are cooking something with onions. I do not recognize the aroma. Do you mind me asking what it is?"

"You must smell the garlic I cook together with onions. My doctor in Germany believes in natural remedies. He told me that garlic and onions are good medicine for my asthma. It seems to help, but when spring comes, I always need additional medicine. Thank you for bringing it." She then walked Janneke to the door and said goodbye.

Janneke wanted to linger. She liked Elizabeth and wanted to ask her about the war, but she had to remember that Elizabeth and the commandant were the enemy, no matter how nice they came across. While crossing the street, Janneke looked around at the free world one more time before she walked through the gate, back into the camp, to resume her duties in the clinic.

* * *

Early in the morning on April twelfth, Janneke woke up to an unusual commotion. Women were running in and out the barracks shouting, "They're gone! They're gone!"

"Who is gone?" Janneke asked, still half-asleep. She dressed in a hurry and went outside. It was the guards who were gone. Janneke rushed to the camp gate. It stood open. No guards were present. She crossed the street and rang the doorbell of the greenhouse. There was no answer. She pushed on the door handle, and the door opened. No one was in the house. The personal items she had seen there just a few days ago were gone. There was no sign of the dog either. Commandant Gemmeker and Elizabeth had moved out.

Janneke started back across the road. For a moment, she thought she was dreaming. Soldiers were coming up the road. And these weren't German soldiers. She ran toward them and was greeted in English, "Good morning, nurse. Do you need our assistance?"

"Yes, we do," she cried. "Who are you?"

"We are soldiers of the Canadian 8th Reconnaissance Regiment. What do we have here?"

"You have found Kamp Westerbork," Janneke replied, her voice trembling with excitement. "Are you here to set us free? And does this mean the war is over?"

"We are here to set you free, but the war is not formally over yet. We have pushed the Germans out of most of the Netherlands, but some areas are still held by them."

"What about the village of Putten, between Amerfoort and Harderwijk? Has it been liberated?"

"I don't believe so. Putten was not on our way north. I know the Germans are still holding parts of the Western Netherlands. We will have more information when the rest of the regiment arrives."

Prisoners were streaming out through the gate now, welcoming their liberators. Janneke went back to her barracks to get Aunt Ellie's scarf and socks. This was the day she could wear the colors of the Dutch flag and the orange socks to honor the queen.

By mid-morning, more Canadian troops arrived from the South Saskatchewan Regiment of the Canadian 2nd Infantry Division. They confirmed that Putten had not been liberated yet.

Janneke wondered what to do. She was free to go home, but would it be safe to make the journey if there still was fighting going on between Westerbork and Putten? She talked to the women she had arrived with at Westerbork. They decided as a group to stay one more night in the barracks and to start walking south early in the morning. They assumed that it would be safe to take the route the Canadian troops had used to reach them. The Canadian soldiers drew a map for Janneke, showing how they safely could reach the city of Zwolle, which they said, would be liberated by the time Janneke and her group reached it.

The group of sixteen women raided the camp kitchen for food items they could carry with them. Janneke found straps in the clinic, which could be used to roll up and carry blankets.

As soon as it was light, they started on their way. The first day, the women walked all day and made it to a small village named Echten, where a farmer allowed them to spend the night in his barn. Janneke asked the farmer if he knew anyone who belonged to the resistance in the area. She told him she was hoping to contact the local resistance about the possibility of a transport by truck. The man replied that he did not, and he added that he would not want to associate with anybody who was in the resistance. Janneke decided not to ask him any more questions.

The following day, late in the afternoon, the group reached Zwolle. The city had been liberated the day before their arrival, and people were still celebrating in the city's main square. They waved flags and were singing and dancing. A Canadian tank was parked in the square, and people were climbing on it to have their pictures taken with the soldiers.

In another part of the square, a stage had been set up. Janneke watched as women were brought onto the stage, forced there by young men who made them sit down on chairs. The crowd around the stage was booing the women and chanting, "Nazi whores! Nazi whores!"

Janneke was stunned as she watched the women being shaved bald. She immediately thought about her cousin Ria. She hoped that Ria had been able to keep the relationship with her German soldier secret. She surely didn't want this to happen to her.

The women asked around about places to stay. A policeman came over to inquire about who they were and from where they had come. After hearing about Kamp Westerbork and their two-day walk, he took them to a hotel on a side street of the square. He explained that two days before, it had been vacated by the Germans and that they were welcome to stay there until they could leave to continue their journey. He apologized for the messy state of the rooms, which of course, the women didn't care about. After all, they would be sleeping in real beds, and more importantly, they could bathe in private. The barracks had shower facilities, but having to always shower with fifty other women and their children in one big open space had not been comfortable. They all felt very privileged and thankful for these rooms. Most of the women, including Janneke, had never stayed in a hotel.

The people of Zwolle brought food to the hotel for them. Apparently, the nice policeman had spread the word about the women that he had put up in the hotel.

Janneke realized that she could not leave for home yet because the Allied troops were at Putten's doorstep and there was still heavy fighting in the area. The same was true for some of the other women who were from Harderwijk, Ermelo, or Barneveld. The people of Zwolle arranged transportation for people from areas that had already been liberated. The rest of them stayed in the hotel for a few more days.

Janneke finally had time to think about everything that had transpired during the past seven months. The thought of Pieter made her very sad. "If he doesn't return, how will I go on without him? And now that the doctor knows about my resistance involvement, will he let me work there again? How many men of Putten will return to their families to help rebuild their destroyed homes? Aunt Ellie had written in one of her letters that men were dying in the camps in Germany. Were Uncle Johan and Cousin Dirk dead or alive? And what about Uncle Hans? Will he make it back to his wife and small children? How are Mama and Papa dealing with the loss of Henk and Gerrit?"

By herself in her hotel room she wept, allowing herself to grieve for all this pain and uncertainty.

* * *

On April eighteenth, word reached Janneke that Putten and the surrounding towns had been liberated. That afternoon, Janneke and six others who had waited in the hotel were driven to their homes in a delivery van. Janneke rode up front with the driver, and the rest of the women rode in the back and sat on empty crates.

The first stop was in Harderwijk, where two women were dropped off. Next stop was Ermelo—two more had made it home. Janneke was next. People were out walking along the roads, waving flags and orange bandanas. Janneke waved her red, white, and blue scarf out of the van's window, excited about going home.

* * *

The driver dropped Janneke off at the end of her driveway. She walked up to the farmhouse and around to the back door. Henk was outside and was the first one to spot her. "Sis," he cried. "You're home!" He picked her up and whirled her around. The back door opened, Mama appeared next. She and Janneke silently hugged, letting their tears run freely. Papa, Aunt Ellie, Ria, Hennie, and the evacuee families all gathered around her. She was finally home, and the war was over.

Epilogue

. . . .

ON THE EVENING OF MAY 4, 1945, the Germans formally surrendered. On May 5, 1945, the war was officially over.

Janneke fell into a deep depression over Pieter's death. He had been executed in Apeldoorn for refusing to give the Germans information about other resistance members. Janneke never felt welcomed in the village again after it became known that she had aided the resistance. The women of Putten blamed the resistance for the loss of their husbands, fathers, and sons, as well as for the destruction of many of their homes. A new forester and his family moved into Pieter's house, so Janneke moved back to the farm and lived with her family until she emigrated to Australia in 1955. She went to school in Australia and received certification to be a physician's assistant. She never married.

Dirk spent six weeks in a hospital in Sweden to recuperate from his harrowing camp experiences. He never regained the use of his right arm. He came home in mid-June 1945 accompanied by Heda, the nurse he had met on the Red Cross hospital ship. They were married at the end of 1945. Dirk's buddy Nick from Kamp Neuengamme came to Putten to be the best man at his wedding. Nick and his parents made the United States their home after the war.

Aunt Ellie, Dirk, and Heda also lived on the farm with Janneke's family until they emigrated with Janneke to Australia in 1955.

Ria's German soldier boyfriend contacted her shortly after the war. She ran away from home to join him in Germany. She was consequently disowned by her family.

Hennie married a Canadian soldier, whom she had met during the liberation of Putten, and moved to Canada with him.

Mama, Papa, and Henk stayed on their dairy farm. Neighbor Jacob also had perished in Germany. Henk took over management of the farm for Jacob's widow and daughters.

For one hundred years, the British government sealed all records containing information about their responsibility for the massacre in the Baltic Sea.

Only 47 of the 601 men sent to Kamp Neuengamme returned, some on foot, others brought back by dignitaries from Putten who went to search for survivors in Germany. Some of Putten's women never learned where in Germany their men perished. The churches of Putten and the village council organized a trip to Ladelund for the survivors to visit the graves of the men that Pastor Meyer had buried and had so diligently documented. Dirk showed his mother and sister where Johan had been laid to rest.

After the war, a statue was commissioned by the village council. On October 1, 1949, *The Weeping Woman of Putten* was unveiled by the new Dutch queen Juliana, in remembrance of the raid of five years earlier.

Until this day, the monument consists of a memorial garden, designed by landscape architect Professor Jan Bijhower, and the sandstone statue, sculpted by Mari Silvester Andriessen, of a woman in traditional regional dress, holding a handkerchief in her hand. She overlooks a garden of 600 squares, which serve as symbolic graves. She gazes in the direction of the Dutch Reformed Church and the square from which Putten's men were taken by the Germans.

A foundation called Stichting Oktober 44 was established to maintain the monument and keep the memory of what happened in Putten alive, including the organization and hosting of trips to various camps in Germany.

In 1992, a memorial hall, exhibiting the story of what happened in Putten in early October 1944, was opened across the street from the statue and the memorial garden.

Annually, memorial services are held in Putten on October 1 and 2.

The village of Putten was eventually rebuilt and became a thriving vacation destination because of its proximity to the woods, its access to the lakefront, and, of course, its immensely important history.

CPSIA information can be obtained
at www.ICGtesting.com
Printed in the USA
LVHW091006080320
649322LV00001B/291